DEATH OF A LIE

A BARBARA O'GRADY MYSTERY

SHARON ROWSE

THREE CEDARS PRESS

DEATH OF A LIE
A Barbara O'Grady Mystery
By Sharon Rowse

Copyright © 2021 by Sharon Rowse

Book cover designed by Sharon Rowse & Three Cedars Press
Published by Three Cedars Press
www.threecedarspress.com

ISBN: 978-1-988037-20-2

ALSO BY SHARON ROWSE

The Barbara O'Grady Series: (in order)

Death of a Secret

Death of a Threat

Death of a Promise

Death of a Shadow

Death of a Lie

Death of a Dream

Death of a Chance

The John Granville & Emily Turner Historical Mystery Series: (in order)

The Silk Train Murder

The Lost Mine Murders

The Missing Heir Murders

The Terminal City Murders

The Cannery Row Murders

The Hidden City Murders

The Dockside Murders

For details on these and upcoming books or to sign up for her mailing list, visit Sharon's website at: www.sharonrowse.com

CHAPTER ONE

MONDAY DAWNED GREY AND MISERABLE, which matched my mood. After a gloriously sunny weekend spent mostly with Nick, the last thing I wanted was to do was drag myself into the office. I knew what waited for me there.

And it wasn't that I was so recently out of hospital, though my arm still ached where I'd been shot. Nor the fact that I had only a few active cases, all of them dull.

Marie started work today.

I went for my morning run, but it didn't clear my mind like it usually did. Even the hot shower afterwards didn't help.

Maybe she'd changed her mind.

I barely noticed what I was eating as I mainlined coffee along with my bagel slathered with cranberry cream cheese. People assume I run for my health. Actually it's what allows me to eat the way I do.

Driving in, I cursed the idiots who thought zigzagging through rush hour traffic in a downpour was a good idea—but with less than my usual heat.

Maybe she wouldn't be there yet.

Even as a bike courier—her former career—Marie had been

notorious for her late starts. I was willing to bet good money that she was incapable of being up and dressed before ten a.m.

I could start my work day in peace.

The ancient elevator creaked its way to the seventh floor. The doors opened. And I found Marie Deslauriers camped on my office doorstep.

Waiting for me.

The black lettering on the door—Barbara O'Grady Investigations—looked appropriately professional. Marie looked like a stranded waif with questionable fashion sense.

"You're serious about working for me," I said. Staring at her. Somehow I hadn't quite believed it.

Marie was the worst client I'd ever had—and I've had some lulus. Twenty-something, with spiky, bright red hair, multiple tattoos, a pierced eyebrow and the fashion sense of a Goth who's discovered neon, she was a force of nature.

And she'd caught me in a moment of weakness—I'm still not sure if it was being shot, or relief at a successful end to a horrible case—and somehow guilted me into her letting her work for me.

On the pretext that she "owed me."

No, she didn't. She'd paid my bill, plus a bonus. If she really wanted to help me, she could just vanish from my life.

That hadn't worked so well.

"Yeah," Marie said with an expression that somehow combined a frown and a smirk. "What did you expect?"

I couldn't begin to tell her what I'd expected. She was such an unexpected character—and quite frankly, such a pain to deal with —that I didn't know where to start. My silence didn't faze her. She glared at me.

"You don't have to look like that, Barbara," she said. "I can help you, you'll see."

Right. Sure she could. I believed her. Or at least, I believed she believed it.

"You'd best come in," I said, unlocking the door. There was no point having this conversation in the hallway.

Besides, given my recent experience with Marie, I suspected I was going to lose the argument anyway. And I'd rather do that in private.

My office is well lit and fairly spacious, but it felt oddly crowded with the two of us in it. I'd always worked alone—well, since I'd set up my own agency, anyway. And Marie's nearly manic energy took up a lot of space. This was never going to work.

"I have a lot of work to do in the next few months," I said. "Sit down, and we'll talk about how you think you'll be able to help me."

I was hoping my approach would be enough to antagonize her and send her stomping out of the room. Probably slamming the door behind her.

I was doomed to disappointment.

Marie flopped down in one of the vintage burgundy leather chairs opposite my desk, and beamed at me.

"I'm so glad you see it my way," she said. "I really can help, you know. Because you've got to finish those paintings for your show in September. And you know they're going to take way longer than you think they will."

I did know. But how did she? As far as I knew, other than the occasional sketch of a tattoo design, Marie had done little or no actual art. Of any kind.

But she was right about one other thing. I wanted that show. And it was going to be a stretch to get another ten paintings finished to my standards while handling everything that being a P. I. involves.

Much less finishing four paintings by the end of this month. Especially if I got another interesting case—and those cases are the reason I do this kind of work.

But the interesting cases always seem to suck up most of my time until they're solved. Which plays havoc with the rest of my life.

And I had four paintings to finish by the end of the month.

Maybe Marie was right. Having a bit of extra help—even hers—might make a difference right now.

Maybe we could make this work? If I brought in a privacy screen to make two sort-of offices. Then another, smaller desk for Marie, a second phone line.

"Let's say I agree," I said. "What are you proposing to do here?"

She leaned forward, tapped a glossy fingernail on my desk. Her hot pink nail polish clashed beautifully with her bright red hair and electric green tunic.

"You need time away from the office," Marie said. "So you can have clear stretches of time to focus on your painting. Which means anything that isn't essential to the work you do, to your detecting, you need to let someone else take care of. Me." And she sat back, looking like the Cheshire Cat.

I stared at her. Again, she was right. And far more rational and logical than the Marie who had been driving me crazy after she hired me to find her kidnapped sister.

Marie had told me that learning her artist mother was a wonderful person as well as an amazing artist—unlike the mean, spiteful aunt who'd largely raised her—had changed her perspective on being an artist herself. And had given her a confidence she lacked. But I hadn't believed her.

Looking at her now, I did.

Even her body language as she sat back in the guest chair was different. Only the spiky red hair and the piercings were the same. And she'd gained a couple more tattoos, if I wasn't mistaken. Intricate ones.

Ones I recognized as being her own designs.

I was torn. Maybe she was right, the part of my brain that was overwhelmed by the work I had to do for my upcoming show said. Maybe this new Marie could help me out. Give me time to do the work I needed to do.

I could use the help. And she'd had it rough, growing up with Anthea Swan. She deserved the chance to feel good about helping someone else, if that was really what she wanted to do.

Still, the idea of working with Marie—as a client she'd been like a train wreck in progress. What would she do to my firm?

Probably she'd get tired of playing my assistant—investigative work is far more tedious than most people imagine. And in the meantime, maybe I could get some extra painting time in.

I sat forward. "Okay, we'll try it. But I'm drawing up a contract of what I expect, and you're signing it."

I half expected her to walk out. But she didn't. She signed.

And I had an assistant. Temporarily, anyway. I had every intention of sending her on her way the minute my show was done.

I should have known better.

Marie may have gained more confidence and a better sense of herself, but she hadn't had a personality transplant. And if I'd had any idea what was ahead of us, and the case she'd get me mixed up in, I'd have turfed her out immediately.

CHAPTER TWO

TUESDAY MORNING I CAME IN at ten, feeling almost giddy, despite the rain that had nearly drenched me as I dashed in from the car. With Marie opening the office, dealing with the mail and any phone calls, I'd had more than two hours free to focus on my painting.

And my work in progress, the one I'd been stuck on, had started to come together. It was going to be good. I could feel it.

I opened the door to see Marie on the phone. She glanced up at me, smiled, and returned her attention to the caller. Walking around the room divider—made of some boringly generic beige fabric—which now divided her area from mine, I saw a the neatly opened mail sitting on my desk in small stacks. And I smelled the coffee brewing.

Since Marie herself won't touch "the stuff" as she terms coffee, she'd made it just for me. I glanced around at the orderly office—not its usual state, believe me—and felt like pinching myself.

Then I tried the coffee.

And choked. What had she done to it? I'd never have believed good coffee could taste that bad.

Okay, I was keeping my job as chief coffee-maker. It was a small thing.

And she'd tried.

The mail was mostly right. Not bad for someone with no previous office experience. Of course, these days actual physical mail is confined to ads for things I don't need, and a few bills. The real work is done by email. Which I was not giving her access to.

Not yet, anyway.

I was half-way through responding to an email from a current client who tended to worry too much when Marie called something from behind the divider. Which did a much better job of muffling sound than I'd have expected. Especially given how little we'd actually paid for it.

With a sigh, I got up and walked around.

"I can't hear you, Marie," I said as I stopped in front of her desk. "You'll have to come around the divider."

"Okay," she said, beaming at me and handing me a small stack of pink message slips. "And your new client will be in at ten-thirty."

"You mean our prospective new client," I said. It was up to me to train her in how the office worked. Oh joy.

"No, our new client. I've made the changes, and she's ready to sign the contract and everything," Marie said brightly.

Contract? Changes? "But how…?" I began.

"She emailed the changes to me, and the copies are ready for signing," my new assistant said, pointing at the color laser printer—which I didn't recognize—that sat on a narrow credenza. Which I also didn't recognize.

"I arranged everything while I was buying stuff yesterday," Marie was saying. "We need to be efficient if we're to save your time. They delivered it all this morning."

I briefly closed my eyes, reeling at the extent of this disaster. Coffee. I needed coffee.

But first I had to make a few things clear. "You do not accept clients, or discuss contracts," I said. "Only I do that."

"But…"

"You set up appointments."

Marie's eyes narrowed. "But…"

"You do not negotiate contracts," I said, ignoring her. "Ever. Am I clear?"

"Yes," Marie said. "But you're not listening to me. I didn't."

"Didn't what?"

"Negotiate a contract."

This just got worse and worse. How much money was this new case going to cost me? "Let me get this straight. You signed a contract that you didn't negotiate?"

"No," Marie said angrily. "Nobody's signed it. I just sent her the contract form. And made the changes she wanted."

Why did I even bother? "You made the changes she wanted. Including to the fee?"

"Well, yes. But I didn't negotiate anything. Not with a fee like that." And she swiveled her chair to grab a few sheets of paper from the new printer and handed them to me.

My eyes went straight to the dollars, and I let out a small whistle.

Marie was right—you didn't argue with that kind of money. But how bad was this case that this client was willing to pay so much?

"What exactly does she want us to do for this much money?" I said.

Marie leaned forward. "The money is fair. But you have to take this case, Barbara. You have to. She needs you. Just like I did."

Given the oddity of Marie's previous judgements, I wasn't liking the sound of this. Not one bit.

Before I could say anything further, the office door swung inwards, and my new client walked in.

———

SHE WAS TALL, and fashionably slim. Almost skinny. Close cropped dark hair, and dark eyes, golden brown skin. A deep burgundy business suit whose asymmetrical closing screamed high end design. No hose—she didn't need them—beautiful burgundy pumps with a heel high enough to flatter her long legs and low enough she could move in them easily.

Expensive, professional and classy—but not boring. Not an easy effect to achieve. I was impressed.

She strode across the office to Marie's desk, her gaze flipping quickly from me to Marie and settling on me. "You are Barbara O'Grady," she said.

At my nod, she held out a hand. "Sonya Lang. Pleased to meet you. Is there somewhere we can talk?"

I gestured in the general direction of my "office", then led the way. I nearly offered her a cup of coffee, then remembered what the coffee tasted like. Which reminded me that I still hadn't had any.

"Would you like some coffee?" I asked. It wouldn't take long to make, after all.

"I haven't much time," she said, glancing at the smart watch on her wrist. "I'd like to get this over with. Can't we just sign the contract, and be done with it?"

For someone prepared to spend as much money as the contract Marie gave me had suggested, she didn't seem very enthusiastic. Just how big was this problem of hers anyway?

I sat behind my desk, the unsigned contract lying on the desk between us. I glanced down at it, then up at her. "I'll need a few details first. Why don't you tell me exactly what I can do for you?"

"Well," she began, sitting back a little. She seemed surprised. Had she expected to walk in here, sign the contract and be done with it?

Her watch chimed and she glanced at it. "This will have to be brief. I have to go. What I need you to..." Her watch chimed again.

She glanced at it, met my eyes. Her own were full of frustration. "I'm sorry, this is urgent. I thought I could explain quickly... but I... There's no time..." She stuttered to a halt. Glanced at her watch again.

To see this confident, self-assured businesswoman so conflicted told me more than I wanted to know about how difficult this case was going to be. I wanted to tell her that I was fully booked—which I almost was—and that I couldn't take her case.

Marie's words rang in my hand. "You can't turn her down Barbara. You just can't."

Yes, I could. But I could at least listen to the details of the case first.

"Just a few quick details then. What do you need from us?" I asked.

I kept my gaze on her, letting the silence stretch on until she looked up.

"I'm a software engineer. Well, I'm the COO, now," she said, and gave a little laugh that sounded forced to my critical ears. "Which means I don't do much hands-on work anymore."

Chief Operating Officer. And she was a software engineer. Probably a startup.

Vancouver isn't the software mecca of Silicon Valley or even Toronto—bio-tech startups are the specialty here. But we've spawned a few good software companies. Just nothing that's really hit the stratosphere. Not yet, anyway.

I wondered what her firm did. "And which company do you work for?"

"I'd… rather not say." She glanced at her watch, looked back at me. "Can we move it along?"

No shortage of attitude there. I let it go. For now. "Do you like your work?"

She looked surprised, then an expressionless mask seemed to descend over her features.

"Of course I do. It's a dream job," she said in a crisp tone that held resonance but no emotion whatsoever.

Her back straightened, her feet aligned neatly on the floor in front of her. She sounded—and looked—like she was doing a TV interview. "Doing challenging work at a fascinating company. Working on cutting edge technology and visionary ideas. Plus it's a huge recognition of my own work, especially as a woman in this field. Who wouldn't love it?"

And she glanced at her watch again, frowning now.

Well, her for one, I was guessing. But why was she hiding behind this very polished public persona? She was here for my help. And she'd obviously told Marie something, in order to engage my wayward new assistant's sympathies so strongly.

"Would you prefer that we finish our discussion in a phone call?" I asked.

I could see the relief in her eyes.

"Yes, I think that might be best," she said, glancing again at her watch, tapping it twice. "I have a crisis in progress. And a meeting —two meetings, actually—very shortly."

"When would be a good time for a call?" I asked her.

"I'll call you," she said, standing quickly and brushing imaginary wrinkles out of her suit. "Thank you," and she stretched her hand across the desk towards me.

We shook hands, she handed me her business card, then strode out before I had a chance to say anything further.

I looked down at her card. Handing it out when leaving a meeting felt like an automatic gesture, especially when she hadn't wanted to mention which firm she worked for, or give me a contact number. Now I had both.

She worked for Xtreme Systems, which even a non-gamer like me knew was a fast-growing local computer gaming company that sold insanely popular games and gaming apps. They'd gone public recently, and raised a lot of money. No wonder she could afford suits like that.

Watching her go, I wondered what she found so difficult to explain. And whether I'd ever hear from her again. She worried me.

Whatever her problem was, I knew I should just let her go. She had "problem client" written all over her.

But at least I could find out a bit about her first. "Marie," I called out.

———

NO ANSWER.

"Marie," I called again. Still nothing. She had to have heard me—the divider wasn't that soundproof. With a sigh I walked around it.

And stared at Marie's empty desk. Now where had she gone?

I needed to stay calm. This was only day two. And it was probably good to have the office to myself right now. I had a couple of calls to make. And I'd rather do it without the possibility of Marie's inquisitive ears listening in.

I reached for the phone. It rang. More bad news?

"O'Grady Investigations, Barbara O'Grady here."

"It's Nick."

Nicholas Markham, six feet plus of broad shoulders and killer grin. Not bad news at all. Nick and I have been seeing each other for nearly a year now. Though not as often as I'd have liked, at least lately.

Nick is an RCMP detective. Since he'd been promoted to a key position on Metro Vancouver's Integrated Homicide Task Force, he often works odd hours, and unpredictable shifts. I could hardly complain, since I did the same. But it meant we saw less of each other.

And I missed him.

Nick had that formal tone in his voice that told me he was at work. "What's up?"

"You free for dinner tomorrow night?"

That was an easy one. "Yes, I am."

Unless this case blew up on me.

"Indian food? At seven?"

"Perfect. The usual place?"

"Of course. And I'll meet you there."

"Done. See you then."

I disconnected, tried again. My first call was to my best friend Andrea. Who runs her own temporary help agency, and is also one of the best sources of business gossip I know.

"Trusted Temps. Andrea Fisher speaking."

"Andrea, it's Barbara."

I could hear my best friend's smile in the tone of her voice.

"Barbara, how are you feeling?" Andrea said. "Are you back at work? And is Marie there?"

Typical Andrea. She's a deceptively petite blond powerhouse, and she likes to operate at ninety miles an hour.

"Slow down," I said with a grin. "Yes, I'm at work. I'm fine. And Marie has vanished. Again."

"Whoa. Trouble already? I thought this was your ticket to getting ready for your show." And she snickered in a very un-businesslike way.

"This was all Marie's idea, as you know full well. But I'm willing to make a go of it. Or at least to work on it."

"I'm impressed. Cory won't be too happy though."

"Cory?"

"You know, your nephew?"

"Very funny. What's Cory got to do with anything?"

"I ran into him at Oakridge mall the other day. He still couldn't believe you hired Marie," she said. "And he didn't think she'd last more than a day with you. I think he had fifty bucks riding on it, too."

"He what?" I said. What was he thinking? "Wait, you didn't take the bet, did you?"

"Of course not. He's only fifteen. What do you take me for?" She paused. "Besides, I thought the odds were in his favor."

"Thanks a lot."

She laughed. "And I think Cory is jealous.

"Of Marie?" She was kidding, right? "Why ever would he be jealous of her?"

"Not of her. Of the job. He seemed to think he should be the one working with you. And your sister—you know, his mother?— she stood there fuming the entire time he was talking to me."

Susanna had barely forgiven me for involving Cory in my last case. A budding computer genius who'd got into trouble for hacking into his school's grading system, I'd only hired him for a few hours of computer work in order to give him a legal outlet.

And I could just imagine how my sister would react to the idea of him actually working here full-time.

Though the way Cory had come through on that case? He could make a computer sing. If I'd had enough computer work—and if he hadn't still been in school—I probably would have tried to hire him full time. Susanna knew it, too.

Which is why she's been giving me these suspicious looks every time I've seen her since.

"Has Susanna forgiven you yet?"

"No. But she has agreed to let Cory do a few hours of computer work for me every week. But he had to agree to a curfew."

"That's it?" I could just imagine Andrea's expression. She knows both me and Susanna too well. "She didn't make you pay too?"

"Of course she did," I said. "I can only hire Cory for ten hours a week, and then only if his homework is done. And I have to clear it with her first if any of the cases look dangerous."

She laughed. "Not bad. How did you manage to get even that much?"

"Cory's been depressed lately, and she was worried. Apparently he was much more cheerful when he was working on that last case."

"I'll bet she loved that," Andrea said.

"Susanna's a good mother," I said quietly. "She might not be happy about it, but she's not fighting it either. Not if it gives him something he feels good about."

"I'm glad," Andrea said. "For everyone's sakes."

"Yeah," I said, glancing at Sonya's business card. Enough about my sister. Time to focus on my new almost-client. "Have you ever done work for Xtreme Systems?" I asked her.

Andrea's temporary help agency is not only the best in town, she's made a bit of a specialty of demanding clients. And an up and coming hi-tech firm tended to expect a lot from all their employees, even the temporary ones. Andrea's people had a reputation for being able to handle it. I was guessing she'd done work for Xtreme.

Turns out I was right.

"Of course," she said. "New client?"

"Not exactly. I just need some general background. Who are they, how long have they been around? What the latest gossip on them is?"

"You can look this stuff up, you know?" She said.

"I know. But it's faster asking you. And your intel is always better," I said.

"Gee, thanks. I think," she said. There was a pause and I could hear a voice in the background.

"Hang on," she said, and I was listening to canned music. Half a minute later she was back. "I have to run, something's come up. Okay if I get you some info tomorrow?"

"Sure. Thanks," I said. "I'll talk to you then."

I pressed the disconnect button, and then listened hard. There was still no sound from the outer office. Marie wasn't back yet. Good.

I punched in my sister's number, but there was no answer. Susanna must be out. I considered leaving a message, then decided that it was likely to just cause more friction between us.

And there didn't seem much point. The job I had in mind for Cory was small and pretty harmless. With a shrug, I sent him a text.

CHAPTER THREE

THREE-QUARTERS OF AN HOUR later there was still no sign of Marie. Muttering under my breath, I was heading to the back to make coffee, when the office door slammed open behind me. I spun around.

My nephew Cory stomped in. Glanced around him. Scowled.

"You have a desk for her?" he said. "Where's my desk?"

Apparently Andrea was right.

"What happened to 'have laptop, will travel'?" I asked him. "Isn't that supposed to be your motto? You can work anywhere. Marie is chained to that desk."

"Yeah?" he said. "How's that working out?" Both our gazes veered to the currently empty desk where Marie was supposed to be sitting.

Sometime attack is the only defense.

"Never mind that," I snapped at him. "I have work for you. And I need it yesterday. Get over here." And strode around the privacy screen to my 'office'.

Cory followed me, a wide grin on his face.

That's what it took to bring him down from a snit? Put him to work? Good to know.

I wondered if Susanna knew that. Probably not. I suspected it only worked for stuff Cory liked to do. Computer stuff, not cleaning his room or loading the dishwasher.

Yeah, I listen to my sister. Sometimes.

My nephew sprawled in one of the guest chairs while I unlocked my desk, got out the Lang file. Glanced across at him.

He seemed to take up more room in the chair than he'd done a few weeks ago. He'd passed my own five foot ten a few weeks ago, and it looked like he'd shot up again. Was he in a growth spurt? At fifteen? It might explain why he was so touchy.

I glanced at my watch. Twelve-fifteen. He was here on his lunch break. And probably hadn't eaten much. I reached into another drawer, tossed him an energy bar.

Watched him rip it open and bite off a huge chunk. Tossed him another one.

"What do you know about Xtreme Systems?" I asked as I stood up. It never hurt to know as much background as possible about a new client. Especially one as challenging as I suspected Sonya Lang was going to be.

Retrieving two bottles of water from the mini-fridge, I put one in front of him and opened the other. Took a sip.

Cory put down the second energy bar, half-eaten. "Xtreme Systems?" he said, his eyes lighting up. "They're like, awesome."

Oh no. "I just need the basics," I said quickly. "Who owns it, how is it structured? Does it make money? Don't dig too deep."

He looked energized.

"Keep it legal," I warned. "And don't talk to anyone there."

"Awww. You're no fun."

"Never mind awww. I have a business to run—I can't afford to have my expensive computer consultant chasing down blind alleys. Even if they're cool," I told him. "Just stick to the facts I need."

As I'd hoped, the "expensive computer consultant" got to him. He nodded, and finished off the energy bar. "I can do that," he said.

But he still looked a bit too excited.

"What time is your next class?" I asked.

"One-fifteen?"

"Want some lunch? On me," I said. Food is usually a good distraction.

"Yeah. Pizza?"

"There's a new place opened up around the corner. Want to try it?"

"Awesome."

And my expensive computer consultant and I headed out in search of the perfect pizza.

———

THE PIZZA WAS REALLY GOOD. By the time I got back to the office—Cory had seconds, and I drove him back to school—it was nearly one-thirty. And there was still no sign of Marie.

I already had my coffee when I heard the outer door slam. Marie came bouncing around the divider screen, and plunked herself into my guest chair. "I'm back," she said.

Really?

"So I see," I said dryly. "What was so urgent that you couldn't wait to have it delivered?"

"Oh, just some office stuff," Marie said. "We needed pens."

Pens? She'd been gone half the morning for pens? I don't think so. She was going to bankrupt me. And this was only day two.

"Look, Marie. If this is going to work, we need to get some routines in place. From now on, you don't leave the office without letting me know first. And you only place orders for office supplies of any kind—and that includes furniture and equipment—once a week. And I need to approve the order before you call it in. Okay?"

She muttered something, but nodded. Her eyes went to the still unsigned contract on my desk. "You didn't sign it?"

"She didn't tell me anything yet," I said.

"Yeah, I heard most of it before I went out," Marie said. "Are all your clients like that? I sure wasn't."

She apparently had a very short memory. She'd been exactly like that.

Oh, she'd told me about her missing sister readily enough, but she held back most of the pertinent details. For most of the case.

And Marie had clearly been listening in on my conversation with Sonya Lang. She must have listened pretty hard to make out anything we said.

I considered a reprimand, then decided to save it for when I didn't need information from her. Sonya Lang was more important now.

"She must have told you something more?" I said. "Or you'd never have faxed her the contract."

Or would she?

Marie's eyes had widened at the question. Then she grinned. "Of course not," she said. "I might not know much about this business, but even I know that. It's only common sense."

I just looked at her, striving for patience. Maybe if I waited, she'd just answer the question?

Or not. The silence stretched between us.

"What did she tell you, Marie?" I asked again, my voice level. Patience has never been my strong suit, and the morning's events seemed to have used up what little I had.

She sat back, looking pleased with herself, as though she'd just won some kind of contest.

I had a feeling our newly formed employer-employee relationship wouldn't last out the day. Not if this was an example of how she intended to operate. Good thing Andrea hadn't taken Cory's bet.

My expression obviously telegraphed some of my feelings, because Marie gave a half-shrug, and started talking. "She's frantic about her sister."

Her sister? Sonya hadn't even mentioned a sister. And sure, she'd been frustrated. And distracted. But frantic?

"That's a pretty strong word," I said. "Exactly what is she frantic about?"

"Well, she didn't actually say she was frantic," Marie said. "But I could hear it in her voice."

Uh huh. "So what exactly did she say?"

"Well, she kept going on about how her sister needed help, how she was getting in too deep, and it was too dangerous for her. And how she—our client, I mean—didn't have the time to figure out what to do. She needed help."

Well, the not having time part fit.

And I could see where Marie might have read frantic worry into all of this. From what I've seen of her, my temporary assistant runs on her emotions. And after what she'd gone through with her own sister's recent kidnapping, Sonya's concern would have struck a nerve for her.

Hell, it struck a nerve for me, too. And I'd been doing this for quite a while.

But Marie's unexpected empathy didn't help me much with whatever Sonya Lang's problem was. "Too deep into what?"

"She wouldn't say."

Of course not. That would have been too simple. "What else did she say?"

"That she would never have let it go on if she'd realized. And that she was afraid it might be too late, but she'd pay whatever it took to fix it. Money wasn't an issue."

The need to protect a sister would be a siren call for Marie, given what she'd just gone through with her own sister. It was for me, too, but I'm more skeptical than Marie—would-be clients lie all the time.

Unfortunately it doesn't stop when they become clients, either.

I didn't know Marie well enough to know how much the promise of unlimited money might have been a factor in her decision to send the contract. She'd been kept poor for most of her life —the fact that she had money now was unlikely to have made much impact on beliefs formed in childhood. Not that it mattered at the moment.

"Let 'it' go on?" I repeated. "What was 'it', did our prospective client say?"

"No."

"Did she say anything that might have given you a hint?"

Marie thought for a moment, then shook her head. "No, she didn't. I wish I'd known to ask better questions. But she was talking too fast to ask much. She sounded really panicked. Or desperate."

Or at least she had to Marie's ears. My experiences to date with my temporary assistant hadn't led me to place a lot of reliance on her judgement. So I still had no idea what Sonya Lang's problem really was.

Just that it had something to do with her sister. And that Marie thought it terrified her.

It would have helped if Marie had been around to tell me some of this before I asked Andrea and Cory for info on Sonya's employer.

CHAPTER FOUR

THE FOLLOWING MORNING THE RAIN had stopped, and as I got out of my car, I stepped out into a bright clear day. I'd been painting for an hour and a half already, and with this kind of light —well, it makes a difference.

I'd fixed yesterday's issue, and had been wrestling with a new challenge on my canvas. But even that felt good.

As I walked from my parking spot to the office, I ran through the events of the previous day. I suspected I'd overreacted—both to Marie's energetic attempts to be my assistant, and to Sonya Lang.

Sonya had been too distracted by a work issue to explain her own problem to me. And she'd been prepared to overpay for what was probably a pretty straightforward job.

I'd seen busy executives who had trouble balancing the demands of their jobs with anything else. Throwing money instead of time at a problem was a pretty common reaction. It didn't mean Sonya's problems fell into the "case from hell" category. Despite what she'd told Marie about her sister.

Sonya was working for a tech company—intense pressure came with the job. How bad could her case be?

The main phone line was ringing as I opened the office door. Which was unlocked.

There was no sign of Marie. Gritting my teeth, I dashed across the room, nearly tripping over a chair in front of Marie's desk—where had that come from?—and grabbed her phone.

"Hello?" I said. "O'Grady Investigations."

"Barbara? I need to see you. Now."

"Sonya?" I said. "Is that you?" Her voice was so ragged with some emotion that I couldn't be sure.

"Yes. It's me. Can you see me?"

"Where are you?"

"Downstairs."

"Yes, of course. Come on up."

Forty-five seconds later my door opened and Sonya rushed in. She must have run up the stairs, all seven flights. The elevator isn't that fast. And she wasn't even out of breath. Her suit was still perfect, as was her makeup. But her expression was distraught.

I'd come around the divider to meet her at the sound of the opening door. Now I led her back into my "office" and gestured towards one of my vintage leather guest chairs.

There was still no sign of Marie. Which was probably a good thing. Sonya looked like she needed the privacy. "What's wrong?" I asked her.

"She's gone!" she said. Glaring at me as if I'd had something to do with it.

"Gone? Who's gone?" And what did she mean by gone? Dead?

"My sister," Sonya said, her breathing choppy. "My younger sister. She kept telling me she was in trouble. And I did know something was very wrong. But I didn't do anything. I did try to tell you, yesterday. I should have told you. But my job..."

I opened the middle drawer and pulled out a box of tissues, put it on the desk in front of her, just in case. My brain was racing and she had my full attention. Her sister was in trouble?

So Marie was right.

And Sonya hadn't even mentioned her sister to me yesterday.

But I'd given her an out—that phone call—when I should have pushed her harder. Usually my instincts click in when clients are avoiding telling me something important. That's when I start pushing them.

Now I was wondering how I'd missed it this time. Is that what having time to focus on painting every morning did to me? Made me lose my edge as a P. I.?

After two days? Wait a minute.

"Sonya, calm down," I said sharply. "Take a deep breath. Then tell me what's going on. Slowly. I need details if I'm going to help you. What happened?"

"I've been tied up in meetings all morning," she began.

It was only quarter after ten. I wondered what time her day had started if ten-fifteen counted as all morning.

"I called her—my sister—a couple times," Sonya said. "Between meetings, I mean. She never answered, and with the way things have been with her lately—well, I was worried. Like anyone would be. And annoyed, too. I didn't have time for another disruption in my day."

She paused, drew in a breath that hitched as if she had something stuck in her throat. "And it had to be nothing, didn't it? But I rescheduled my next meeting, and went over. To her place, I mean."

Sonya's choppy sentences and disjointed thoughts were far from the polished professional woman I'd seen yesterday. It told me just how upset she was. But not why.

"And?" I prompted her.

"And she wasn't there," Sonya said, her voice cracking. "She was gone."

Please tell me this wasn't another kidnapping case. I couldn't handle another kidnapping case, not so soon.

"What are you afraid has happened to her?" I asked, keeping my voice neutral with an effort of will.

"I don't know," she said. It came out choppy, almost harsh. She sounded like she wasn't getting enough air.

Clearly I needed a different approach. "Why did you go to check on her? What are you worried about?"

"She has been talking wildly," Sonya said. "Sounding unlike herself."

I started taking notes. "What kind of wild?"

"She talks about threats, a conspiracy. Talks about being afraid, of 'them' finding out about her."

"Them?" I asked. "And who are they?"

"That I wish I knew," Sonya said. "She has never really said. I tried to get her to talk, but she would not. Once she said she didn't want to put me in danger too."

There were so many things wrong with that statement I didn't know where to start.

So I started at the beginning. Where I should have started the day before. I was going to be kicking myself for that failure for a long time.

———

"WHAT IS YOUR SISTER'S NAME?" I asked Sonya.

"Anna. Anna Lang."

"Do you have a photo of her?"

Sonya nodded, and pulled a photo out of a snakeskin wallet. The edges weren't even creased.

I glanced at it. Anna Lang looked to be in her mid-twenties, with shoulder length dark hair, solemn brown eyes under well marked brows and a very bright smile.

"How old is she?"

"Twenty-four."

"And is she married?" I asked.

"No," Sonya said with a slight frown. "She is single."

"What kind of work does she do?"

"She works at an art gallery. Over on Granville Street. Zanthus."

I knew it well. Very high-end, had been around a long time. Most of the art they showed was very modern.

The Zanthus Gallery had a reputation for spotting talent in up-and-coming artists and showcasing both the art and the artist. Combined with an impeccable sense of what would sell well both locally and internationally, the gallery was both high profile and highly profitable.

Then it registered. This was another case connected to the art world?

I suddenly recognized a question I should have asked the previous day. "How did you choose my agency?" I asked her. "Did someone refer you?"

"Margaret, the co-owner of the Courtland Gallery," Sonya said. "She's a friend."

And the woman expecting me to deliver another ten paintings in time for the solo show of my works she was putting on in September. I wondered if Margaret knew that a case this confused was guaranteed to cut into my painting time when she made the recommendation. I was guessing not.

Not that I didn't appreciate the vote of confidence. But her timing sucked.

"And does Margaret know Anna?"

"Of course."

Reminding me yet again what a small town Vancouver can be, for all its growing international status. And when you're involved in the art world, it's even smaller, and more tightly knit.

I'd never met Anna Lang, though. Not that I remembered, anyway. Of course, I've been pretty out of touch with the art world over the last few years, since my focus was on my second career. You know, as a P. I.—the one that paid the bills.

Fleetingly, I wondered if my upcoming one woman show might change all that.

Then I wrenched my focus back to the case, annoyed at my own lack of focus. Anna's disappearance might have something to do with the art world, but then again it might not. It was far too early for me to make assumptions.

And I couldn't afford to any more distractions. Trying to get paintings ready for my show was already enough of one.

"When did your sister start talking about threats and a conspiracy?"

"Maybe six, seven months ago," she said. "It wasn't much at first, just the occasional hints she would drop. As if she couldn't help herself."

"What happened next?"

"She started looking—worried, I guess is the best word. And tired, as if she wasn't sleeping well. When I asked her about it, she said it was nothing. And she was distracted. I'd be talking to her, and she wasn't really paying attention, as if she was preoccupied with some concern of her own."

"But she didn't tell you what was going on?"

"No. Just dropped a few details, here and there. Nothing helpful. I could see how worried she was, though. And that worried me. It's not like her to worry like that. Anna has always been light hearted. Oh, she'd laugh it off at first, and then later—it was as though she wanted to talk, but kept stopping herself. And she was afraid."

Sonya tightened her lips and laced her hands together, gripping them tightly. "I could see her fear. I think that was the worst of it. I could see her fear, and she wouldn't even admit it to me. But the more I asked about it, tried to probe, the more afraid she got."

"So your questions made her more afraid?" I asked. "Were you getting too close to something?"

Sonya shook her head. "No, the opposite. That's when she said something about it not being safe for me to know, and tried to change the subject. She wouldn't talk at all."

"And did she ever say what the threat was? Did it relate to her work at the gallery? Or something else in her life?"

"She never said."

"You must have some sense of what she was worried about?"

"Nothing. She wouldn't tell me anything concrete."

"Did her habits change? I'm assuming she was still working at the gallery the whole time?"

"Yes, she was. In fact, she got a promotion."

"A promotion? At the gallery?"

"Yes. She had been a sales associate. They promoted her to assistant manager. It was a job she'd been angling for a long time. But—she didn't seem pleased. She just looked more tired, and more scared. Every time I saw her."

There was something there, obviously. "When was she promoted?"

"I think—eight months ago."

I'd have to follow up on that. "When did you last talk to her?"

"Last night. But she broke it off short, without really telling me anything. And she didn't sound right. That's why I was so concerned about talking to her this morning."

"And when you went to her apartment? Was there any sign of a struggle?"

"No. Only her usual mess."

"Did it look as if anything was missing?"

She blinked at me. "No, I don't think so. I didn't really look."

"So you don't know if she'd taken any of her clothes?"

"No. I never thought to check."

"Then why are you so sure she's gone?"

"Because her phone is off. She never turns that thing off. And she told me she'd be working from home today. She had stuff to catch up on."

"And she's not answering her calls?"

"No." It was nearly a wail.

"Does it go to voicemail?"

"Nothing. She must have turned voicemail off, because there's no message at all. It just keeps ringing."

Who did that, turned voicemail off? Someone on the run.

Or worse. "Did you try texting her? Or emailing?"

"Both. When I couldn't even leave a voicemail, I sent both," Sonya said.

"And?"

"And nothing. No response at all."

This wasn't sounding good. "Maybe she lost her phone

somewhere."

"Then why is voicemail off?"

And that I didn't have an answer for. "Good question. What was she working on? Do you know?"

"No idea."

"And was there any sign of files or anything else she might've been working on? Did it look like she'd been interrupted?"

"No, I don't think so. But I was so upset Anna wasn't there—I didn't think to look. And she still wasn't answering her phone. "

"Was her phone there?"

"I don't…" She paused, squinted a little as if picturing something in her mind. "No. No, it wasn't."

She still could have lost her phone. Or turned it off for some reason her sister didn't know. "Did Anna leave a note? Email or voicemail on your phone?"

Sonya's eyes went wide. "I'm so stupid," she muttered as she pulled out her phone and scanned rapidly through it.

"Nothing," she said. And she sounded defeated. "No voicemail, no text or emails."

She drew in a deep breath, visibly composing herself. "And I didn't see a note at her place, but…" She shrugged one shoulder apologetically.

But she'd been frantic. Too frantic to think straight. Marie had been right about that. Which struck me as very out of character for this lady.

"Then we'll start with her apartment, see if you can tell if anything is missing," I said. "Do you have time now?"

"No. But I'll call in and reschedule everything for the rest of the morning. My sister is more important. And I should have taken the time to help her earlier. I knew I should have. And I didn't," she said quietly, almost to herself. "I just didn't."

I felt for her.

"Then we'll need to get your contract signed," I said, taking it from the folder where I'd stuffed it the previous evening.

I hadn't been prepared to sign it then. I was now.

CHAPTER FIVE

ANNA LANG'S APARTMENT ON COMMERCIAL and Eleventh in East Vancouver was untidy, but it looked lived-in, not tossed. What furniture there was, was either well-maintained vintage—and not the expensive kind—or up-cycled with high-sheen paint in primary colors. Big windows caught the sunlight, and intensely white walls didn't detract from the few large abstracts carefully displayed on feature walls.

I looked more closely at the art. Really nice abstracts, in fact. I glanced at the dates. All of it was early works of artists that were now garnering acclaim.

She must have bought them when the artists first showed at Zanthus. Or maybe she'd gone to art school with them. She had a good eye for promising new artists.

No wonder she'd been promoted.

Anna Lang either had a very good mentor, or a fine-tuned appreciation of what made art sell. I glanced at the dates again. And she'd been making good choices for quite a while.

But it had taken her employers four years to promote her. I wondered why.

While I was thinking about art—and searching the small desk in the hallway between the living room and the bedroom—Sonya was slowly wandering through the apartment, looking at everything.

"Have you found a note?" I asked her, while taking another look at the small painting over the desk.

Not an abstract, this one. A small village, somewhere tropical—but you knew you were looking at the aftermath of war. It was powerful…

"No." Sonya said, but her tone caught my attention. She'd regained her professional demeanor on the drive over, but her terse answer told me at what cost.

"I don't see anything missing, either," she said after a moment. "And her phone definitely isn't here. Even the charging cord is missing."

It was an astute observation. "Check her closets," I said, and followed her into the bedroom.

The grass green chest of drawers might be old, but it had beautiful lines. And the piece's glossy new color tied in beautifully with a riveting abstract on the opposite wall.

I glanced at the signature and nodded. I'd thought so. A very early Jayson Ho abstract, still showing faint traces of his false start in realism. She'd been buying art for quite a while. And my opinion of Anna's art sense had just gone up several notches.

Her small closet looked full, the clothing I could see mostly black, and tight-fitting. I'd have to ask Sonya for a list of Anna's friends.

And I needed to talk to Margaret Courtland. Who would undoubtedly nag me for more paintings. I didn't need the distraction, but I did need whatever information Margaret might have on Anna. And if I was disconnected from the local art world these days, Margaret was my polar opposite. If Anna's threats and conspiracies were somehow connected to the art world, Margaret would have heard about it.

Sonya had bent over and was tossing things out of the bottom of the closet. Her sister seemed to have used it as a catchall for anything that didn't fit elsewhere. After I'd watched the flight of what looked like several seasons worth of boots, shoes and bags, I gave in. "What are you looking for?"

"Her suitcase," Sonya said. "Anna has both a small suitcase and, I think, a large tote bag that she kept in here."

"They're both gone?" I asked, my interest sharp. Maybe Anna had run?

But from what? Or should that be from whom?

More boots and shoes came flying out, followed by three more black handbags. Finally a much less immaculate Sonya emerged.

"I think they're both gone," she said. "I can't find any sign of them. And Anna never throws anything out. Says she's not making enough money yet—and that odd combinations make great outfits. She's probably right about the first, but we'll never agree on the second."

I looked from Sonya's edgy designer style to what I could see of Anna's wardrobe. She was right about that. "So what else might be missing? Can you tell?"

Sonya stood up, ran a hand through her short hair and smoothed her suit. Expensive tailoring fell obediently into place. She looked immaculate again.

I've never been a fan of suits, but if I had one that good, I'd probably wear it all the time, too.

She walked to the dresser, started going through drawers. "I don't know everything, but Anna doesn't actually own a lot of clothes." She waved a hand at the bulging closet behind her.

"She just doesn't have good storage. I've told her it's worth the cost, but as you can see, she doesn't often listen to me." She looked irritated.

"It shouldn't be hard to see what's missing, though." She banged open a few drawers, muttering to herself.

It felt like a familiar pattern, an argument the sisters had played through many times. I suspected Sonya was losing herself in it now to escape from the fear that had been consuming her earlier.

"There's underwear missing, enough for three or four days, I think," she said at last. "Some t-shirts, a couple pairs of jeans. Her favorite ratty jacket. Black leather, naturally. A couple of baseball caps and maybe some scarves. An old pair of Doc Martens. That's about it."

She looked up at me. "Thank God. She isn't dead. She's gone into hiding."

I suspected she was right, but couldn't let the statement go unchallenged. "What makes you say that?"

"Because the clothes she's taken are ones she rarely wears since she started work at Zanthus. Maybe on an occasional Saturday when she's not going anywhere. She says they no longer fit her image."

"You said she's had her eye on the assistant manager position for awhile. Is that why she changed her image?"

"I suspect so. It happened not long after she started work at the gallery."

"So she's going back to—or at least assuming—a version of herself that existed before she joined Zanthus?"

"Yes," she said, leaning forward. "I hadn't made that connection. And I should have. Because it means she's hiding from people at the gallery."

That was one possibility. But it wasn't the only one. And it was way too early in the case to be making assumptions. "Why?"

Sonya gritted her teeth in frustration. "You mean why is she hiding from them? I have no idea. And I seem to be saying that far too often."

"No, I mean why does her choice of clothing mean she's hiding from someone at the Zanthus Gallery?"

Sonya looked startled. "I—well because she's going back to a former persona. Hiding the person her colleagues at the gallery would know. Doesn't it follow that's who she's running from?"

Right. I'd have to ask Cory a bit more about what kind of games Sonya's company specialized in. "Did she ever say anything concrete that might have led you to believe that? Any details? Or a name?"

She thought for a moment. "No," she said slowly. "I can't think of a single specific."

"So you don't know anything for sure?"

Her lips tightened. "I know she was afraid. But no. Nothing concrete."

"Have you any idea where she might go?"

"No. I wish I did," Sonya said. She looked a little calmer than she had earlier. "But at least she chose to go. She wasn't taken. Or killed." She choked a little on the last word.

"Does she have a car?"

Sonya shook her head. "No. She takes the bus."

Not much to go on. "Someone must be looking for her, for her to have vanished like this. Who?"

"I don't know."

She had to know something. "You have to admit, taking only clothes she won't be recognized in and leaving with no word to anyone is a pretty desperate move."

Sonya looked away.

Uh oh. "Sonya? What did I get wrong?"

"Well, she might have left word. Just not with me."

"With who then?" I demanded.

"With James. Her best friend."

"And have you called James today?"

"No. I haven't."

"Why not?"

"He won't take my calls," Sonya said. "I'm hoping he'll talk to you.

Well, at least I had a lead. And a lot more questions.

"I'll need his contact info," I said.

———

JAMES KOWALSKI AGREED to meet me at a nearby coffee shop at eleven. The Urban Grind is a local favorite, with lots of communal tables. Students with their laptops mixed in with entrepreneurs of various types in hurried conversations on their smart phones or bent over their tablets. There was a low-level buzz of conversation, and the air was rich with the smell of good coffee.

I spotted James immediately. Mostly because he was the only one there wearing all black, and sporting a trendy haircut. Art World R Us. He looked up and saw me in the same moment, raised a hand in greeting. I wondered if I looked like a P. I. to him. Or maybe this was "his" coffee shop, and the others were all regulars.

"James?" I asked.

He nodded, gestured me to a chair.

"Thanks for meeting with me," I said.

"Yeah," he said, dismissing it with a funny wave of his hand. "You mentioned Anna? Have you heard from her today?"

I felt my stomach tighten. "You mean you haven't?"

"Not since last night."

"What time did you speak with her?" I asked.

"I didn't," he said. "She left me a bunch of texts and a couple of voice messages. By the last one she sounded really frantic. But I had my phone turned off. Didn't check it until I got home at two this morning."

He shrugged. "By then it was too late to call. And this morning, she'd turned her phone off."

His best friend sounded frantic and he thought it was too late to call? What was with this guy? "What time did Anna's last message come in last night?"

He frowned. "Just a minute."

And pulled out his phone, flipping through screens with practiced eases. "That one was a voice message. And just after ten."

"How long after?"

He gave me an odd look, but answered. "Seven minutes after. Why?"

I ignored the question. "Did she say what she wanted?"

"No, she didn't. Just for me to call her."

"And were you worried about her?"

"Yeah. It wasn't like her. And with her situation at work…"

Now we were getting to it. "What situation at work?"

"She'd been seeing some things there that made her nervous. Though she was never specific about exactly what she'd seen. I'm guessing she'd found some anomalies in the books."

He shrugged again, a quick impatient movement. It seemed to be a sign of nerves with him. "And after she was promoted it got worse. She started to wonder if she'd been given the promotion just to shut her up."

"This was at Zanthus?" I asked, just to be sure.

He nodded.

"And you believed her?"

"I believe she saw something. And I know it worried her. But the art world…" His thin shoulders rose and fell. "Well, it's like any business. Most of them are honest, but everyone cuts corners. And some of those corners are shadier than others."

"Anna didn't see it that way?" I guessed.

"No, she didn't. She's light-hearted, a lot of fun. But she can be a bit of an idealist. She'll learn."

I hoped she had the chance.

Wait a minute. I had only Sonya's fears to suggest that Anna was in any real danger. And Sonya was her big sister. It's a big sister's job to worry. As I knew all too well.

"Anna seems to have disappeared," I said. "Do you have any idea where she might have gone?"

"Gone? Did she run?"

Now why would he assume that? "I was hoping you might know."

"Me? Why me?"

Interesting. He'd twice answered a question with a question. Did he really not know, or was he hoping to distract me? "According to Anna's sister, you're her best friend."

He managed to look flattered and appalled at the same time. "Really? Me? Sure, we talked all the time. We are in the same business."

Seeing my blank look, he said, "I work at a gallery too. We like to talk about what's going on. And there's never any shortage of industry gossip to share."

I could just imagine. "But you didn't talk about your own life?"

"Oh sure, all the time. But not the really deep stuff, you know? And she wouldn't tell me anything concrete about whatever it was she was worried about at her gallery."

"Why not?"

"Professionalism. Anna takes most things lightly. But when it comes to her work, she's a real professional. She'd never tell me anything specific about their business practices. But I could see it eating at her more as the weeks went by."

"I'd like to listen to the voice messages she left you yesterday," I said. Hoping he'd agree. And that I could hear something in them that he'd missed.

James frowned. "I'm sorry. I already deleted them."

"Even though she sounded frantic? You didn't think they might be important?"

He shrugged. The mannerism was beginning to annoy me. "No. Sorry. I have a cheap phone plan—only saves up to three voice messages. Deleting them is a habit for me."

I wasn't sure I believed him, but I let it go. For now. "Do you have any idea what might have spooked her yesterday?"

"No."

"What about where she might have run to?"

"I wish I did."

"Is there anyone you can think of she might have run to? Anyone she's close to?"

"Not her sister, that's for sure."

"Why not? Didn't she trust Sonya?"

"Oh sure, she trusted her. But Anna felt judged. And she wanted to prove herself so badly. If she felt any of her choices and her actions were at fault in whatever she was worried about, there's no way she'd tell big sister."

Yes, I could see that. I had only James' perspective on all of this, of course, but that definitely rang true.

My younger sister Susanna was much the same.

And we're so different, she probably had a point. I'd never have made some of the choices she makes. And she's pretty vocal about what she thinks of some of mine.

But I often wished I could protect her from some of the consequences of her choices. Futile, I know.

"Anna was oddly protective of Sonya at the same time," James said. "She'd never have told her something that might put her in danger."

That caught my attention. "You think whatever she was worried about could put someone else in danger, too?"

His lips twisted. "I think she thought that. But I'm just guessing here, remember? From the very little she did tell me."

He'd still only half answered my first question. "Who else might Anna have gone to?" I asked again.

He pursed his lips. "I can't think of anyone."

"What about her other friends?"

"Sorry, can't help you there. Like I said, we were work friends. Not the real kind."

Interesting distinction. "Thanks for your time. And please let me know if you think of anything." I handed him my business card.

I still wasn't sure how much of the truth he was telling me. Or what he might have to hide, if anything.

So far, I was no closer to finding Sonya's missing sister. Or understanding what it was she had run from. I needed to know more about Anna, and where she fit in the art community.

It was time to talk to her employers at the Zanthus Gallery. But first, I needed to talk with Margaret Courtland. Much as I'd like to avoid it.

CHAPTER SIX

MARGARET COURTLAND WAS PLEASED TO see me. She showed me into the large, sunny front room of her gallery, which was being painted for its next show. And our conversation started off pretty much the way I'd been afraid it would, with her asking how the paintings I still owed her were coming along.

I was thankful I could tell her that I was making progress, and that I was confident I'd have them finished in good time for her to get them framed for the show. All thanks to Marie, though I left out that part.

I didn't tell Margaret I had my fingers crossed, either.

She had to break off and deal with her sales associate about the exact color to paint one wall, and where she wanted a spotlight to go. Then she turned back to me. "But what can I do for you, Barbara?"

"You referred Sonya Lang to me, I understand. Which I appreciate, by the way." Mostly, anyway.

"Oh, yes. And you're welcome, dear. I've been impressed by your professionalism."

"Oh. Thanks." I felt oddly embarrassed. Probably because I didn't feel like I was exhibiting anything of the kind as an artist.

But I was there as a P. I. "Sonya hired me because she's worried about her sister, Anna Lang. I have a few questions I hope you can answer about Anna."

"I don't know how much help I can be…"

I was on familiar ground now. "Just tell me what you know about her."

"Not a great deal, actually. Anna came to the gallery often as a student, and really paid attention to the shows, and to the few nuggets I was able to tell her."

"You must see a lot of students coming through." Including me. Which thought I buried as soon as it came up.

She laughed a little at that. "Yes. I do, indeed."

"But Anna seems to have been memorable?"

She looked thoughtful. "Yes. You notice the interested ones."

"Oh?"

A nod. "So many are focused on themselves—what their art is, or isn't, how to make it better. It's rare to find artists at that stage of their career who can truly appreciate other artists."

She paused, thought about it for a moment. "And are prepared to listen to opinions other than their own," she added tartly.

I had to laugh. She'd nailed it. "Guilty as charged," I said.

"Oh not you, dear. You were one of the better ones," she said.

That was nice of her. But it was Anna I needed to know about now. "And Anna?"

"She was rather exceptional. Not necessarily as an artist. She was a bit of a slow developer, there. Though I'm very interested in what kind of artist she'll be five or ten years from now, if she continues to develop her own art. As I hope she will."

I knew where this was going. "You're saying Anna had an eye for promising work by others." I wondered if she'd tried to hire Anna.

"Well, yes. But that's not really what I meant."

"No?"

"No. Anna had a sense for where an artist, or a school of art, even, fit into the history of art, the development of it. She was developing an ability to spot the wrong turns well before the critics did."

She was? "Anna would have made a good academic, then?"

"Oh, not at all. Far too dry for her. In fact, I can think of few things worse. No, Anna's understanding was more dynamic than that. I suspect her skills would see her end up running a very high end art gallery or a significant museum."

Huh. That wasn't at all what I'd expected to hear. "Why?"

"She had a fear of debt, especially student loans. She apparently knew a few too many artists too buried under their loans to practice their art."

Smart woman. "And Anna herself? What do you think of her as a person?"

"Oh, she's delightful. Though almost too principled, too honest, for the world she's chosen."

Got it. Did that have something to do with why she'd run?

"Have you heard from her recently?" I asked.

"No, not in several weeks," Margaret said. "Why? Is something wrong?"

"She may be missing. But only since this morning, so it may be nothing. Please keep it to yourself."

At Margaret's nod, I continued. "Any idea where she might have gone? Or why?"

"No to both, I'm afraid. But if she has disappeared, she would have had good reason to do so, I'm sure."

"Disappear? You think she left of her own choice, then?"

"Well, of course."

"What makes you think so?"

"She's a very strong minded young woman. And an independent one. If she is missing, I can only assume that she has reason to be so."

"Not that something might have happened to her?"

"She hardly lives a risky lifestyle," Margaret said. "And Anna is an astute young women, for all her naiveté on certain topics. I'm certain she would have made a rational decision to disappear for a time, for her own good reasons."

This struck me as distinctly odd. I wondered what she wasn't saying. And what she knew. "Did she ever say anything that might suggest what those reasons could be?"

"No, I'm afraid not. I wish I could be more help," Margaret said.

"Have you heard any rumors about Zanthus that might suggest there were problems there?"

"Of course not." She looked a bit annoyed with me. Why? Did gallery owners not gossip about each other?

"Or anything else in Anna Lang's life?" I asked.

"Not a thing." While her voice was still polite, her attention had clearly shifted to the work that was being done behind us.

And that appeared to be that. While I had the distinct impression that Margaret knew more than she was saying, I couldn't think of anything I hadn't asked. And she had clearly said all she was going to.

For now, at least.

So I thanked her for her time, and left. But I made a mental note to check back with her when I could ask more pointed questions. And to check Margaret's perceptions of Anna herself—which struck me as oddly idealized, given how hard-headed Margaret tends to be—against those of others who might have known Anna a little better.

Starting with Anna's employer.

———

THE ZANTHUS GALLERY was located on South Granville Street, along that section known as Gallery Row—seven good to great art galleries spread along a four block stretch. Once a cutting-edge gallery known for finding edgy new artists and launching their careers, Zanthus has been around so long now that it's firmly part of the establishment.

Those formerly edgy young artists are now the acknowledged

masters, but Zanthus has never lost their knack for finding the best of the hot young artists. Everyone who is anyone in our small world marks Zanthus launches on their "must-see" calendar.

The building's architecture reflected cutting edge design—in the 1970s. It still held up pretty well, all white concrete with huge show room-style windows, and cleverly angled skylights that bathe the public areas of the gallery in natural light, while still protecting increasingly valuable paintings from sunlight.

Inside everything was white or neutral—walls, ceilings, floor—except the paintings, which were explosions of color carefully spaced along the walls for maximum impact. The rooms were spacious with plenty of room to stand back and truly feel the impact of each painting or sculpture. The gallery was quiet, with that hushed feeling you only find in churches, good museums and really good art galleries.

Their salespeople were good, too. You knew they were there, but they were careful not to come between the potential client and their contemplation of the art.

The sales desk—a large uncluttered expanse of white quartz—was discreetly located at the back of the first big room. There were no cash registers or Visa machines in sight, nothing so mundane here.

Transactions now took place on smart phones equipped with the latest and safest security technology, handling large dollar transactions and relieving wealthy collectors of their money quickly and discreetly. There would be printers hidden somewhere for the inevitable paperwork.

I did a quick tour of the two large rooms, just because I was there, and I hadn't seen this artist's most recent work. It was amazing. But I had a job to do.

As I walked towards the back of the room, I noted that there were three sales associates visible, all black clad with trendy hair-cuts. Two seemed to be male and the other female, but I wasn't entirely sure. The androgynous look is popular again.

I knew that the manager's office was tucked in behind the sales staff, but there was no sign of him. When I identified myself to the tallest of the sales associates, and said that I'd like to have a word with the manager, he barely blinked. Just accepted my business card and vanished behind a partition wall, returning moments later with a lanky, well-tailored man in tow.

"Barbara O'Grady," Don James said as he came forward with an outstretched hand. "What a pleasant surprise. I haven't seen you in years."

"Don?" I said in surprise. "I didn't know you were managing here."

Don and I had taken a number of the same art courses during the five years of my fine arts degree. I'd liked him.

He'd grown up poor, was there on a scholarship and worked harder than anyone I'd met, but sometimes he seemed overwhelmed. Talented but a bit naive, he'd struggled with the politics of the art world.

I guess he'd found a way to deal with it.

Since those days I'd painted for a few years while temping in various offices to pay the bills, before turning a long-term assignment at a security firm into a permanent career by studying for my private investigator's license.

Don, on the other hand, had painted on the side while working in a couple of different galleries. I'd heard he was doing quite well, but then he fell off my radar.

Probably around the time I stopped painting, come to think of it.

Now I had an upcoming show, and here he was, manager at Zanthus. It was quite a coup for him. Though maybe not so much if James was right about Anna's concerns about the gallery.

Those concerns didn't match with the Don I remembered. Still, I hadn't seen him in nearly fifteen years. A lot can change in that time.

And James' impressions weren't necessarily accurate. Or true.

"I've been here just over a year now," Don said. "But what can I do for you?"

That long? I'd really fallen out of touch with what had once been my world. Now it was coming back to haunt me.

"I have a few questions about a case I'm working," I said. "You've heard that I'm a P. I. now?"

"That's right—I'd heard that about you."

"Is there somewhere more private we could talk?"

"Of course," he said, leading me towards his office in the back.

I glanced around, curious. The last time I had seen this office, the previous—and long-term—manager had been here. The furniture had all been Danish modern, but there was a lot of it and the room had felt crowded, stacked with papers in crazy piles.

Magazine articles and reference books with everything from paperclips to torn strips of paper stuck in them to mark a relevant section had cluttered every available surface. It had smelled of stale cigarette smoke, despite a high-end air purifier that ran constantly. I'd found the smell off-putting and the white noise distracting.

Now the office felt clean and spacious, and smelled faintly of lemon. It had been freshly painted a flat white. There was no paper in sight, and the magazines were neatly stacked on an angled bookshelf that looked like it was floating on air.

The desk was a slice of honed white marble without drawers, and it had nothing but a large screen iMac sitting on it. A large Jayson Ho abstract in greens and gold covered one wall.

Don waved me to a round white table in one corner. "Have a seat. But what's this about?"

"You have an employee named Anna Lang?" I said, watching him closely as I sat down. The sculptural wire mesh chairs were actually comfortable, which was a surprise.

"Anna? Yes, we do—our assistant manager. She's a rock star," he said with enthusiasm. Then he made the connection, and gave me a worried look. "Has something happened to Anna?"

He glanced at his watch. "She is running late, but not by much. She's normally here by now, though."

I looked at my own watch. It was past one, and the gallery had opened at nine. "She doesn't open the gallery for you?"

It was common practice to have the assistant manager open the gallery, leaving the manager free for meetings and such. And, I'd always suspected, to sleep in.

"No. I'm a bit of an early bird, so it works for me to open the gallery in the morning. Anna does the closing, and stays on afterwards to finish off any urgent paperwork for the day."

Interesting. "So you are expecting her in today."

"Yes. Is there any reason I shouldn't be?"

He didn't look or act as if anything was wrong. Was it possible that Sonya was simply over-reacting? And that James was imagining the worst from the—admittedly little—information Anna had given him?

"I don't know yet. Her sister is concerned about her," I said. "When did you last see Anna?"

"Last night," Don said, with no apparent hesitation. "We had some business to discuss, so I stayed on and we met for about an hour after the gallery closed."

Which would have been before the messages that James said Anna had left him. Too bad I only had James' word for that.

Not that I necessarily believed James was lying about those voice mails—but I did want to know why he'd deleted them. I made a mental note to check into his phone contract. "And after the meeting?"

"Anna said she had somewhere to be, and left."

"She didn't say where she was going?"

"No, and I didn't ask. It was none of my business."

It sounded like he didn't encourage closeness with the people he managed. But he hadn't needed to tell me that. So why had he?

Perhaps he only wanted me to think he kept a distance from his employees? Especially if Don turned out to be the last person who'd seen Anna. "What time was this?"

"Seven? Probably just shortly after."

"You didn't leave together?"

"No, I had some work I wanted to finish. She got her coat and her sunflower umbrella, and gave me a wave as she left."

The umbrella was a nice touch—a sunflower umbrella created an immediate visual image. A strong one. And it had been raining last night.

I hadn't seen a sunflower umbrella in Anna's things. She probably took it with her. Which might help people remember her.

But a sunflower umbrella? It struck me as both too cheerful and too clichéd—it didn't fit the image I'd been forming of Anna. And Don was an artist, or had been one, anyway. He knew the importance of visual symbols.

Enough to invent a sunflower umbrella to lend a sense of truth to his statement? I wondered. Wishing that my over-developed suspicions didn't keep landing on people I liked.

"What was Anna wearing yesterday?" I asked him.

"Wearing?" He stared at me. "I don't know. Why would you ask that?"

I was getting tired of people who didn't know anything. "Just bear with me for a moment. Shut your eyes and just picture the last moment you saw her. Was she in a suit? Wearing yellow, to match her umbrella?"

Don gave me a strange look, then did as I asked. "Yellow? No, she was wearing black, just like usual. Boots, straight skirt, black sweater with some kind of zipper things everywhere."

For an artist, he didn't have much of an eye for clothing styles. I made a note. "Was she carrying anything? Besides the umbrella?"

"Umm… she has one of those small, flat purses. Black. With zippers."

"No tote bag? Or gym bag?"

"No. Nothing big like that."

If he was telling the truth, Anna must have gone back to her apartment sometime after she left work. Which probably cleared Don. Unless he was lying, of course. "Thanks, that helps."

"It does?"

"At this point, even small details can be important. Anything you can remember," I said. "Did Anna have any time off coming to her? Or any vacation days booked in the near future?"

"No to both. She's dedicated, doesn't take much time off. And we're too busy now, in any case. I rely on her, and couldn't spare her right now if I wanted to—I can't afford to."

I made another note, then passed him my card and stood up. "Thanks, Don. Please call me if she comes in, or if you think of anything else."

"I'll do that," he said, reaching the office door before I did and opening it. "I'm sure it's nothing, and she's just running late this morning."

"I hope you're right," I said. Though I knew he wasn't. Anna had already packed and gone. And I was getting a niggling feeling that something was very wrong indeed. I hate it when that happens.

"Don't be a stranger, Barbara," Don said as he saw me out.

CHAPTER SEVEN

I WAS OUT OF LEADS.

I went back to the office, opening the door with some trepidation. But all was quiet.

It actually looked pretty good, with the small reception desk facing the door, and the privacy screen hiding my larger, messier desk. But there was no sign of Marie. Again.

Dealing with my temporary assistant's inconsistencies—not to mention her abysmal business practices—made my head hurt. I put the coffee on, then checked my emails. There was one from Cory, which seemed to mostly consist of links to various gaming sites.

It looked like he had fun doing the research on Xtreme Systems. I clicked on a couple— mostly reviews and specifications on various games. Those could wait.

But there were also a couple of links to financial sites, from when Xtreme Systems had gone public. I clicked on those first. And they gave me a pretty good overview of the company's structure.

Down at the bottom of the email, Cory had added a comment. "Seems like Xtreme Systems is in pretty good shape," he'd written. "And their stuff sells like hotcakes. But I think their structure is kinda weird. I know a couple of their programmers, from online games. Want me to see what I can find out?"

It was probably irrelevant, given what I'd learned that morning. There seemed to be no connection between where Sonya worked and her missing sister. But you never knew what was going to be useful in an investigation. And what could it hurt?

"Sure. But be careful. Don't dig too deep," I sent back.

Thought for a moment. Added, "And can you look into the Zanthus Gallery, too? Who owns them? How solid is their business? Who do they work with?—which artists, and which galleries? Same cautions as with Xtreme Systems."

That should do it. I hit send.

———

I WAS JUST ABOUT to pour my coffee—finally—when I heard the outer door open. A client?

I used to be able to see visitors from anywhere in the office. But now I couldn't see who it was around the privacy screen. And Marie wasn't there to greet them. This just wasn't working.

Schooling my features into what I hoped was a pleasant expression, I went to greet the visitor. But it was Marie.

"Finally. And just where were you?" I asked her.

"Where were you?" she countered.

We were so not doing this. I kept my gaze steady on her.

She glared at me from eyes ringed with long green eyelashes. "I had to register. For my class."

"You mean you really are starting art classes?" I said.

She nodded. "Told you I was."

She had. I hadn't entirely believed her. But it was good news—the sooner she started seeing herself as an artist, the sooner she'd stop trying to pretend she was an investigator.

The irony of that thought didn't escape me, but I ignored it. It wasn't enough to distract me, either. "You can't just go out and leave the office empty for half the day. And you didn't lock up."

"No. Ms. Lang said she was coming in. I told her I'd leave the office open for her."

I was almost at a loss for words. "You can't just leave this office empty…

"But it wasn't empty," Marie said. "Ms. Lang was here."

"Not yet she wasn't. And you can't leave a client—any client—on their own in the office, either. That's even worse. Not only is it bad customer service, she could potentially have access to all our files. Which are confidential."

"But our file cabinets are locked."

"Yes, but those are not the most secure locks in the world," I told her. "And it's simply bad business. Don't do it. Ever."

"Fine," she said. "I won't. Is there anything else?"

I held onto my patience with both hands. "Did you at least spend some time in the office this morning?"

"Of course," she said. Frowning at me with an injured air.

"And?" I said.

"And what?" She looked at me as if I was making no sense.

I wasn't the one with the problem. "Were there any messages? Any new clients. Anyone come in?"

"Oh," she said. "Let me see." And pressed the play button on the answering machine before I could stop her.

There were four messages. Two of them from Sonya, sounding increasingly frantic. The other two were previous clients, asking me to get in touch.

Marie looked at me. "Oh," she said. "I guess I should have listened to those first thing, right?"

I held onto my temper through an act of will. Yelling at her was not going to help. But she was done here. "Yes," I said in a very level voice.

Too level, apparently.

"I can't just sit here with you towering accusingly over me," Marie said as she leaped up. She skirted her desk to stand inches away from me.

"Look, I know I'm screwing up," she said, so fast the words

almost ran together. "And that it doesn't look like I know what I'm doing. I'm a fast learner, honest. And I need to do this."

She put her hands on her hips and scowled at me. "And you need the help, whether you want to admit it or not."

I wasn't listening to this.

She gave me a shrewd look. "You're not buying this, are you?"

I didn't answer. But apparently I didn't have to.

"How much painting did you get done this morning? Before you came in?" she asked. Then went in for the kill. "And how did that feel?"

It had been a gift. A real gift. And clearly, she knew that.

"Okay, fine," I said. "You get one more chance. But you have to at least pretend you know how to work in an office. You can't just vanish. You can't do things whenever you happen to feel like it. Not if I'm going to stay in business."

She muttered something under her breath. I caught the words "office work". Obviously she wasn't a fan. I couldn't blame her—I wasn't either.

But that didn't mean I'd let her run my business in to the ground. "I mean it," I said.

"Fine. So now what?" she asked.

"So now I'm going to return those client calls," I said. "And you're going to stay here, and do your job. The job you asked for."

"What about Sonya?" she asked.

"I've already met with her," I said. "The investigation is underway. If Andrea or Cory calls, please put them through."

"Underway?" She said. "Is that all you're going to tell me? If I'm going to work here, I need to know what's going on."

I just looked at her.

"So I can help you," she said belligerently. Even she knew that was a little weak, because she didn't meet my eyes as she said it.

"You'll need to prove yourself first, I said. "Investigations are confidential."

And I wasn't letting her anywhere near them. Not until she proved I could trust her.

And I didn't think she had it in her, good intentions or not.

CHAPTER EIGHT

HALF AN HOUR LATER, I walked through the door of the Omega Gallery. A fruitless twenty minutes reviewing my notes on the Lang case had convinced me that I needed to dig up some new leads.

Ian Wong seemed pleased to see me. If he was surprised, he didn't let it show, coming forward with outstretched hand and what for him was a big grin.

"Barbara, how nice to see," he said. "I'm surprised you have the time—I hear you're very busy preparing for your show."

It was a bit of a dig. After I'd signed with the Courtland Gallery to do a show of my new work, Ian had got in a few sly comments about how I hadn't even considered showing with his gallery.

Which had stunned me.

I had no idea that he'd even be interested. And in fact, from what I knew of Ian, if the Courtland hadn't offered me a show, I'm not so sure he would have been interested.

But he was now. I had to shove back a little bubble of pride. This meeting was about Anna Lang.

The missing Anna Lang.

"I'm actually here on business," I said.

"Painting business?" he asked. "Or investigative business?"

"Investigative, I'm afraid," I said.

"Oh, don't be. Your investigations are always interesting. And the last one netted us some lucrative new business."

He gestured me towards his office in the back. "Perhaps you'd prefer to talk in private? But first, would you care for an espresso?"

He'd said the magic words. "I would indeed."

He raised an eyebrow towards a discreetly hovering sales associate, then ushered me into his sleekly functional office. In short order we each had a small but fragrant cup of espresso steaming in front of us, and one of his sales associates was gently closing his office door behind her.

"So how can I help you?" he asked.

"I'm looking for anything you might know about the assistant manager at the Zanthus Gallery," I said.

"Anna Lang?" he said, sharp surprise coloring his voice. "She's a lovely person—and an ambitious one. I suspect she'll go far."

He sipped his espresso. "She has all the right instincts," he added. "And she knows her stuff. I, for one, would hire her in a heartbeat."

Coming from Ian, that was high praise indeed.

His chin thrust forward in a gesture I'd seen him use before when he'd found something interesting. "But why are you asking? Is something wrong?"

"She seems to be missing," I said, downing my espresso.

"Missing?" Ian's voice had gone very smooth. He leaned back in his chair, sipping at his espresso.

What was this? I tried to read his body language. Was he pretending he didn't care? Distancing himself from whatever was going on? What?

"Yes. She seems to have left town last night, and no-one knows where she is," I said, watching his face closely.

"Maybe she needed to get away for a bit." His expression gave nothing away.

"She was due to work at Zanthus this morning."

"Ah." He finished his espresso, then reached over and tapped a few buttons on his desk phone. "I'm sorry to hear that. But I'm not sure why you've come to me about it."

I wasn't either. It had been a gut instinct, and, I was beginning to think, a good one.

The news about Anna Lang's disappearance had thrown the usually imperturbable gallery owner, and he was working too hard to hide it. Ian knew something.

Now I just had to get it out of him.

———

"I WANTED to get a feel for what the latest word is on Zanthus," I said, choosing my words carefully. "And with your connections, Ian, you are the person who is most likely to know."

"Why me?" Ian asked.

"Because from what I've seen, you have the broadest knowledge of what goes on in Vancouver's art world, especially at the other galleries. And I was hoping you'd share a little of that with me now," I said. "Anna's family is very worried about her."

"I'm afraid you'll be disappointed," he said, "As I don't know nearly as much as you're suggesting. But I'll help you as much as I can."

He paused, rubbing his smoothly shaven chin absently. "Zanthus has been around for quite a while, and they're very well established. And well-regarded."

He glanced at me. "As you already know, I suspect. In any case, Anna did well to take a position there, and very well to earn her promotion so quickly."

"Even though you say she has an eye for which new artists will sell? Isn't that like a license to print money for a gallery?" I asked, curious.

He nodded. "Even so. It is not so rare as all that, and the training she would have been getting at Zanthus was worth a great deal."

Which probably explained why sales associates are paid so little.

It was regarded, at least by the gallery owners, as a sort of apprenticeship. But one with no assured graduation to the next level.

"So?"

"So she should have been looking for a promotion in another year or so. Most likely at another gallery, since there was little room to move up once they hired Don."

I gave him a surprised look. "Are you suggesting you interviewed her? For a position here?"

He nodded.

"When?"

"Two weeks ago."

Wait a minute. Two weeks ago?

Before I could frame my next question, the same sales associate as earlier appeared with two fresh cups of espresso. She put them in front of us, cleared the empty cups and vanished without a word.

So that's what he'd been tapping on his phone. I wasn't sure if I was impressed or appalled by that level of service. But I was glad of the caffeine. This was going to be a long day.

After a grateful sip of the smooth black brew, I looked up and met his gaze. "You said she should be looking in another year or so. Was she ready to make this move?"

"In my estimation, no."

"So you turned her down?"

He was too savvy to show any reaction to my question, but he didn't kick me out, either. Of course, the second espresso suggested that he might not have, anyway. I wondered what he wanted in return.

"Not exactly. She was most impressive."

"You're telling me you hired her?" I asked.

"Not exactly."

"What then?"

He smiled. "Patience, Ms. O'Grady. We were in the process of discussing various options. Just between you and me, Anna wanted to leave Zanthus. Quite badly, it would seem. I wanted to hire her, but not into a position above her current level. And I have no opening for an assistant manager. So it was an ongoing discussion between us."

I focused on the first part of his statement. "Anna wanted to leave Zanthus? And badly?"

"Oh yes. Quite badly, as I said."

"Did she actually say so?" I asked.

"Not in so many words. But we both knew what we were talking about."

"And what was that?"

"Zanthus was no longer the place for her."

"Why not?"

"Again, she didn't say." He sipped his espresso, considering me from behind the tiny cup with an amused look. "But I could speculate, if you like."

I gave up. This was going to be played his way. "Please do."

"Do you know Don James?"

"We're acquainted," I said.

"Mmmm. Acquainted? It sounds as if you know him rather well."

He ran an assessing eye over me. I would have been more irritated if I'd thought he saw me as anything other than a 3D painting.

"You are rather his type. Though I gather he isn't yours?" He quirked a carefully shaped eyebrow at me.

This wasn't where I'd expected the conversation to go. "No. He isn't," I said. No hesitation at all. He'd polished up some, but he was still the same Don.

"He wasn't Anna's either."

Wait a minute. "He made a play for her?" Was this what Anna had been concealing from her sister?

"So I gather. And implied her choice could affect her career."

"I see." Yes, he'd be in the power position. The scum.

This wasn't the Don I remembered. But then it had been a long time ago. "Did she tell anyone else?"

"She didn't exactly tell me," he said smoothly. "Though I rather doubt it. She was very professional—and very careful—in what she said and didn't say to me. Leaving me to read between the lines, as it were. And I doubt she would have said more to anyone else."

"I wonder if she'd been applying elsewhere," I said, mostly to see his reaction.

He shrugged one elegant shoulder. "I rather doubt it. She gave me the distinct impression that I was her first choice."

The woman was good. "Do you think she would have run to get away from Don?"

He frowned. "No, I don't. If she was that desperate, she would have accepted my offer."

Interesting. Something else was going on then?

"And what were you offering?" I asked. Other than keeping her in an associate's position as long as he could get away with it.

I was under no illusions about the career path for those working in art galleries. It was why I'd taken a position as an office temp to earn money while I tried to build a career, rather than working in a gallery. The pay was much better, for one.

And it came with less attitude.

"That's confidential," he said. "But I would have promoted her quickly enough. I like to test my people."

Uh huh. I wondered how they felt about it. "And Anna knew that? That you'd hire her immediately, but on your terms?"

"Of course," he said. "And she was determined to negotiate for her own terms. Even if it took longer."

He gave me a sly smile. "It was one of the things I liked about her."

I could imagine. And she'd probably thrive here, if she was that good, and didn't hesitate to stand up for herself. I'd noticed before that Ian respected people with talent and strength.

Not necessarily in that order, either.

"Was it entirely Don's behavior that made her want to leave Zanthus?" I asked. "Or were there other things happening there?"

"Other things? That's a very broad category," he said. "Can you be more specific?"

"Not at the moment, I'm afraid," I said, letting his assumption that I knew more than I did stand. "What can you tell me?"

"She didn't say much. Oh, there were a few hints thrown out, but nothing I could say for sure. And nothing that would suggest she might run."

Right. "And did those hints fit in with anything you already know about Zanthus?" He had to know something, surely.

But I was wrong. Or he was being discreet.

"No," he said blandly. "They don't. I wish I could be more help. Anna really would be an asset here. And she'd grow a lot more quickly here than she ever will under Don's management."

He seemed to mean it.

"I have to find her first," I said. "Anything you might think of about Zanthus's practices or her employment with them would be a help." And I handed him my card.

He accepted it with a funny little nod, and showed me out.

"Find her, Barbara," he said as he turned away. "She's too good to lose."

CHAPTER NINE

AS I WALKED OUT OF the Omega Gallery, I glanced down Granville Street towards downtown and the North Shore mountains towering behind it. Rush hour was in full swing, lines of brake lights in both directions. No honking horns, though—a blessing which still surprised me. When had honking your horn at the idiot in front of you become rude behavior?

Standing still, I'd become an obstacle to pedestrians striding towards home, as well as to those racing to catch a bus. I stepped back out of the way, and glanced at my watch. Nearly six.

And I was only a dozen blocks or so from home. The idea of going home and immersing myself in my current painting was overwhelming. I could probably finish it in another three, four hours.

But so far I'd gotten nowhere on Anna's disappearance. I didn't know why she was running, or where she might have gone.

Pulling out my cell, I called Sonya. "Have you heard from Anna?" I asked when she answered.

"No, not a word," was the answer. "Have you found anything?"

"Not much," I said. "And so far I've found nothing that suggests she didn't leave of her own choice."

I could hear Sonya's indrawn breath. "Kidnapped? You think she might have been kidnapped? What would make you think that?"

I stifled my irritation. "I just told you that I don't think that. It's generally a remote possibility, and nothing points to it in this case."

But it isn't something that can be ignored, either, when someone disappears. I didn't tell her that. Sonya was already panicking enough.

"So what can I do?" she asked.

"Have you filed a missing person's report yet?"

"No I haven't," she said. She sounded more shocked than I'd expected. What was that about?

"You're already looking into it," she said quickly. "And I thought I had to wait forty-eight hours before I could file, anyway?"

That probably explained the shock. But I still wondered if there was something more behind her reaction. In cases like this one, you never knew.

I'd learned to be cautious. The hard way.

"They likely won't act on it any sooner," I explained. "But you can at least file it now. Unless there's some reason you'd rather not do so?"

"No, of course not. I'll go there as soon as I get off work."

"Tell them you've hired me to look into it, too. And let me know if you hear anything," I said and disconnected.

Then I headed for my car and back to the office, my mind made up. There was no way I could shift back to painting yet.

———

AS I CLIMBED the stairs to the seventh floor, I expected my office to be dark. But all the lights were on and Marie was still at her desk. Which surprised me.

She looked surprised to see me too—and so she should, given that she was going through a stack of files.

"And just what are you doing?"

"Familiarizing myself with how you work," she replied, just a hint of snippiness in her tone.

If I hadn't been trying to set a good example—which was going to get old really fast, I could tell—I would have rolled my eyes. "Those are confidential."

"Which is why you had me sign a confidentiality agreement, remember?"

Definitely snippy. I decided to ignore it. For now.

"Fair enough," I said. "Let me know if you have questions. Were there any messages?"

She seemed taken aback that I hadn't taken what had obviously been bait. I wondered who she usually played that dynamic with. Her sister Celeste?

"Andrea Fisher called. And your nephew."

"And?"

She handed me the pink slips. "Andrea said she'd call back. Cory just muttered something."

I glanced at the two messages—yup, that's exactly what they said. Well, being literal was a useful quality in an assistant, right?

"Thanks. And Marie? I'm not your sister, I'm your boss. Try not to forget that," I said.

And enjoyed her stunned expression far too much as I walked back to my desk.

Then I picked up the phone and called Andrea. Who answered on the second ring.

"Andrea Fisher here," she said crisply. "Oh, Barbara. Can you hold on a second?"

She must have someone with her, judging by the formality of her words and the murmur of voices I could faintly hear. Andrea had a bad habit of holding the handset against her shoulder instead of just putting a call on hold.

One day it would backfire on her, when a caller managed to overhear something she didn't intend them to. But she wouldn't listen to me.

I put my own phone on speaker and began entering the notes I'd made in my last few meetings.

"Okay, I'm back," she said before I'd finished. "I gather you're returning my call?"

I picked up the handset and cancelled speakerphone before Marie could hear any more, while wondering if I'd ever get used to having an assistant of any kind in the office. Not that I needed one.

"You gather right." I said. "Have you got something for me?"

"Not a great deal," she said. "Xtreme Systems uses our services all the time," Andrea said. "They're great clients because they want the best staff available, and don't care what it costs them. And they pay on time."

"Mmm. Cory told me they went public. Presumably that makes things easier?"

"Not exactly," Andrea said. "Now they're under incredible pressure to produce effective products with impressive results before investors get tired of constant losses and the bottom drops out of the share price."

"A lot of pressure, then."

She laughed. "You got it. And it's why they'll pay a lot for my temps. The place is a pressure cooker to work in—long hours, and insane expectations—and if you want good people to keep coming to work and keep producing, you have to pay them."

"And you get your cut," I said.

My mind was turning over what she'd said, and thinking about my client. Sonya Lang worked in that environment, and obviously thrived there, judging by her current position. No wonder she'd been in such a rush to get back to her office.

But under that kind of pressure, how would she have dealt with a younger sister who was having problems she refused to talk about?

Ignore her until it was too late? Judging by her panic earlier, that's what Sonya thought she'd done.

I'd give a lot to know what Anna thought.

Doodling idly on a blank page in my notebook, I considered Ian

Wong's odd reaction to the news of Anna's disappearance. He'd seemed neither shocked nor worried by the news. As if he'd half-expected her to do something like this.

I had to wonder. Was this case really a case at all? Or was I dealing with a high-tech star who was close to burnout? And a younger sister who didn't tell big sis everything.

"Barbara? Are you there?" Andrea was saying.

Apparently I'd been thinking about that one a little too long.

"Have you ever dealt with Sonya Lang?" I asked Andrea.

"Not directly," she said. "I know who she is, though. And she'd need to hire programmers, not support staff. But I've placed my people in her department."

"And?"

Andrea paused. "You're asking for a lot of information. It's going to cost you."

Of course it was. "What is it this time?" I asked with a fake sigh.

"I haven't seen much of you lately," Andrea said.

"I've been busy," I said.

"Busy," she said slowly. "Like you're the only one. But I return your calls…"

"Don't you think this is a little juvenile?" I said, glad she couldn't see my grin.

"It's the only way we get to spend much time together, between your job, your painting and your boyfriend."

I hated that she was right, but I was having enough trouble just trying to juggle work and painting, never mind romance or anything resembling a social life.

People who thought living a balanced life was possible were deluding themselves. "Okay, what do you want?"

She laughed. "It's not that bad. I'm thinking cocktails. I hear the Meridian has a new bartender, who is quite the talented mixologist."

Which was hardly a sacrifice, but no way was I admitting that. "As a bribe, that's a pretty good one," I said. "Since I'd rather go to Luigi's, and I prefer to drink red wine."

I had to put up at least a token resistance.

"Stop whining," Andrea said. "You need to get out of your rut once in a while. If you want the information, then you and I will be enjoying cocktails on Friday night. Unless you're already seeing Nick then?"

"Nope. I'm seeing him tonight."

"Then you have no excuse. I'll see you on Friday."

"Fine, then," I said. "But I get another question."

"Done," Andrea said, a laugh in her voice. "You have a pen ready?"

"Of course. Now give."

"Sonya's department is supposed to be a great place to work, not least because she demands a lot and pays even better. The programmers are good, really good. They expect a lot of my people, and rely on their temps to provide the structure so they can focus on programming."

"Sounds like a lot of stress on the lady in charge."

"I've never met her," Andrea said. "What's she like?"

"She's…" I started to say, then remembered she was a client. "I wouldn't know," I said.

"Uh huh. So what's your other question?"

"Have you heard anything about the Zanthus Gallery and their current manager, Don James?" I said. I'd known Don at university, but I didn't think Andrea had met him then.

"We haven't done any work with that gallery," she said. "But his name rings a bell. Let me check and get back to you."

"No more bribes," I said in a warning tone.

She laughed, as I'd intended.

"And thanks, Andrea."

"Anytime. I'm looking forward to Friday."

"Me too," I said.

SO HOW GOES it with your new employee?" Nick asked.

We were sitting at our favorite table at the Heaven and Earth Curry House in the slightly less pricey section of Kitsilano—huge, old style menus and decor, wonderful food. And lots of space between the tables for a private conversation. How could we resist?

In answer I crossed my eyes and stuck out my tongue. He laughed that deep laugh of his. I grinned back at him.

"Let's just call it a work in progress, shall we?" I said. "Although she did bring in a new case today."

"Well, that sounds helpful…" he said, watching my expression. Waiting for the punch line he knew was coming.

"One who is likely to be a far worse client than Marie ever was."

"Ouch," he said, reaching over and topping up my glass of house red. "Well, at least it should keep things interesting?"

"That's one way of putting it," I said, and proceeded to fill him in on the complexities of Sonya's case, leaving out any details that might identify her.

I trust Nick implicitly, but we both work in confidential businesses. We've worked out a kind of shorthand that lets us talk about our cases in a way that allows the other to give helpful feedback, without giving too much away.

I'm amazed, sometimes, how much I've come to rely on that outlet. Especially for the difficult cases.

You know, the ones I'm supposed to be avoiding while I get my show together.

"Why do I get the feeling I'm not going to be seeing much of you over the next few weeks?" Nick was saying.

"Past history?" I suggested. "We do have a tendency to get involved in cases that take most of our time and attention, both of us. But somehow, we manage to keep seeing each other."

I raised my glass in a mock toast. With a grin Nick clinked his against it.

"True that," he said.

There was a pause while the server brought our order—steaming plates of chicken vindaloo, seafood in red curry, chana masala, daal and fragrant rice. It all smelled amazing, and I was suddenly starving. We passed dishes and heaped our plates.

I was just tearing off a section of warm naan bread when Nick put his fork down and looked at me. "I think I have a solution," he said, in a too casual voice.

"For eating these mounds of food we seem to have ordered?" I asked, glancing at the still-half full serving dishes. "We always do this, you know. Order too much."

"And somehow we always manage to eat it," he said. "Even if it's for lunch the next day. But Barbara…"

And there was a note in his voice that made me nervous. I tried to change the subject. "Maybe we should just order double portions of everything in future. Cut out the shopping and cooking part for days."

"Maybe we should live together," he said in the same tone.

I looked at him in shock. "What?"

"Look, we both have crazy schedules. Sometimes we barely see each other for weeks on end. If we lived together, at least we'd see each other every day, even if it's only in passing."

I stared at him in shock. "We'd only see each other in passing most days. And not even that some of the time," I managed to say as I struggled to process what he was asking.

He reached for my hand. I gripped his, tightly.

"I love having you in my life, Barbara," he said. "I'd like more of that."

Leaving me with nothing to say.

And no coherent thoughts in my head. Just the frantic feeling that it was too soon, I wasn't ready. And I didn't want to lose what we had.

Or change it.

But Nick is coming to know me too well. "We don't have to talk about it now," he said, squeezing my hand. Then releasing it to top up my wine again and his own.

"Just keep it as a possibility," he said. "We'll know if the time is right."

Yeah, like I was going to be able to stop thinking about it, now that he'd stuck it in my head. I grabbed for my wine glass, my mind finding distraction in the full, rich taste and the red depths the low lighting brought out.

"So, what's happening with the Murder Squad?" I asked.

He laughed at my nickname for the task force. Raised his glass to me. And accepted the change of topic.

Is it any wonder I love the man?

Even I have trouble admitting it.

CHAPTER TEN

THE FOLLOWING MORNING WAS CRAZY. Nick had spent half the night wordlessly convincing me that we should live together. I woke up tired but upbeat, and nearly told him yes during our joint shower.

But somehow we ran out of time…

By the time I got to the office, I was feeling better than I had since this case started. I'd even managed to squeeze in half an hour to sketch an idea I'd had for a new painting—the next in the series. It wasn't quite ten as I opened the office door, so I felt like I was caught up, despite the late start. Good thing, too.

I stepped into pandemonium.

Marie was standing behind my desk, yelling at my nephew Cory—what was he doing here?—the phone was ringing, the printer was beeping.

And Sonya Lang stood in the middle of the chaos muttering into her cell phone, a look of panic on her face. Who was she talking to?

And why was she here?

At the sound of the door opening all three of them swung to face me. Sonya waved me away and focused back on her phone, while Marie and Cory converged on me, both talking at once. I stopped dead and held up my hand.

"Not now," I said firmly. "Marie, get the phone. Cory, can this wait?"

He shook his head.

It figured.

A glance at Sonya told me she'd be occupied for a bit.

"Can you shut that printer up?" I said to Cory. "Then come into my office and you can tell me whatever it is. And then get back to school, before I get another call from your mother."

He gave me a sheepish grin, and hurried to solve whatever problem the printer was having.

Suddenly it was silent, except for Sonya's low tones as she talked into her cell phone. With a silent sigh of relief, I strode to my desk. I'd just managed to get organized when Cory hurried over.

"Aunt Barbara, there's something wrong at the Zanthus Gallery," he said quickly, hovering over my desk. He seemed to be trying to get the words out before I stopped him and sent him back to school.

Usually he'd have been right. But this I needed to hear. "Wrong?"

"They aren't showing any of your paintings, are they?" He sounded worried.

"No. But what kind of wrong?"

"Not sure," he said. "Everything looks fine. Their press releases say they're doing better than ever. But they doesn't seem to have booked as many shows for this year as they did in any of the last three years. I don't know much about the art world, but that doesn't make sense. At all. Does it?"

"No. It doesn't," I said, waving him to a chair. "Show me. But quickly."

He pulled out his laptop.

———

WHEN CORY HAD LEFT some fifteen minutes later, I stared at the notes I'd made. He'd been right about there being something off at Zanthus. And I couldn't figure it out either.

Not only were the number of shows down, but they hadn't yet announced the big name shows for next year. Which was odd. Usually those were booked, and announced, well in advance.

As assistant manager, even though she'd been recently appointed, Anna would definitely have been aware of the change. Maybe even concerned about it. But it shouldn't have led to her disappearing.

Even if she'd asked Don some questions, she wasn't at a level that should have mattered to him.

Had it?

I'd have to figure out who to talk to. Obviously it wasn't going to be my old buddy Don James. Not yet, at least.

That was when I heard the sound I'd been waiting for. Sonya made farewell-type sounds and her low-voiced conversation ceased. I stood up and walked around the privacy screen to intercept her before she headed for the door.

"We need to talk, Sonya," I said.

"Later. I have to get back to the office," she said. "I've been away too long as it is."

"Did you Skytrain here?" Our largely elevated rapid transit system was usually the best way to get downtown on a weekday. Except when it wasn't.

She nodded. Downtown traffic and parking being what it was, that didn't surprise me.

"This won't take long," I said. "I'll walk with you." Which was no hardship—it was a sunny May day, Vancouver at its best.

Sonya looked like she wanted to argue, but what could she say? She set off towards Chinatown Station with a ground-eating stride, which I matched.

"What is it you want?" she asked. "Your assistant already told me you have no news of Anna."

How helpful of her. Not.

"No, but we are making progress," I said. "I've spoken to a number of Anna's colleagues, and I'm beginning to wonder if her disappearance might be linked to something other than her work. Was there any other area of her life where she was frustrated or upset? Even afraid?"

"No. It is as I told you. She only talked about her work."

"Did she talk to you about her personal life much?" I asked.

She drew penciled brows together. "No. She is very private."

"I see. How often did you see your sister?"

"We had lunch or dinner once a month, most months. We were both very busy."

For some sisters, that was pretty good. Though I saw Susanna more often than that, and I wouldn't have said we were close. Not anymore.

We stopped at the light on Beatty Street. "Do you have parents still living? Or other siblings?" I asked carefully.

"No siblings. Our parents are in Germany," she said. "I haven't seen them in some years."

"And Anna?"

She gave a strained little laugh. "Oh, she went home last summer. She said she enjoyed it."

I wondered what the story there was. And if it mattered now.

"Could Anna have gone to visit your parents now?" I asked her, keeping my voice low enough not to be overheard.

Not that any of the other pedestrians were paying any attention to us. Most of them were in business attire, and judging by their focused expressions either late back to the office, or in the middle of a critical call on a headset.

She looked taken aback. "To Germany? I suppose it is possible. But why would she? And without saying anything to me?"

"If she thought she needed to vanish for some reason, would she go to your parents' home?"

"Maybe. Few people know about them—neither of us talks much about the old days. But why would she want to vanish? If that is even what she's done."

"It's certainly one possibility. You have to admit that."

She pressed her lips together in a stubborn look, but said nothing. I ignored her and pressed on. Chinatown Station was in sight, and I was running out of time. "Do you know where she kept her passport?"

"No. I suppose it would have been hidden somewhere. I didn't see it."

I hadn't either. "Does she travel under a German passport or a Canadian one?"

"It could be either. She has both."

Interesting. "If Anna did decide to vanish, you still have no idea what might have driven her to it?"

She shook her head.

"Or if she might have confided in someone other than James or yourself? A girlfriend? Boyfriend?"

"No. She is very private. She tells me only of her work life. No more."

I wondered why the two sisters lived such separate lives. And why Sonya was estranged from her parents. But my time to ask questions had run out. I walked with her into the glass lobby, and stopped at the Skytrain fare gates.

"I'll let you know as soon as I have information on your sister," I told her. "And please let me know if you think of anything more."

She gave a quick nod and vanished into the throng. I had to be satisfied with that.

CHAPTER ELEVEN

SO ANNA HAD A GERMAN passport. I wasn't sure what, if anything, that told me. But I was sure Sonya's reluctant revelations were making my life more difficult.

Muttering under my breath, I grabbed a coffee at the new—and far too temptingly good to fit my budget—coffee shop on the corner, as well as an energy drink for Marie. Who seemed a little stunned that I'd brought it for her. And very pleased.

Apparently it didn't take much. Which reminded me of the harsh woman who'd raised her, and suddenly I was feeling empathetic towards Marie again. I'd probably pay for that.

She handed me my phone messages with no comment. I nodded my thanks and went back to my desk, glanced through the messages and went back to reviewing my notes. The ones that were getting me nowhere.

The phone rang and Marie put a call through to me before I could get too frustrated. Andrea's voice said, "I don't know how you do it, Barbara."

I had no idea what she was talking about. "Do what?"

"Find cases that are likely to threaten either your career or your health."

My best friend really does like a good story. But she usually restrains herself when it comes to my work. "Andrea. You aren't making sense. What are you talking about?"

She sighed. "Let me close my door."

That was a decidedly bad sign. I mentally ran through my current cases. Nothing there that should have set off red flags for her.

Over the phone line I could hear a door softly closing.

"You wanted any information I had on the Zanthus Gallery and Don James?" Andrea said.

I still didn't get it. "And…?"

"I don't have any notes on the gallery, but Mr. James is a different story. Him I had a separate file on."

Uh oh. Andrea doesn't set up separate files on very many clients. They have to be either really good, or really bad to earn themselves that kind of attention from my very busy friend.

"I didn't recognized his name at first," Andrea was saying. "Because when I knew him, he went by Jasper, not Don. He signed checks as D. Jasper James. And he was in a different industry. It took me awhile to figure it out. You owe me."

"Yeah, yeah. So what about Don?"

"He is seriously bad news," she said. "You need to stay away from him. A long way away."

This was my old art buddy Don she was talking about? My earlier conversation with Ian had already shaken my perception of the man he'd matured into, but this…?

"I need details, Andrea."

"I don't know if you know anything about this guy," she started.

"We took a few of the same art classes when I was in university," I said. "Then I lost touch with him."

"You and everyone else," Andrea said. "That's because he left the art world for a dozen years or so."

So had I.

"That's not so bad," I began.

She talked right over me. "Not now, Barbara. I don't have much time, and you need to hear at least the gist of this."

"Go on." I grabbed my coffee one hand, a pen in the other.

"Don James is dangerous. Slippery. He's one that will make sure nothing lands on him, no matter what the issue. If he has a conscience, I'll eat my file on him."

Fifteen years later she still had a file on him? I knew for a fact she only kept most of them eight years after they'd last done business. "You kept his file?"

"On this guy? Oh, yeah. None of my people were ever going to work for this guy again. Especially not if he'd had a few years to work on his M.O."

I'd rarely heard my friend so adamant. "Tell me."

"I don't know where he was or who he worked for between then and now, but about ten years ago he was at Bright Financials, working as an investment adviser. He hired a series of temps from my firm, including a personal assistant."

Uh oh. Given what Ian had said about Anna, I suspected I knew where this was going.

"I had to replace all of them. Several times," she said. "And these were some of my best people."

"Just spit it out, Andrea," I said. "I've heard a bit about his tomcatting."

"That's not it," Andrea said. "Well, it is, but it isn't the worst thing. He hung my people out to dry!"

"What? How do you mean?"

"Don James would do anything to make money, take any risk. And he made bad decisions all the time. Whenever he got called on it, he'd blame my people and get them fired. Different ones each time. Then come right back to me for a replacement. After the fourth time, I figured out what he was up to and gave him a warning."

"Let me guess. He didn't stop."

"The next person he fired, I refused to fill any more contracts for him. And he tried to blame that on me—told several people that

I'd been stalking him, and this was my response when he turned me down."

She sounded so aggravated that I had to bite back a laugh. It takes a lot to get Andrea this angry.

"I can see why you wouldn't work with him again," I said. "But that doesn't mean I should be wary of him. Lots of people blame everything they do wrong on someone else."

"I know," Andrea said, sounding more than a tad irritated with me. "But from what my people told me later, he was more con artist than adviser. A lot of his advice to his clients was borderline, if not outright illegal."

She drew in a frustrated breath I could hear over the phone. "Yet he was considered an up and comer at Bright Financials, and making very good money, from what I heard. Then suddenly he's gone, and no-one seemed to know why, or where he'd gone. I'm guessing he left one step ahead of the law."

Put like that, she had a point.

"I'll be wary of him. But he's a possible suspect, at best an information source. I doubt he's a danger to me, or my investigation."

"Until you start looking harder at him," Andrea said. "Then wait for it."

"Wait for what?"

"Whatever he'll do to make himself look good. It wouldn't surprise me if he hit you with a lawsuit."

"A lawsuit?" I repeated, not sure I was hearing right. "For what?"

"Anything he can think of. I saw how he works. Stay away from this guy, Barbara," she warned. "He's dangerous."

That hadn't been my experience, but Andrea knew people. It was her business, and her gift. That she still felt so strongly about what had really been a minor interaction more than a decade ago… It meant I had to add her perspective to my own on Don James.

"Just be careful, okay?" she said.

"I will," I promised, adding a few notes to my file on the case.

Now I really needed to know more about why Anna wanted to

get a job elsewhere. Ian had hinted Don was the reason she'd disappeared.

I wondered what had made her leave so suddenly. What had Don done? Threatened her with something, maybe? More than the obvious, I mean.

And why had Don taken the job at the Zanthus Gallery, anyway? Given what Andrea had just told me about his earlier career, it didn't make any sense.

"Has this guy asked you out yet?" Andrea asked. Her mind had obviously gone off on another tack.

No, but Don had made a point of inviting me back to Zanthus. "I hardly see…" I'd begun, when she interrupted.

"I knew it. Stay away from that man," she said.

"You know I'm still seeing Nick," I told her. "And very happily, too. I'm hardly likely…"

"You don't see him often enough," she said shrewdly. "Are you two okay?"

Concern in her voice.

I wasn't ready to tell my best friend that Nick had suggested moving in together. Despite how wonderful last night had been. Maybe because of it.

Truth to tell, I still didn't quite trust the way Nick made me feel. Jayson had been able turn my knees to water too, in our early days. And look how that had turned out.

Andrea, of course, would tell me I was being silly. I could hear her voice in my head—"You're comparing Nick to Jayson? Really?" I could even hear the exact tone she'd use. And she'd be right.

Which is exactly why I wasn't going to give her the opportunity. In real time, I'd lose the argument with her. And I wasn't quite ready to do that.

I needed a little more time to be sure it was right.

"Work," I said. It was all the explanation she needed. Luckily.

"Well, just avoid Don, okay?" Andrea said. "He's poisonous."

"And I'll treat him that way," I said. "You don't need to worry."

"Close this case fast, and I won't," she said. "And if you end up looking into him, whatever you do, don't let him find out about it."

Right. "Andrea, I know my job."

"And you think I'm over-reacting," she said, reading my mind again. "Fine, but I've never run up against anyone who is so good at twisting things to make himself look golden. And everyone else look like lead."

"I hear you," I said. Trying to remember what the young Don James had been like.

Enthusiastic and awkward was the way I'd remembered him. I'd helped him out a few times, when he was clearly out of his depth.

More than a few times, come to think of it. He'd just seemed so helpless. Had he been manipulating me even then?

No, I just couldn't see it. He'd been young. And hapless.

Which wasn't the Don I'd seen the previous day. The mature version of him was polished and confident. I'd been impressed at how far he'd come.

Even Ian's revelations hadn't tainted that view much. Because I'd remembered the eager young painter, in love with art, that I'd known then.

Andrea's warning was timely. Especially if Don really was a suspect.

At the moment, I still wasn't sure there was a crime. Just a missing person. Who might or might not want to stay missing.

"Thanks, Andrea. I'll pay attention."

"See that you do," she said. "Oops. I've got to go—client's waiting."

And she disconnected, leaving me thinking about the question she hadn't—quite—asked. What was going on with me and Nick?

And what answer was I going to give him?

———

THIS MORNING'S ENTHUSIASTIC "YES!" had morphed into this afternoon's caution.

Maybe Nick was right. Maybe it was time we moved in together. There were decided benefits. My lips curled up at the memory of those benefits.

But it seemed too soon.

And my current lifestyle suited me. I couldn't imagine how we'd combine our lives so that both of them would still work.

I pictured my apartment—barely big enough for me, when I had the second bedroom set up as a studio. I had good fans, and acrylic dries fast, so the paint smell wasn't bad. But painting took up a lot of space, and lately it had tended to overflow into my dining room when I needed a change of light. Or perspective.

How would Nick deal with that? Or my occasional all-night painting sprees. I don't know if he even knew about those.

Why would he? They never happened on nights he stayed over.

And where would we live? Neither of our places would easily accommodate two. I grimaced at a James Thurber-ish sketch of an apartment bursting at the seams I'd just drawn.

I was avoiding the real issue, and I knew it. But I wasn't ready to deal with it yet, either.

So I turned back to my notes on one Don Jasper James. Trying to make sense of them was easier than thinking about relationships. Unfortunately, it wasn't any more effective. There was too much I didn't know about this case.

Okay, then. I turned off the computer and grabbed my purse.

I'd been hired to find Anna. It was to do so.

CHAPTER TWELVE

MY FIRST STOP WAS THE URBAN GRIND, which happened to be six blocks north of Zanthus. Two of the sales associates I'd seen at Zanthus sat at a small table near the back, coffees and muffins in front of them. A third one joined them as I walked in. They obviously recognized me, too.

"Have you found her?" the trendy blond string bean asked, tugging a nervous hand through his very clean dreadlocks as I approached their table. "Do you know where she went?"

"Not yet," I said, sitting down and handing each of them one of my cards. "That's why I wanted to meet with all of you. I need a better picture of Anna and her work at the gallery. There may be things you know that will lead me to her."

"We don't know anything," the dark-haired girl said, her bangles clashing as she leaned forward.

"Tell me anyway," I said. "You may well know something that you don't think is important. But that detail might just help me find her."

"Fine. But you have to keep this quiet," the kid with the shaved scalp and strongly marked dark brows said. "Don would probably kill us."

"I'll keep your confidences," I said. "I promise."

They eyed me skeptically for a moment, then the guy with the dreads squinted at me. "I don't know your face," he said, as if that was a bad sign. "But didn't I hear Don say something about you having a show?"

"Yes. At the Courtland, in September."

The woman glanced at my card. "Barbara O'Grady," she read. "OMG! You're the one having a one woman show at the Courtland in September!"

Now all of them were leaning forward, and skepticism had changed to something like adulation. It made me uncomfortable. "That's right. Now, about Anna…"

It wasn't enough to distract them.

"But why don't I recognize you?" the guy with the dreads said. "I know every local artist. And you're local," he said accusingly, waving my card at me.

"Where have you shown?" the other guy asked.

I gave up. Clearly I was going to have to answer their questions —establish my artistic creds—before they'd tell me anything.

"I haven't shown before," I said. "Well, not since I did my degree."

"Fine arts?" the woman asked.

I nodded.

"And you haven't painted anything since?" she said with a squeal.

"Of course I have. Just not shown anywhere."

They looked at each other, glanced back at me. Leaned back in their chairs, putting distance between us. Now what?

"Just like Don," Mr. Dreads said. "He hasn't shown for years, either."

And if I was like Don they weren't going to trust me? Now we were getting somewhere.

"And where is Don showing now?" I asked quietly, making no move to close the distance between us.

"He isn't." The guy with the shaved head narrowed his eyes at me, as if to let me know he was onto me, and not falling for any tricks.

I narrowed mine back. "And have any of you seen his recent work? Any of it?"

They looked at each other, communicating wordlessly.

"No," said the dark-haired woman, looking back at me. "And I haven't heard him talk about his own paintings since he started at Zanthus."

"But you'd consider him part of the art world?"

"Oh yeah," the guy with the dreads said bitterly. "He's at every function, front and center. Schmoozing it up with the best of them. Everyone knows Don."

"But you don't know me," I said. Leaving them to draw their own conclusions.

It didn't take long.

"She wouldn't have an upcoming showing at the Courtland if she wasn't good," the second guy said to his coworkers. "The Courtlands have high standards."

"And I've watched Margaret Courtland go out of her way to avoid Don," the woman said. "More than once."

Three pairs of eyes turned back to me, considered me. I waited.

Which was hard. I didn't have time for this. Anna didn't have time for this.

But if I could gain their confidence, I'd be more likely to get the information I needed. On Don as much as on Anna.

Something was going on at Zanthus, and these three undoubtedly knew at least a part of it.

I needed to know what they knew.

———

AFTER WHAT SEEMED like forever the three of them stopped staring at me and looked back at each other. Then the dreadlocked blond, who seemed to be their spokesman, leaned forward. "I'm Drew," he said. "And this is Sharla and Ramon."

"Barbara," I said.

"What do you need to know?" Drew asked.

"Tell me about Don," I said. "Why are you so wary of him?"

Then before they could go back to glancing at each other, I said, "You can trust me to keep your confidences. I know the art world runs on gossip, but I don't."

After a sharp pause, Drew nodded. "Don hasn't been there that long, but he keeps making changes. Says he's determined to make his mark on the place."

"But some of what he's doing doesn't make sense," Sharla put in. "Not if he's trying to promote artists, anyway."

"Give me an example," I said.

She shrugged. "We had a show of Giardo's work last month. The sculptor?"

I nodded. "I like his work," I said.

Sharla leaned forward a little. "He's good, yeah? And we did all the usual stuff for him. The opening, the press. But something was missing."

"Yeah. Don," Ramon said with a heavy edge of sarcasm in his voice. "He was at the opening, all right, but nowhere near his artist."

They didn't much like Don, that was clear.

Drew was nodding. "We did what we could, of course. But Don's the manager. He's the one who needs to treat his artists like stars, needs to shine the spotlight on them. And he doesn't."

I was making notes as they talked, but something in Drew's voice had me looking up. "And you think you know why," I said.

"I pay attention," he said softly. His glance roamed the room. "And I notice people. That guy pretending to drink coffee over by the window? He's been waiting awhile for someone, and she's late. He's afraid she isn't going to turn up, and now he's wondering if he'd look stupider if he left now or kept waiting."

I glanced over my shoulder, assessed the guy he'd noticed. Drew was right. I turned back, gave him a quick nod.

He grinned.

"Wait, how do you know he's waiting for a girl?" Ramon demanded. "He could be waiting for anyone."

"He keeps patting his wallet, making sure it's there," Drew said. "He's probably planning on buying her coffee. Or lunch. Then he neatens his hair, and checks his wallet again."

"That's good," Sharla said. "Most guys don't notice stuff like that. Why do you?"

"I just watch the customers a lot," Drew said with a shrug. "If you want to sell art, you have to know which ones are buyers, and what they're looking for. Some are just looking, some are collectors, some are looking for status pieces, or to match their color scheme."

She was nodding. "And some really love it. That's good."

He ducked his head. "Thanks."

Drew was interested in Sharla. I glanced at her. And she hadn't noticed yet. Interesting. But it had nothing to do with why I was here.

I turned back to Drew. "So you notice things others might miss. What have you noticed about Don?"

"That he spends a lot of time with people who have nothing to do with the art world," Drew said.

"How do you mean?" I asked.

He shrugged again. "Well, at the opening Sharla was describing, he spent most of his evening with a couple of parties. One was two men, South American, I think, judging from their clothes and their accents. Ramon might know."

We all looked at Ramon, who looked startled, but nodded. "Sí. Probably from Colombia."

"And the other group was from Hong Kong. Smooth, expensively suited businessmen. Neither group were customers, nor were they people I'd seen before. And they had zero interest in Giardo's work."

"I noticed him with the Hong Kong group too," Sharla said. "They had money, you could tell. And a lot of our biggest buyers are from Hong Kong lately. But I'd never seen these three before.

She glanced at her co-worker, smiled slightly. "And Drew is right—they never once looked at anything on display. I wondered at first if they were in the wrong place. But Don talked with them for at least twenty minutes."

Drew nodded. "Exactly. It's out of character for who he pretends to be—the connected gallery manager who's focused on getting the best artists and putting on the best shows. You don't keep the best artists as clients by ignoring them and their sales."

"Was his behavior at that show unusual for Don?" I asked.

"No," Drew said bluntly. "It's how he works. He spends more time in his office than he does on the floor. And when he is on the floor, he spends more time talking to people who don't seem to have any interest in the work than he does anything else."

"So what is he up to?" I asked. "You must have some idea."

"No," Drew said. "Not really. I have some pretty wild guesses. Want to hear them?"

"Yes."

"They range from running some kind of non-art business on the side to using the gallery for smuggling or running drugs. But they aren't based on anything I've actually seen him doing."

"You're judging based on what he isn't doing," I said.

"That's it."

"And do either of you know anything that might argue for—or against—Drew's guesses?" I asked Sharla and Ramon, looking back and forth between them.

Both shook their head slowly.

"I wish I did," Sharla said. "But no. Nothing."

"Nothing," Ramon said.

"Did Anna say anything to any of you that might tell me why she's run?"

More head shakes, this time from all three of them.

"Did she confide in any of you? Sharla?"

"No," said Sharla. "I could tell something was bothering her, but she wouldn't say anything."

"She's too professional," Drew said, and Ramon nodded.

"Did she ever talk about Don?"

"She is too professional," Ramon said again. The others backed him up.

"She'd consider it gossip," Sharla said. "Once she was promoted, anyway."

"And before that?"

"Oh, before that Don was on his best behavior," she said wryly. "Besides, he promoted her pretty soon after he started."

But when I pressed them, none of them could—or would— tell me exactly what had changed.

"It's an atmosphere thing," Sharla said vaguely.

Time for another approach. "Tell me about the last day Anna worked at the gallery. What happened that day?"

"You mean Tuesday?" Drew asked.

"Yes. Tell me everything about Tuesday, from the moment you got to the gallery."

"It was a pretty normal day," Drew said. "We didn't have any artist meetings booked, and no big clients."

"Was it busy?"

He grinned at me. "It's always busy. We have an active website, and we ship a lot of stuff around the continent. There's always stuff we need to be doing. And the gallery itself needs to be kept spotless. Which isn't easy with that much glass, so we're always keeping an eye out for anything out of place."

"But there were quite a few visitors that day, too," Sharla said.

"Does anyone stand out for any of you?" I asked. "Any of the visitors, anyone else who might have come into the gallery."

They looked at each other, then shook their heads.

"What was the mood in the gallery that day?" I asked.

"Mmm, focused, I guess," Drew said.

"And how did Anna seem?"

"The same as usual," he said. "She was friendly—we work as a team, all of us. But she doesn't show much of what she's thinking."

"She is a good manager," Ramon said, and Drew agreed.

"So it was a normal day for all of you," I said.

Sharla giggled. "Except Don went out for several hours in the afternoon, remember. The gallery was empty. And we were all cracking jokes."

"What about?"

"I can't really remember," she said. "Nothing, really."

"Did Anna join in?" I asked, trying to get a feel for the missing woman.

"Yes, she did. She came up with a couple that had us in stitches," Sharla said.

"She has a wicked sense of humor," Drew said.

"She is very funny," Ramon said.

"And what do you remember Anna doing that day? What time did she come in? What did she do? Who did she talk to?"

"Ummm," Sharla said thoughtfully. "She got in at her usual time, around eleven."

"Isn't that late?"

"No, Don likes to open up."

So he'd told me, but it was good to have it confirmed.

"So how did her day start?"

"She met with Don for half an hour, like usual," Sharla said. "Then I think she was getting a shipment of new prints ready. Checking they were what we'd ordered, checking them against our current inventory, setting the prices, like that."

"She handled a couple of inquiries for possible large purchases," Drew said slowly. "Around lunch, I think. She'd brought her lunch, so she ate in the back room and worked on the sales from the previous day."

"The rest of the day she was either on the floor with us when we were busy, or phoning other galleries about works our clients were interested in," Sharla said.

"And Don?" I asked. "What was he up to all day?"

"Mostly in his office with the door closed," Ramon said. "We never know what he does in there."

"He did come out on the floor for an hour or so in the afternoon," Drew said. "After he got back from wherever he'd gone."

"And he was there when we arrived in the morning, of course." Sharla said. "He opens up at nine, because the first half hour nothing ever happens. We get there by nine-thirty, and stay until six."

"And Anna?"

"Stays until seven, or even eight. It depends how much paperwork there is to do, and whether Don wants to do a planning session."

I made another note. "Were any of you there when she left on Tuesday?"

"No," Ramon said. "She was planning to work late, I think, because she was going somewhere downtown at eight."

The other two nodded.

"Where was she going?" I asked.

Three blank faces looked back at me.

"She never told us. Anna kept her private life quiet," Sharla said. "She shared more before she got promoted, but after…"

"The professional thing," I said.

She nodded.

It made sense. It wasn't very helpful, but it made sense. "So when did you last see her?" I asked.

"She was on the floor at six when the three of us left," Drew said.

"You left together?"

Another round of nods. "We were going to the art gallery—the Mashup exhibit. It's free on Tuesday nights, so we often grab a bite and head down."

The Vancouver Art Gallery. They'd have video if I needed to check these three were telling the truth. "Anna never joined you?"

"Not once she was promoted."

Right. "Is there anything else you remember from that day?"

They exchanged glances, slowly shook their heads.

I gave up. Thanking them, I bought them another round of coffees. I took mine to go, and told them to call me if they thought of anything.

There was no point talking to Don James now, so I headed back to the office. Still feeling like I was getting nowhere.

CHAPTER THIRTEEN

WHEN I GOT BACK TO the office, Marie was diligently working away on—something. I nodded at her as I went by, making a beeline for my office. It just felt wrong to have her sitting there all day. No matter what I'd said about her being there to answer the phone.

I'd used a service in the past, and it had worked out just fine. But they hadn't been sitting across the room from me, watching my every move.

Still, it was only for another four months. And I could paint every morning. It was worth it. I could do this.

Trouble was, I didn't much believe it.

But hey. It was only week one. Things would get better, right?

Sure they would. Not. With a grimace, I turned my attention back to my case.

So far all I had was a worried sister, and a missing gallery worker. And a lot of people who didn't trust Don James. Basically, a whole lot of nothing.

So what was up with Anna? Had she vanished on her own, as it appeared? Or was there something more nefarious at play here?

If the sales associates' story was even remotely true, and not an exaggeration of annoyed employees, then it sounded like Don might be using the gallery as cover for something else.

Which could explain his sudden career shift, the one Andrea had questioned. And if Anna, working late, had seen something she shouldn't have…

She could be in real trouble. Even dead.

Except that supposition wasn't based on anything even resembling facts. And no one had even hinted that Anna was worried about something that big.

Well, except her sister. But Sonya's worries were surprisingly non-detailed. And I was beginning to get an odd vibration on the sisters.

Whatever their relationship was, it wasn't a close one. I wasn't sure how far I could rely on anything Sonya told me. Or said that Anna had told her.

I contemplated my notes for a minute. I had collected quite a bit of opinion, but very little in the way of facts.

Had Anna confided in no-one at all? It was certainly beginning to seem that way.

The ringing of my private line distracted me from my useless speculation.

"Barbara O'Grady," I said.

"Aunt B., we need to talk," Cory said. "Are you in the office?"

"Yes, but where are you supposed to be?"

He laughed. "Mom thinks I'm studying with my friend Jeff. I'll be right there."

And disconnected before I could protest.

My sister was going to kill me. If she found out, that is.

In the meantime, maybe I'd finally get some facts on Anna Lang.

———

I SHOULD HAVE KNOWN BETTER.

Twenty minutes later Cory was unfolding his laptop on the

other side of my desk. "You're going to have to see this," he said. "You'd never believe me if I just told you about it."

He swiveled the computer so I could see the screen, too.

I blinked. It looked like a mess of numbers, in no apparent pattern. "Is that code?" I asked.

"Way to go, Aunt B. Yup. Really old-style. Pretty great, huh?"

Not the word I would have chosen. "What am I looking at?"

"I have no idea," he said cheerfully.

Okay, then. "So why are you showing it to me?"

"'Cause of where I found it."

I waited.

He said nothing. Just grinned at me.

He might be some kind of computer whiz, but he was still a teenager. "And where did you find it?" I asked.

"Turns out your missing girl has a blog. And this was on it."

That didn't fit. No-one had mentioned that Anna was into programming. I hadn't even thought to ask if she had a laptop.

I'd never pictured the missing woman as a techie—everything about her home screamed old-school artistic. No reason the two interests couldn't be combined, especially these days.

But I hadn't even seen Wi-Fi at her apartment. Was she running a blog from her—currently missing—smartphone?

"Is it something she put there?" I asked.

"Doubt it. Too sophisticated. And everything else she had is all about art."

"So this was just posted somewhere on her blog?"

"Nope. It was hidden. I went a couple of layers deeper on her site. Which wasn't hard—there's not much there. She isn't a sophisticated user. But I did find this."

"So why was it there?"

"I've no idea. Yet. But that's not the really weird thing."

"No?"

He grinned at me, enjoying this game. "Nope."

"Okay. So what is?"

"I found something similar on her boss's site." And he was suddenly serious as he brought up Don James's blog."

"Wait," I said, putting a hand on his wrist as I peered at the screen. "This is the gallery website. Don does a blog there?"

"Yup."

"And Anna's blog? Is it on the same site?"

"No, and that's the weird thing. She has her own website. But if I click through to Don's blog..."

He did so. "I'm still on the gallery site. But then I look for that same funny symbol."

He clicked on it. "And I get this."

More code. "That looks pretty similar," I said.

"Nope, not really. But it seems to work the same."

"And does Don have a personal website?"

"Uh uh. Just this blog."

"And is Anna's website linked to the gallery site?"

He gave me a thoughtful look. "No. Why?"

"Not in any way?"

"Nope. Not something I'd miss. Why?"

"Because often several employees will blog on a gallery site. Visitors come for the different perspectives, and it's good publicity for everyone," I said.

In fact, it was very odd that Anna's blog wasn't even referenced on Zanthus website. Had she made a conscious decision to keep her own views separate?

Or had her blog not been welcome on the gallery site? Something else to find out.

"Are there any other blogs on this site?" I asked him. "Or employees who have blogs that aren't here?"

"None that I could find, either way," Cory said.

"Huh. So what do these pages of code do?"

"Good question."

Okay. "And how did they end up on these sites?"

"An even better question."

"Cory," I said warningly.

"Sorry, Aunt B. I'm not trying to be difficult. I just don't want to say too much and be wrong. I don't have answers yet. It would help to see her computer."

"I'll see what I can do."

"Good," my nephew said, impervious to irony. "But even without it, I think I know what I need to do."

I bit back a sigh. "You're not thinking of anything dangerous?"

"Nope. I have a buddy who's a whiz with esoteric programs, will probably help me figure out what's going on with this. Without letting whoever put these here know that we're onto him. Or her."

"You think it's the same programmer?"

"You're pretty quick for an aunt," he said with a sideways look. "Yeah, I do. But I could be wrong."

I nodded. "See that you don't put yourselves in danger, whatever you do."

"Yes, Aunt B."

The grin he gave me was less reassuring than his words.

"Your mother will ban you from working here—ever—if you end up hurt or in trouble, you know," I told him. "And you're still a minor."

That took care of the grin.

"While you're researching exactly what this program is, though," I said. "Can you give me a hint of what you think it might do?"

"I think it's collecting information," he said. "I just can't figure out what information. Or why. These are pretty boring blogs."

"Maybe to you," I said. "But they matter to some people."

I glanced at Don's latest blog post. "I'll have a look at both blogs later tonight, see if I can see any connection, or anything that someone in the art world might care about."

"Just be careful," he warned, clearly enjoying the irony. "Don't click on those marks." His last words were serious.

"Don't worry. I don't want to give away our hand."

"Good." He glanced at his watch. "Gotta run. Ron's mom is serving spaghetti. She makes really big portions. And her sauce is awesome."

"Have fun," I said. "And Cory? Stay safe."

He rolled his eyes, and was gone.

And I was emailing Sonya to ask if her sister had owned a laptop. And if Anna knew anything about programming. Wishing I'd thought to do so yesterday.

———

I'D BARELY SENT the email off when my cell phone buzzed. I glanced at the display. Sonya? That was fast.

"Barbara O'Grady," I said.

"You got me out of a meeting for this," Sonya snapped. "What do you mean, does Anna know anything about programming? Anna hates computers and everything to do with them. I don't understand why you'd even ask."

"My technical expert found something on Anna's blog," I said.

"Blog? Anna doesn't have a blog."

"Apparently she does." I'd loaded it onto my screen, was scanning it as she spoke.

Anna's blog was pretty good, too. She had a lively, personal tone to her posts. And the last one had been sent the morning she'd vanished.

"She blogs a few times a week, on the local art scene and art in general," I added. "Somewhere there must be a computer to go with it. Either a laptop or a tablet. And I need to see what's on it."

"I don't know about any computer. Or any blog." Sonya sounded irritated. "Send me the URL."

If Anna was hiding her computer from her sister—maybe there was even more tension between the sisters than I'd picked up on? I emailed the URL to Sonya. "And there's coding hidden somewhere on the site. If you find it, don't click…"

Which was as far as I got.

"I hardly need you to teach me my business," she snapped. "I do know a little about security."

Okay then. "I'll need to search Anna's apartment again for a computer," I said. Maybe I'd missed it the first time. Somehow.

"Fine," she said. "I have to go. I will look at this blog you say Anna writes."

I wouldn't want to work for her. Though to be fair, family matters can be enough to make most of us a little strange.

I began scanning through Anna's blog, making notes as I did so.

She seemed to have started it around the time she joined the Zanthus Gallery, though she never referred to Zanthus or her position there in any way. Which was strange in itself, given that both her job and her blog focused on art.

It was a very personal blog, full of opinions and personality, but it was professional at the same time. It showed a lot of who Anna was, but without revealing much about her life, except where it touched on art.

And even there, I found no mention of the artworks she must have purchased during the period covered by the blog. Nor of artists she'd have met personally through the gallery.

Somehow she'd managed to be both social and private. That wasn't an easy line to walk. Probably the reason I had a very utilitarian website for my business. Not only did it fit my line of work, but I'm just not comfortable being quite so exposed online.

I suppose I've just seen too much in my line of work. It's made me wary.

Though it did raise the question of what kind of online presence I planned to have as an artist, once I got closer to my show. The thought made me cringe. Maybe I could just hire Anna to build a website for me. Clearly she had a gift for it.

Of course, I'd have to find her first.

———

TWENTY MINUTES LATER, I was back in Anna Lang's apartment, looking for a computer. Or more specifically, looking for a tablet. Given Sonya's reaction to the idea of Anna even owning a computer, I was guessing Anna wasn't a fan of computers. A tablet seemed to fit her style better than a laptop.

The logical assumption was that she'd have taken a tablet with her. Even without a car, it wouldn't have added much weight to her bag.

But Sonya had said Anna had taken only the items that pre-dated her work at Zanthus. And that didn't include her blog. Or, most likely, her tablet.

So there was a remote chance she'd left it behind. Though it wasn't likely. She still had her phone, after all.

If Anna's tablet existed at all, and I wasn't just stretching what little I knew too far.

I walked slowly from room to room, concentrating on any spot that might hide a very slim tablet. There were a surprising number of them. All empty, of course.

Until I found a couple of loose boards in the floor of her clothes closet—under all those bags. With a high-resolution tablet computer tucked neatly inside.

I was tempted to stop and go through it, but I knew Cory could find things I'd never even think to look for. And if the tablet was compromised in some way—she had left it behind, after all—I didn't want to mess it up.

I texted Cory that I had the tablet, and that I'd drop it off for him. Then I locked up and headed for the car.

CHAPTER FOURTEEN

ON FRIDAY MORNING, I AGAIN woke late and groggy. I'd stayed later at the office than I'd meant to the night before, trying to make sense of Anna's disappearance. Instead of my usual six a.m. start, it took Cat nudging at me with a paw and muttering to wake me.

Cat belongs to my neighbor—who named him Buttercup—and I refuse to call him by such a ridiculous name. Apparently Cat thinks he owns both of us. I think otherwise.

Not that it's done me any good.

After a second nudge with a paw, I opened a bleary eye, knowing the carefully extended claw came next. Then I caught sight of the clock.

Eight a.m.? How did it get that late? And what happened to my alarm?

I scrambled out of bed, dislodging Cat in the process. Which didn't amuse him.

After several cups of coffee for me, and half a can of tuna for him, it was clear it was going to be one of those mornings. I was tempted to skip my morning run and get in a bit more painting time. Bad idea. I needed those endorphins I get from running. And I needed them now.

By the time I got in it wasn't quite ten. Marie was there, thank goodness, with a stack of pink messages in front of her. Uh oh.

"Are those from Sonya?" I asked.

She nodded, biting back a smile.

"All of them?"

"Not quite all. One's from Andrea. And Cory said he was coming by." She paused, chewed on her lower lip. "Ummm, Barbara?"

"Not now, Marie," I said as I accepted the messages from her and escaped to my 'office'.

The first message from Sonya wanted to know why my cell phone was forwarded. Flipping quickly through them, I found increasingly terse messages from Sonya to call her. By the last of them she was calling every five minutes.

Guiltily I un-forwarded my cell phone. It promptly rang.

"Barbara…"

"Where were you?" Sonya demanded.

Okay, this stopped now. Guilt or no guilt, I was a professional, and I expected to be treated with professional courtesy.

"Good morning, Sonya," I said. "How may I help you?"

"You…" she said. It was almost a screech. Then she stopped, and I could hear her take a breath. Then another.

"My sister," she said then. "Is missing. I hired you to find her."

"Yes," I said. She hadn't asked a question yet.

"I am paying you an inordinate amount of money to do so," she said. "Because she is in trouble. And I have neither the time nor the skills to help her."

So Sonya was feeling guilty too. No wonder she was so mad at me. And she still hadn't asked me anything.

"I see," I said. Maybe she just needed someone to listen to her.

"Is that all you can say?" she asked. The screech was back.

Apparently she didn't just want someone to listen to her.

"Sonya, I found your sister's tablet. It's being analyzed now."

Well, I hoped it wasn't being analyzed this very minute—Cory was supposed to be in school. And I didn't need more problems with my own sister. Not while I was trying to track down Sonya's.

"Well why didn't your assistant say so, the first time I called," she muttered.

"Because most of the elements of this investigation are confidential," I said. "Need to know only. And my assistant doesn't need to know."

I heard a snort from the front of the room. I ignored it.

"I'm sure she told you I would be available at ten," I said. Holding my breath in case Marie hadn't told her.

"She did," Sonya said.

Phew. "Then what's the problem?"

I'd managed not to ask what her problem was. Just. Clients like this one annoy me.

They seem to think that their money buys the right to dictate exactly how I investigate a case. And it doesn't. Quite the opposite.

"I looked at her blog," Sonya said abruptly.

"And?"

"And it isn't secure at all," she said. "I'm surprised she didn't ask me to help her with it."

I wasn't surprised at all. Not after this call.

"Anyone could hack it," Sonya was saying. "She left herself too vulnerable."

"Vulnerable?" It was a very specific choice of words. Especially when she was talking about a woman who had vanished.

"Vulnerable to what?"

"To any nut that's out there," Sonya said.

There was something wrong with her tone on that last statement. It was too strong for what she was saying. And the words didn't fit with the earlier comment.

She knew something. Or she was hiding something. Something was off, anyway.

I just couldn't figure out what. Or why.

"So you agree it's Anna's blog?" I said, in an attempt to get her to stick to the facts.

"Of course it is," she said in clipped tones. As if I was an idiot for asking.

Right. "And did you find anything that might explain her disappearance? Or anything I should know about, that might help me find her?"

"No. Nothing. Just empty prattle about art."

She sounded disgusted. And hardly supportive of Anna's career. Which made me even more curious. What was going on with these two sisters?

But I had something more important to deal with. "Sonya, I've checked, and there is no sign of Anna's passport anywhere. I suspect she took it with her," I told her. "So I need you to call your parents, and ask if she's with them. Or if they know where she is."

"Call them? In Germany? But I don't want to worry them," she said.

"Then make it casual. But find out. If she's there, then you have your answer."

"Can't you call them?"

"Yes. But having a P. I. call with questions is more likely to panic them than your calling will."

"So." She was silent for a moment.

"Then all right," she said, as if it was a momentous decision, making me wonder just how bad her relationship with her parents was. And why.

"I will call. And I will let you know what they say. It may take some time to get through, though. The time change. And they are getting older. They do not always choose to answer the phone."

"Just let me know as soon as you hear," I said. "I'm afraid…"

"I must go. I have a meeting," she said, and disconnected on me.

Fine. Just wonderful.

———

I DUMPED the pink slips that were Sonya's calls in the trash. Which left me with the one from Andrea. Who hadn't said what she was calling about.

I punched in her number. Voice mail.

Of course.

I left a message, turned back to my notes, and realized I'd never followed up with on the missing persons report Sonya had filed about Anna. It wasn't likely they'd found anything we hadn't, but I still needed to check.

I called Cathy Yip in Missing Persons. I'd worked with her on a previous case. She wasn't in.

I left a message, hoping that I'd have more luck than the last time I'd left messages for her. That had been in the middle of Marie's sister Celeste's kidnapping. To say Ms. Yip didn't take me very seriously would be a serious understatement.

By the end of the case, however, she'd come around. Mostly. Hopefully this time she'd at least return my call.

I disconnected, and was just making a note of the date and time in my follow-up list, when the front door banged open. Then I heard an odd thumping that I'd learned meant a teenager had just flipped up a skateboard and leaned it against a wall by the door.

Judging by the noise and the heavy footsteps headed my way, that would be Cory. Who was apparently in a growth spurt that had misaligned his mind's communication with his body. Which had to be frustrating for him.

He didn't seem to mind, though. He put Anna's tablet on my desk and flung himself into a guest chair with a big smile.

I glanced at the clock. "Which class are you missing now?"

Resignation in my tone. Picturing my next showdown with his mother.

"It's a study block. I'm good," he said. "And you'll never guess what I found on this thing. Which is a piece of junk, by the way. No security at all."

Funny, that was what Sonya had said about her sister's blog.

Maybe she and Cory should meet. Except that she'd probably try to hire him, once she realized how good he was.

And then my sister really wouldn't forgive me.

"What did you find on it?" I asked him. "And how did you find it so fast?"

"I had some time this morning," he said. "And it wasn't hidden very well."

I decided I didn't want to know. I was probably going to need the deniability when Susanna caught up with us. "You're remembering our deal, right?"

"Yeah, I know. I only get to work here if my grades stay up."

"Right. So what did you find?"

"This," he said, opening the cover and tapping down a few levels. He pointed to an app. "It's monitoring software. Spyware."

"So what is it doing there?"

"It's watching her. And sending the information back to another machine."

Okay, that was creepy. "Like a keystroke logger?" I asked.

He looked impressed at the question. He shouldn't have been. I make the effort to keep up, even if my knowledge base is pretty shallow.

I'll never be an expert, but it helps if I know what's possible. Then I can hire the expertise I need.

"No, not a keystroke logger," Cory said. "Whoever this is, they're not interested in her routine transactions. This thing doesn't look for her passwords or her accounts. It seems to be waiting for her to visit particular sites."

What? "Which ones?" I asked.

"I don't know yet. The way this is written, I risk alerting whoever put it there if I go digging any deeper. I need to get some help before I can tell you anything."

"Anything? What kind of anything?"

"What exactly it's watching for. What information it's relaying. And if we're lucky, who the information is being sent to."

That sounded good. "So how long will all of this take?"

"Hard to say. I'll let you know soon as I figure it out," he said. "Who had access to this tablet, anyway?"

"I have no idea," I said.

"It probably doesn't matter. If my guess is right, it was a remote hack anyway."

He glanced at his watch, turned the tablet off and stuffed it into his backpack. "Gotta go. See you, Aunt B."

CHAPTER FIFTEEN

AS I DROVE INTO THE office on Saturday morning, it was overcast, and raining lightly. Traffic was heavier than I'd expected, since the clock on the dash said it was only nine-thirty. My painting session had been cut short this morning—a combination of one too many cocktails last night with Andrea, and a nagging guilt about Anna. Whom I still hadn't managed to find.

Andrea's concern about Don hadn't helped matters any. She was still convinced he was Super Villain. Capable of anything. And I didn't have any proof either way, so I couldn't even argue with her. Not yet.

Which left me facing just how bad it could be for Anna by now —if Andrea was right. If Anna hadn't chosen to disappear under her own steam.

And if she had? If she was hiding somewhere, she seemed to be doing a pretty good job of it. But if she'd gone into hiding, why not tell her sister, at least, where she was going? She must have known Sonya would be frantic.

If Anna was in hiding, it was already clear I wasn't going to find her easily.

Maybe it was time for me to put my search for Anna on hold—

since it wasn't getting me anywhere in any case—and find out what was really going on with Don James. If Andrea and the gallery's sales associates were right, it meant I'd need to do a whole different kind of investigation than what I'd managed so far.

And if Andrea was wrong? Then I'd be taking a hard look at Sonya and Anna's relationship.

My instincts said something was off there, and I still wasn't sure what it was. But I wasn't discounting the possibility that Anna's sudden disappearance had more to do with her relationship with Sonya than with anything else.

Except that wouldn't explain her leaving Zanthus with no notice—a move that could endanger a career she clearly loved.

Only Anna seemed to have made sure that people in the art world knew she wanted to leave Zanthus, and hinted that it was because of Don James. Which gave her an excellent excuse for vanishing.

And from the sound of it, she already had another position lined up and waiting for her—all she had to do was accept Ian's terms and she'd be working at the Omega Gallery. With a solid career path in front of her, too, given the hints Ian had been dropping.

If Anna had planned to disappear for awhile, but in a way that only impacted her current employer—and her sister—but not her career, she'd done an exceptional job of it. She'd been able to vanish, and only her sister was worried.

Which sparked a sudden thought. I did a quick online search, made a call. Yes, Anna's rent was paid up to the end of the month, and she'd also left a post-dated check for the next month. Which she didn't usually do.

It seemed her departure really was that well-planned.

Or was it just made to look so?

———

I PARKED, and took the stairs, impatient to get started. The office was client-free, and Marie greeted me with a scowl. "You're early."

I had to laugh. "Isn't that a good thing?"

"For business, maybe. But you'll never get that show ready if you keep this up."

"Thanks for the concern, but I'll be fine. Are there any messages?"

"Nope," she said, still scowling.

It wasn't easy to keep a scowl going that long. I wondered how she managed it.

"I hope you know what you're doing. You'll end up broke if you don't get more clients," she added.

"Didn't you deposit Sonya's check?" I asked.

"Of course I did."

"There you are, then. I'm not going broke."

"Maybe not now. But with that attitude, you will."

She was a riot. Especially given her previous feckless lifestyle as a bicycle courier, with most of her expenses funded by her older sister. "So which is it? I need to paint more? Or I need more clients?"

"Both. If you had more clients, I could do more for you. And I wouldn't be sitting here waiting for the phone to ring."

Now we were getting to it. She thought she was a P. I. "You can't investigate without a P. I. license."

"Not investigate," she said. "Ask questions. I can be subtle."

I looked at her combination of chartreuse and hot pink—and was that a purple streak in her hair?—and had to bite back a smile. I could just imagine what her version of subtle would look like.

"Asking questions is what most investigations are about. I don't run around with a gun, you know."

"Well, you should. You got shot, you know."

Yes, thanks to her. But I refrained from rubbing it in. For once.

I'd decided it was worth having her around until after my show. I did seem to be getting more painting done. Despite everything. And I was happy with the results, too. Mostly.

No artist I've ever met has ever been fully satisfied with any work in progress. Sometimes we like them when they're done. Usually we're just focused on making the next one even better.

"If I carried a gun, I'd be more likely to get shot again," I said. "I prefer to avoid guns entirely."

I just wasn't very successful at it. People always seemed to be waving them at me. In fact, I was lucky I'd only been shot twice so far, and both times only winged.

I might not be smart at times, but I am quick.

Maybe Marie was right, though. Maybe I should be carrying a gun.

I didn't much like the idea of shooting someone. And it's beyond foolish to carry a gun if you aren't prepared to use it if you need to. I'd rather be smart—and careful—about exactly how I investigated.

I could just hear Jerry laughing in my head. My old buddy, Jerry Hawald—now a Vancouver police detective—thinks I walk straight into trouble, every time. And once in a while, he's right.

But I have him beat on the averages, because most of the time, he's wrong. It's just that the few times he's been right have been memorable.

"Well, can I at least help you with something this morning?" Marie said, apparently giving up on the argument. "What are you working on, anyway?"

Maybe she could help at that. "I'm looking into the manager of the Zanthus Gallery, Don James," I told her.

"Did he kill her? Anna?" she said, in horrified tones that didn't quite hide her fascination.

"We don't know she's dead," I said. "I'm operating on the assumption that she's alive and running. And that she has reason to want to hide. I don't know who she's hiding from,"—though I couldn't shake the notion it was her sister—"so I'm looking at everyone. Starting with her current boss."

"Oh," she said.

"And that doesn't mean he's why she ran, either. Or that he's guilty. It just means that we're looking at him."

"Oh," she said again.

I didn't like the sound of that second "oh."

"Marie," I said. "We have to be very careful here. It would be all too easy to let something slip that could be seen as derogatory towards someone we're looking into. And neither of us can afford a lawsuit."

"I can," she said.

I rolled my eyes.

"No," I said. "You can't. Even if you had the money," —and she probably did. Her mother's paintings had gone sky high in value, and Marie and her sister still owned more than a few of them—"it isn't just about money. It's about this firm's reputation. A slander suit would ruin me."

I paused, decided a little career counseling here wouldn't hurt. "And it wouldn't do your reputation in the art world any good either. This is a small community. Don't forget who Don James is."

"I thought I'd go for "Angry Young Artist" as my brand," she said, scowling and striking a pose. "D'you think it would work?"

I had to laugh. Marie? Making light hearted fun of herself? That was a first.

"I think it's been done," I said. "I thought you wanted to be cutting edge?"

She grinned back. "Then I guess I'd best be careful what I ask. What did you want me to do?"

"Can you go online, and get copies of any articles that mention Don from local newspapers as well as from international magazines?"

"Well, I doubt I can ruin your reputation doing that," she quipped, making a note. "You mean the art magazines?"

"Start with the local newspapers," I said. "My sources tell me that Don has spent a lot of his working life in various corporations, and only recently rejoined the art world. He did his degree in fine arts."

"Just like you," she said.

I nodded, surprised she knew that much. "Same year, too," I said. "I knew him a little, back then, but we lost touch."

"Huh," she said. "So I'm guessing that it'll be business journals I'm looking in."

I was a little surprised. "That would be my guess. But he might surprise you. And for some of that time, you might find him listed as D. Jasper James rather than Don James."

She gave me a look I couldn't read. "D. Jasper? Really?"

"Really. Can you do it?"

"Yeah."

Now I was impressed. "Send me copies of anything you think is important or significant."

And I'd print them for my personal files. I was trained to have paper backups. Of everything.

She beamed. "Okay. I'll start digging. I should have an update for you by lunch time."

"Great. Call me if you need me," I said, and went to make coffee.

CHAPTER SIXTEEN

TWO HOURS LATER I'D GONE through half a pot of coffee, had a headache—which I swore had nothing to do with the coffee—and had drawn a blank on my old friend Don.

No-one I'd talked to knew much about him. None of them—mostly artists and denizens of the local art world—knew much about what he'd been doing between his degree and his current gig at Zanthus.

With a sigh, I admitted defeat. It was time to call Gossip Central —Cassandra Stone. Cassandra's another former university friend who is on staff in the Fine Arts Department at Vancouver University, and she thrives on gossip. If she didn't know all the dirt on Don, no-one would.

But first, I needed more coffee.

I'd just got up to pour another cup when Marie gave a squeal. "Barbara, you have to see this," she called.

Intrigued, I grabbed a fresh cup and ventured around the partition that separated us. "What do you have?" I asked her as I stood beside her desk.

She turned her computer screen so I could see it. "You were

right about the D. Jasper bit. He used that a lot, mostly overseas. Look," she said.

It took me a moment to recognize what I was looking at. She'd started with a copy of Don's CV, and added information from there as she found it. She'd created a list of dates and places, as well as which name he'd been using, with a column for comments. I ran my eye down it. "This is where Don has been?"

"Yup."

No wonder she was excited. It was amazing how many of his prior jobs hadn't found their way into the official version of his CV. And the creative way some of his experiences had been presented.

My first thought as I compared the two was to wonder what he was hiding.

"Marie, this is fantastic," I said. "What made you think to lay it out like this?"

"My first searches kept leading to other searches, and the information was in articles from all over the place. Different times. Different companies. I couldn't keep track of it.

The only thing constant was that Don James was involved somehow. So I started putting stuff in date order, with as much detail as each reference gave me."

She pointed at the screen. "And that's what I ended up with."

I was still reading it, paging down several times. The many and varied nature of the jobs he'd held made my head spin. Investment adviser for a mutual fund firm. Stockbroker. Then he'd made an abrupt shift overseas, and found work as a travel adviser, then concierge for a luxury hotel in Geneva.

He'd gone back to the art world for a short time, working in several galleries. Then he'd worked with a fine arts consulting firm, but had specialized in jewelry, not painting.

He'd even worked with a couple of security firms, but Marie hadn't been able to pin down details. And he'd lived all over the world while he pursued—whatever it was he was pursuing.

"I don't see anything related to painting on this list," I said.

"That's because I didn't find anything. If he's been painting at all, he's kept it pretty quiet."

I nodded, still reading. "No wonder no-one I talked to had heard much about him," I said when I came to the end of the list.

"He hasn't worked as an artist for well over a decade. And he hasn't worked in the art world for most of that time, either. In fact, he's done everything but, from what I see here."

"What I don't get is why he'd want to come back," Marie said. "To Vancouver, as well as to the art world. He's had some pretty lofty positions. Probably made some decent money."

It was a good question. "Maybe he made enough that this job is a hobby of sorts."

She snorted. "If he's rich enough to have a hobby instead of a job, then why isn't he painting? Isn't that what he studied?"

She was right. Interesting. I hadn't expected Marie to be so good at this.

"Yes. It is. And it's a good question. Why come back? And why to Zanthus?"

Unless he had another reason for being there?

I remembered what Drew of the blond dreads had told me about the customers who never bought anything, the ones Don paid special attention to. And ran my eye down the list of his varied positions again. Don had worked in a variety of fields that could be considered useful knowledge for his present position.

Or for a fine arts consultant.

Or someone who advised collectors on how best to leverage and protect their collection.

Or for a smuggler.

The shipment of fine arts was a not often discussed but effective way to smuggle in small items of great value.

Like stolen jewelry.

Or drugs.

"I have a few more calls to make," I said to Marie. "Keep digging."

I was suddenly looking forward to my chat with Cassandra, the Fount of all Gossip, as I liked to call her.

————

"CASSANDRA? IT'S BARBARA O'GRADY," I said when she answered.

"Barbara!" she said with a squeal that sounded uncomfortably like the one Marie had let out earlier. "How lovely to hear from you. And how have you been? Painting all hours, I'm sure, with your show and all."

Was there just a bit of envy in that remark? I hoped not. Now that she's a tenured professor—and set for life—I shouldn't be much competition.

She'd certainly seen it that way when she'd learned I was a P. I. And information had flowed from her. She was too valuable a source to lose.

Even if I generally needed a deep breath and a large cup of coffee to deal with her.

"It's taking much longer than I'd hoped," I said, playing it down. "And it's a relatively small show."

"Yes, so I heard," she said smugly. "But Margaret Courtland told me she has real expectations for the show. And for your career," she added generously.

That was the first I'd heard of it. My career? I was a P. I. Full stop.

Just one that had the chance to revive an old dream—having a one-woman show of my paintings.

"But how can I help you, Barbara?" Cassandra was asking. "What are you working on now? Oh, you can't tell me, can you? Never mind. I'm happy to help."

"Thank you," I said, meaning it. Mostly. "What can you tell me about the Zanthus Gallery?"

I knew better than to mention Don by name. She'd seize on it as the focus of my investigation, and trying to deny it would only make her more convinced she was right.

"Zanthus? Oh, but that's where poor dear Anna worked before she vanished. Is she your client? Oh, no, she can't be, can she? Not when she's disappeared."

I started to answer, but Cassandra wasn't finished.

"Still, I suppose that your current investigation has something to do with poor Anna. Good. It means she'll be found."

Really? Cassandra—of all people—had that much faith in me? I doubted it, but I thanked her anyway.

"For now, all I can tell you is that any information you can give me on Zanthus could be critical to this investigation."

I knew I was laying it on a bit thick, but I was confident she wouldn't notice. And she didn't.

"Zanthus, is it?" she said, her voice thoughtful. "Well, let me see, Barbara."

Then her tone changed. "Is that the time? I must run. And I need to do a little digging before I can tell you what you need to know, anyway. Why don't we have lunch and I can fill you in? Or, I know! What about tea? I know this divine little teashop on Broadway that serves exquisite afternoon teas. I'll make a reservation for us. How is Sunday? At three?"

I glanced at my calendar. Tea? In a divine little shop? I shuddered.

I could only hope they also served decent coffee. But I needed her help. "Sunday is good," I said. "Address?"

She gave it to me.

"I'll see you then," I said.

"Lovely." And she was gone.

Leaving me staring at my empty page. I hadn't learned a thing. Maybe Marie had.

I went back out to find that she'd filled in more of her list. Looking over her shoulder, I could see that it had grown to three and a half pages, most of it detail about exactly what Don had been responsible for in his various positions.

"Can you print a hard copy for me, then email me a copy?" I asked her. "I want to use it as a basis for my own questions."

She beamed. "I can do better than that. We're both set up on your server now, so I've created a master document there. Both of us can update it, so it'll be complete."

I had to admit it was a good idea. "Show me," I said, and leaned forward, watching her fingers fly.

———

BY THE END of the day, Marie and I had pieced together a fairly complex overview of what Don had been up to for the last fifteen years or so. And he'd been a very busy boy indeed.

What I couldn't figure out was why.

Very few of his jobs flowed logically from one to the next. If he was on a career path, I couldn't see it. Maybe it was simply a result of the ups and down of the economy—which had been all over the map for the last fifteen years. Just like Don himself.

In retrospect, though, he'd been assembling a pretty unique set of skills. All of which would serve him well in his current role. Of course, they'd also serve him well if he'd decided to specialize in international art theft or smuggling.

To be fair, it could just be that one newly acquired skill naturally helped him find the next job, which then helped him with the one after it. And so on.

But it just seemed too pat to be believable. Especially remembering the awkward kid I'd known.

After all, if you lost a job as a stockbroker in 2008, as he and so many others had, the odds were you'd be looking for a new career. So that made sense.

But the skills he'd developed in authenticating fine art should have been portable. If he couldn't find work in one city, surely he could in another. Especially since he'd moved constantly, leaping not just from city to city, but from country to country in the process.

But no. His next job after that one was a security position. Still working with fine art, but in a much more technical role. I couldn't figure it out. Not without suspecting that he had ulterior motives.

Well, not unless he'd been incompetent. Maybe he got fired, and couldn't find more work in that field.

"Marie," I called.

"Yeah?" she said as she bounced around the partition.

"Any chance he got fired from any of his positions?"

"Don't know," she said. "I can look, if you like. But I doubt it, because he keeps getting quoted as an expert, even when he's no longer working that particular job."

Odd. "See what you can find," I said. "And if he ever explains any of his career choices."

"Will do," she said cheerfully. "Shouldn't be too hard. The guy does like to talk about himself."

Which was a trait that hadn't changed from when I'd first known him, I remembered. Maybe he hadn't changed all that much, after all.

Maybe it was my ability to read people that had improved. In my current job, I'd had no choice.

Just like Anna had no choice except to leave Zanthus?

I glanced through the list again, felt my eyes start to cross. I needed more coffee. Or maybe to stop trying to do work that Marie was clearly capable of doing. And doing well.

I could be out looking for Anna. Who was still missing, without a trace, nearly four days later.

So where had she gone? And what kind of trouble was she in?

The ringing of the phone interrupted that thought. And it was Sonya.

"I finally reached my parents," she said. "They have not heard from Anna. Nor is she there. But they aren't worried. Apparently she told them she was going on a buying trip for her job, and would be unable to call them for at least four weeks."

Four weeks? Why four weeks? "When did they talk to her?" I asked.

"Monday night," she said.

"And Anna told you nothing of this?"

"No." Her voice was a slammed door.

Right. "It sounds as though Anna planned her departure very carefully. I'd say she left of her own free will. Do you still want me to keep looking for her?"

"Yes. I want her found," Sonya said. "Call me when you have something to report."

And I was listening to a dial tone.

I glanced through my notes on Anna. Everything seemed to confirm that she'd disappeared on purpose. More, that her disappearance had been carefully planned. And I had no leads that might tell me where she had gone.

Who else might know? No-one that I'd learned about so far.

So if Anna had left on her own initiative, what did that tell me? I read through my notes again, item by item. Contemplated the crack in the opposite wall. Even if Anna had chosen to leave, her behavior was odd.

What could have triggered it?

Was she in danger? Running from someone or something?

For someone who was running, she seemed to have planned her disappearance very carefully. And in a way calculated not to worry anyone.

Except her sister. And the people she worked with at Zanthus.

Why them? Was it her sister she was hiding from? Her coworkers? Don?

All of them?

I glanced at my notes again. Grimaced. I'd come to a dead end on why she'd left. I had a lot of speculation, but no clear answers, and I seemed to be out of leads.

Time to focus on how she'd left. Maybe that would give me a direction.

I grabbed my purse. "Marie," I said as I rounded the divider.

She looked up. Her hair was standing on end, as if she'd been pulling at it while she searched various databases, but there was no trace of her earlier scowl. "What's up?"

"I'm going looking for Anna," I said. "When you've dug up as much as you can on Don, see if you can find a copy of Anna's CV. And any articles by or about her—especially the ones relating to her career."

"Same thing I did for Don?" she asked.

I doubted there would be anything like as much information on Anna—her career had been shorter, for one thing. But you never know. "Sure. Anything that seems relevant to you."

She grinned. "Will do."

Mentally crossing my fingers, I left her to it, and headed to Anna's apartment for another look.

CHAPTER SEVENTEEN

ANNA'S APARTMENT FELT EMPTY. SHE'D been gone less than a week, but already it had taken on an abandoned air. A fine layer of dust lay over every surface, and the air was stale. The clothes Sonya and I had pulled out of Anna's closet in our search looked like flotsam, thrown up on some lonely beach.

I scowled at my own thoughts. Apparently painting regularly was bad for the hard edge I'd cultivated as a P. I. It's hard to be taken seriously if you're seen as too soft.

Which, given the emphasis placed on the importance of emotional intelligence these days, is the kind of contradiction that makes me crazy.

I opened a window to let in some fresh air, and walked slowly around the apartment. I wasn't looking for anything in particular— I'd already done that. This time, I was trying to get a feel for who Anna really was, something that might tell me where to look next.

Everything I knew about her I'd been told by other people, especially her sister Sonya. In the last few days I'd grown wary of Sonya's biases when it came to her sister. And I couldn't afford to let other people's perceptions cloud my thinking.

Not if I wanted to find Anna.

And I did want to find her. I'd feel the same even if Sonya wasn't paying me. Something was off. Despite the evidence that suggested Anna had carefully planned her flight, I still had a bad feeling about what had happened to her.

I wandered slowly from room to room, taking in the bright, edgy artwork, the eclectic, but obviously comfortable, furnishings, the textured wall coverings that didn't detract from the artwork, yet was as far from the stark white you'd find on a gallery wall as it was possible to get. It felt like a home. An abandoned home, at the moment, but still a home.

I had the feeling that I'd like the person who lived here, who drew sustenance from these surroundings. So why had the woman who'd created this home for herself fled from it? And where would she have gone?

I strolled through the apartment again. Looking for something —anything—out of place. Anything that might give me my next step.

In the bedroom, a collage on the wall beside the bed caught my eye. It held what looked like pages of a journal, dog-eared and sepia-toned; a small brass key; a few strands of dried grass; a pressed violet and a lock of short dark hair. It was beautiful, and evocative, and looked very personal. Looking closer I could make out Anna's signature in the bottom left corner.

I stared at it for a long moment. It was well-done, but it was student work. Nothing like the quality of the rest of the works that hung on her walls. So why was it here?

Clearly it held sentimental value, but it didn't fit the style or the feel of anything else in the apartment.

Putting on disposable gloves to preserve any fingerprints, I carefully lifted the frame down from the wall, and carried it into the bathroom, the brightest room in the apartment. I turned on all the lights, and began to examine the images and items that made up the collage. The individual items that made up the collage told me very little. Except for the pages, covered in pen and ink writing—and probably "aged" with tea. Despite the careful antiquing, I could just read what I'd assumed were journal pages.

They weren't.

They were pages from a contact list of some kind, with abbreviated notes in some kind of code, and series of numbers that were too long to be phone numbers. All of it was written in a flowing, slightly old-fashioned hand, by someone who was right handed—no ink smears—and had been schooled in Europe—the sevens were crossed.

I checked my notes. According to Sonya, Anna was left-handed.

I held the collage closer to the lights, angling it so that the lights didn't reflect off the glass covering it. Peering closer, I tried to decide if the document was actually old enough to be this faded, or if it was an artistic effect that had been added. But I couldn't tell. Not while it was framed and under glass.

I reached for my smartphone and snapped several pictures, reviewing them until I had one in which the writing showed clearly. Then I turned the frame over to examine the underside.

It had been professionally framed, the entire underside covered by acid-free brown paper, to protect the work from dust. The upper left corner had been peeled back slightly, then stuck back in place in what appeared to be a hurry.

I took the work back into the bedroom and laid it face down on the bed. Then taking off my right glove, I picked at the loose edge with a fingernail while holding the frame steady with my gloved left hand.

For a moment I felt resistance and thought I'd torn it, but then something—probably the glue—let go, and a fairly large section of the paper lifted up and away from the frame. Putting my right glove back on, I carefully picked the collage up by the edges of the frame, then angled it toward the light from the bedroom window. Trying to see what the paper had covered.

At first I saw only the back of the board the collage had been mounted on, but as I tilted the frame, I heard a very soft sliding sound. I tilted it back the other way. There it was again.

I turned the work over, and looked carefully at the elements that made up the collage. This time I was looking to see if they were all securely anchored. They appeared to be, but there was only one way to know for sure. Holding my breath, I turned the collage over, and then turned it upside down and on an angle, so that the upper left corner was facing straight down.

Again I heard the soft slithering sound. I placed the collage on the bed, half leaning it against the wall to keep the angle, and steadying it with my left hand. This time, when I lifted back the loose corner of the backing paper, I could see whatever had been concealed inside the frame. It appeared to be a small, thin notebook —about two inches by three.

I held my breath while I slowly maneuvered the tiny notebook out from inside the frame. Once I'd done so, I put the framed collage back flat on the bed so it couldn't fall. And opened the notebook.

I found the same old-fashioned pen and ink writing I'd found in the collage itself. Not as faded—but a careful tea staining would account for that. It appeared to be page after page of similar lists.

I flipped through the small book. There were no missing pages. So where had the pages Anna had used in the collage come from?

Obviously this was the lead I'd been looking for. But what did it mean?

I wasn't even sure where to start. Other than the obvious.

I snapped photos of all the pages, carefully checking each to make sure they were entirely readable. Then I slipped the little notebook into the back of the collage again, and re-sealed the backing with a gloved finger and just a little water from the tap.

Once everything was back in its original place, I locked up and left.

CHAPTER EIGHTEEN

WHEN I GOT BACK TO the office, Marie was just finishing up her list on Don James. Which had turned into a comprehensive CV with comments and hyperlinks. I was impressed. So, apparently, was she—judging by the big smile she greeted me with.

"You have to come and see this," she told me, oblivious to the fact that she was ordering me around. But I was too curious to comment.

Standing behind her, I peered over her shoulder as she scrolled through several pages. "This is where it gets interesting," she said, stopping at an entry for a staff position at an obscure little gallery in Munich.

I looked carefully, but couldn't see anything remotely interesting about either his position or the gallery itself. What had she seen? "Go on," I said.

"He's working here with a woman," and she clicked on a link, then highlighted the result. Mona Gruen. "See, in this article, she mentions the same gallery. And the dates are the same."

I checked. She was right. "However did you find that?" I asked. Neither document referenced the other, as far as I could see.

"Oh, one link led to another," she said.

"So what's so significant about Mona Gruen?"

She grinned up at me. "Not a thing. On the surface. But when I dig into the next place he worked..." Several more clicks, and she was opening another website. "I'm finding Mona Gruen working as a consultant for the same people."

"At the same time?" I asked. That would be entirely too much of a coincidence.

"No. Several months after he left."

That could be still be coincidence. "Most of these jobs have at least something to do with the art world. Which is pretty small. A lot of it runs on word of mouth," I said. "It's all about who you know."

"Hmmm," she said, clicking rapidly again. "Yet here he is, doing security. And she's there too."

More clicks. "He's working for an investment group of some kind. And she's a consultant for them. And over here, he's working on security plans for Larimer and Sons."

"Let me guess. She's working there too?"

"No. Now she's an adviser for one of their major clients."

Don's resume on its own was odd, with an unusual career path and too many moves. But if Marie was right, and this Mona Gruen's working life had run parallel, then something was fishy. Unless...

"Any sign they're romantically involved?" I asked.

"Not so far, though it's a good guess, I'd say," Marie said, still peering at the screen. "But here's where it gets really weird."

This I had to hear. "What did you find?"

"Two, maybe three more names. They each worked with either Don or Mona during at least part of these dozen years. Sometimes they overlapped, sometimes they showed up a few months earlier or later. All three spent some time at different firms from each other and from Don and Mona, too."

"Okay," I said slowly, trying to piece it together in my head. And having a hard time doing it. "But at least some of that is to be expected."

She nodded. "Yeah, that's what I said, too. At first. But the more I dug for those five names, the more almost-connections I found."

"Almost-connections?"

"Same place, different time," she said. "Or same time, connected places. But despite all that, I never found any of their names linked, not anywhere."

"Doesn't that argue that they didn't know each other, then? Or at least that they weren't significant in each other's lives?"

"No, it's like some vast secret web, where they're all…" She must have caught sight of my skeptical expression, because she stopped talking and ran her hands through her choppy hair, tugging at it in apparent frustration. "This is too hard to explain."

I looked back at the jumble of words and links on her screen. One thing was clear. Whatever she'd seen—or thought she had—in the data she'd been digging up all day, it wasn't going to be easy to explain to someone else.

"Can you print that out?" I asked her.

"Yeah, sure. Why?" she asked, setting the printer humming with a couple of clicks.

"It's time for a low tech solution," I said. "Whiteboards."

I grabbed the bucket of colored pens while she stared at me blankly. "Come on. Let's move this divider."

———

AN HOUR LATER, the office looked much more colorful. We'd hung two of my three huge whiteboards on one side of the divider, and moved the divider so that both Marie and I could read it. Then we created a bigger version of her diagram.

Soon the whiteboards were covered with scrawls in six colors, and I was prepared to admit that Marie was definitely on to something. We had years along the bottom, Don's various jobs running along the middle in blue. Then we'd added Mona, with a purple timeline that almost mirrored Don's.

Dotted lines connected the two timelines when Mona was

working at a different company than Don, but there was a connection between their employers.

Then we added the other three with their own timelines, popping in and out of Don's timeline and each other's, each in their individual colors.

Shown that way, you could see the patterns made by the connections between the five of them over the last dozen years. They were too clear to be random.

Both Marie and I were having far too much fun with colors and patterns, and we kept it up long after most people would have decided they had enough data and stopped. We kept going back to Marie's master list, then adding connections as we found them: dotted lines, or sometimes a fine solid line, with different colors to help us keep it all straight.

By the time we were done, I'm not sure the riot of color on the white boards would have made sense to anyone else. Walking in cold, it probably looked like someone attempting to freehand a Spirograph drawing. Lines of color shooting off in every direction, creating overlapping half circles and odd shapes. It was kind of pretty.

But more to the point, it had clarified in my head—and in Marie's, judging by her satisfied expression—that whatever Don had been up to the last few years, he hadn't been doing it alone.

At that moment, Marie glanced across at me. I must have been wearing an identical expression, because she grinned at me. "We need more colored pens," she said. "I can order some tomorrow?"

"Good plan," I said. "You'll probably have to hunt for them, though. I don't know that I've ever seen them in more than five colors and black."

"Don't worry, I'll find them," she said.

I had no doubt of it. I wasn't sure if she was a shopaholic, or had just lived too long in poverty, much of it in a forgotten town with no shops left.

"Just make sure they're whiteboard pens," I said. "Or our future efforts will be indelible."

She nodded. But there was a gleam in her eye that worried me. "If you want to do whiteboard art, buy your own whiteboards," I said.

I was joking. Mostly.

Marie laughed, still contemplating our work.

"Where is Mona Gruen now?" I asked her. Partly to distract her, but mostly because it had just occurred to me. If Don was in town, was Mona here as well? "Have you found her?"

She shook her head. "I haven't really looked yet," she said. "I wanted to get as much detail as I could on what all of them had been up to…"

Her voice trailed off, and she gave me a panicked look. "Did Anna trip over some of this? Is that what happened to her?"

"I think we need to know where all of them are now," I said quietly. "Probably urgently. But between them, they have some interesting backgrounds, and I have to assume they might notice if someone is looking for them online."

I was thinking out loud, but my gut told me I was onto something. "You did most of these searches in journals and newspapers, didn't you?"

She nodded.

"That's probably safe enough. It's readily accessible, anyway. And it's out of date."

I waved at the whiteboards. "There's nothing here more recent than two years ago, and a lot of it's five years old. Or more."

Marie looked worried. "Should I have been checking the recent stuff?"

"No, I'm glad you didn't." I paused. "I don't know enough about what a computer expert can do to know if your searches could have triggered anything. Do you?"

She shook her head.

"But if these patterns represent some kind of criminal activity —" I said, waving towards the whiteboards, "—and I think we have to assume that it does—then they won't want it known. To be safe, let's assume for now that one of these five is either a computer expert themselves, or has hired one to build them some safeguards."

"I could just..." she began.

"No. I need to call in someone who at least knows what we need to watch out for."

"Good idea," she said. Then stared at me. "Oh no. Not your nephew..."

Funny, that's pretty much what I expected my sister to say.

But I wasn't going to allow Cory to do the digging himself. Too dangerous.

We needed an expert. And I suspected he'd know just the person.

———

HE DID.

It took a lot of persuading, though. Cory wanted to do the work himself.

We texted back and forth for a bit, neither of us willing to move on our positions. I finally had to put my foot down and threaten to fire him.

I'd never seen anyone sulk via text before. He was pretty good at it, too.

But I had a name. And Cory's promise that he'd set up "the meet" as he called it.

"Badger won't know you. I'll take care of it," he'd texted.

With a grin, I agreed. By text.

At his age, I spent all my time on the phone with Andrea. If something didn't take at least half an hour to explain, with a lot of "no way"s involved, it wasn't worth talking about.

Smiling at the memory, I went back to have another look at our whiteboards. And this time I focused on where everything had taken place.

Was it just a coincidence that the first incidence Marie had been able to find of Don, Mona and the three I'd begun calling the Three Stooges had been in Germany?

And that Sonya and Anna Lang were from there?

I suddenly wanted to know exactly where the Lang's had lived. And when they'd left. And why?

I got up to ask Marie if she had found a copy of Anna's CV yet. She looked up, hit a few keys, then waved towards the printer.

I picked up two pages. "No problem," she said, as I glanced through it.

The document didn't show Anna working in Germany at all. It seemed as if she'd come to Canada to study for her Bachelor of Fine Arts. Her earlier schooling wasn't listed. No help there.

"What about Sonya?"

With a shrug, Marie handed me another two pages. "Harder. This was it. I couldn't find anything earlier."

Sonya's CV didn't list her education at all. Nor any jobs she might have held before she arrived in Vancouver ten years ago. "Nothing else?"

"Nope. Want me to keep digging now?"

I glanced at the clock. After six. "No, go on home."

"I don't mind. Really."

She was really fired up about this. It was nice to see, but I was worried where it might take her online, given what we'd found so far.

"Thanks, but why don't you just hold off for now. At least until..."

"Yeah, I know. Until Cory the Wonder Boy gets here."

It appeared Marie was about as fond of Cory as he was of her. I still wasn't sure what had set them off, but they needed to get over it. Soon. I didn't have time for this.

"He's setting up a meeting with our expert consultant. I'll let you know the timing."

She muttered something. I pretended I hadn't heard her.

CHAPTER NINETEEN

ONCE MARIE HAD LEFT AND I was alone, I hauled out my phone and enlarged and printed out copies of the scans I'd taken in Anna's apartment. I had to darken them a few times until they were readable. Then I spread them out on my desk.

When that wasn't big enough, I locked the office door and taped them to the third whiteboard, moving them around until I had them in the order they'd been in the notebook. I referred back to my scans to be sure.

The page that had been in the collage was the hardest to fit in. Did it come from another book? There hadn't been any missing pages in the one I'd found.

Then I realized that it had to have come from the middle, and that I was looking at one of four pages that had originally been in the center of the booklet. The booklet was saddle stitched, so pulling out the four middle pages would have left no ragged edge.

I wondered if all four pages were in the collage, folded so that only this one showed. Which would mean this was either the first or the fourth page of the four. The other three might be blank. Or they might be critically important. It was impossible to know, too early even to guess.

I hadn't wanted to take the collage apart when I first saw it. Still didn't. It was an original—and clearly very personal—piece of art, and a rather appealing one.

Even though collage clearly wasn't Anna's area of expertise, it was still her work. And it went against everything I valued to destroy someone else's work.

I'd take it apart if I had to, though. Depending on what I found here.

Although it might not help—I had no idea what kind of glues Anna used to make her collage. Normally you'd never use an original document in a collage, because it destroyed it for any other purpose. This might be the only page still readable.

Or it might not be.

Leaving that ethical dilemma for now, I moved my copied pages around to leave the one from the collage in the middle, with an empty space on either side of it. Then I stood back, and tried to make some sense of it.

I didn't have much luck. All the pages were written in the same hand. All seemed to contain the same or very similar type of information, laid out in columns that seemed the same from one page to the next.

There were a few numbers that were easy to recognize, but the rest of it was letters that must use some kind of cipher, because they weren't words in any language I knew or had ever seen. Not much to go on.

I took the pages down from the whiteboard, careful to keep them in order, paper-clipped them together, and locked them in the safe. I sensed they were important, both to Anna herself and to my search for her, but I still had no idea how or why.

I didn't get the chance to be frustrated by that realization, because just then the doorknob rattled on the outer door.

I jumped. Then cursed.

It was only seven-thirty or so, and still light out. I'm not the nervous type. But with the information Marie and I had been working with this afternoon...

My phone chirped at me.

I glanced down. I had a text. Cory.

"Are you there, Aunt B?"

With a wry laugh I went to let my nephew in. And Badger as well.

Who turned out to be a stocky girl with platinum hair and kohl-rimmed eyes. I wished I'd had time to cover our whiteboards, as her eyes moved quickly from board to board.

As did my nephew's.

I cleared my throat.

Cory looked guilty. Badger just turned that look on me.

I found it unsettling. Which should have amused me—she couldn't be more than twenty-one or twenty-two. But the challenge was clear.

It was equally clear that I needed to meet her challenge if I wanted her help. My gut told me I needed that help.

Cory looked from Badger to me. And back. Swallowed.

"Ummm, Aunt B., this is—this is Badger. And this is my Aunt Barbara. O'Grady. She's the P. I."

"Ms. O'Grady," Badger said. Face neutral, voice flat. Square chin thrust forward.

She was good. I was starting to like her.

"Ms. Badger," I said.

"Heard you needed some help."

"I do. And Cory here says you're the one that can help us. I trust his judgement."

He looked pleased.

Badger looked from him to me and back again. She grimaced. "I make my own decisions. Most jobs aren't worth my time."

Good for her. Most people took years to reach that conclusion.

"Fair enough," I said. "But the work here is confidential. You'd have to sign a confidentiality agreement."

"Fair enough," she said.

I couldn't tell if she was mocking me, or simply liked the phrase.

"I have a missing persons case. It's too early to tell if she's been abducted or has chosen to vanish. We've been doing some fairly basic background searches, but putting them together suggests some connections that worry me," I said. "I've no real evidence yet, just gut feel."

Nothing I could take to the police, in other words.

"But if I'm right, there's a rather clever criminal mind behind this. Someone who would have safeguards in place."

"In case someone came digging for exactly the kind of information you've found," Badger said, her eyes going to the two colorful whiteboards.

"Exactly," I said.

————

BADGER GAVE me another considering look. Then she walked to the wall and wandered the length of the two side-by-side whiteboards. And back again.

She did this several times in silence, while Cory and I watched her.

Glancing sideways at my nephew, I could see he was watching her intently. Trying to get inside her mind, and figure out how she did what she did?

Whatever that was.

Growing tired of what was starting to feel like a staged display, I opened my mouth to ask what she thought of our diagram. Only to be stopped by my nephew's hand on my arm and an admonitory look.

He'd done me a favor by bringing her here. That gave him some rights. I could be patient. Right?

Luckily for both of us, Badger chose that moment to speak. "Someone dug out all this information?" she said. "Online?"

Well, duh. I managed not to say it, after a glance at Cory's face. I suspected he knew what I was thinking. Probably Badger knew it too, though her face showed absolutely nothing.

"My temporary assistant, Marie, found most of this," I said in a neutral tone. "Mostly on news sites and job boards."

She nodded, and stood back far enough she could see the whole timeline, which by now ran across both whiteboards. Stared at it for a long moment. Then looked over at Cory. "This why you called me in?"

"Yeah," he said, a little gruffly.

"Good call," she said, and he beamed. Until he remembered he was a fifteen year-old male, and scowled instead.

If Badger found that as funny as I did, she did a commendable job of hiding it. On the other hand, she hadn't shown anything I could have classified as an emotion since she got here.

She surprised me by turning to me. "Your gut's right on this one. You need help, and now. If this assistant found all this on the net—when? All at once?"

"Yes. Today, in fact."

"She found all this information today?" Badger said. Finally a hint of emotion in her voice. Alarm.

Which didn't make me feel any better. "Yes."

"Diligent of her," Badger observed. "And unless these folks are totally incompetent, which I doubt, she's lit up red flags everywhere."

"So what do I do?"

"Hire me," Badger said. "And let me get started on her computer."

"Umm," Cory said.

Both of us turned and looked at him. "You should probably know..." he said, looking at Badger.

"What?"

He reached for the backpack he'd dumped earlier and pulled out Anna's tablet, turning it on and flipping through a few screens so rapidly it made my eyes hurt.

"The missing person?" he said. "This was on her computer." Holding it out to Badger.

Who snatched it from his hand with a scowl. "Why is this the first I'm hearing of this?" she asked.

"I was going to call you in on it, but I haven't had a chance," he said. "It seems to be watching for her to access particular websites, but I couldn't chance going any deeper."

"That's smart, at least," Badger said, her fingers flying over the tablet. "How did you protect yourself?"

His explanation lost me in a hurry, starting with anonymous IP addresses and bouncing signals, then descending into gibberish from there, but she seemed satisfied.

"You didn't dig into any of the sites?" she asked.

"No. I know better," he said.

Was that wounded pride I heard in his voice? Probably. The dynamic between the two of them was fascinating.

I couldn't tell if my nephew had developed his first crush on an older woman, or if it was one hacker's admiration for another who was badder than he was. Probably both, knowing Cory.

Badger seemed tolerant of his crush, or whatever it was, despite her lack of expression. Or at least she wasn't stepping on it.

And I suspected she was more than capable of that.

Badger had been listening to Cory and flying through screens on the tablet at the same time. Suddenly she froze, and stared at a screen. Cory and I both craned to see over her shoulder.

She immediately powered down the tablet and turned to me.

"Who did you say this belonged to?" she asked.

"I didn't," I said. "Not unless it's necessary. And after you sign the confidentiality agreement."

She waved it off. "Do you know who might have had access to this tablet?" she asked.

"No. But I can see if I can find out," I said.

"Do it," she said.

"You mean physical access?" Cory asked. "But—the spyware I found could have been downloaded over Wi-Fi. Which means any coffee shop in the city. Do you mean there's something else on there?"

Judging by her actions, there was definitely something else on there. And I really wanted to know what we were dealing with here.

"No questions," Badger said. "Not yet."

And to me she said, "Just find out."

I nodded. Glanced from Cory to Badger and back again. Was I going to do this? Oh, what the hell. I had no time to waste.

"Give us a moment," I said to Badger. "Cory? You're with me"

And I led him out into the hall, closing the office door behind us. Badger watched us go, no expression at all on her face.

"How well do you know Badger?" I asked him, leaning in and lowering my voice to a whisper.

He looked surprised. "Why…"

"We don't have time. Do you trust her?" I asked him.

"Yeah. I wouldn't have brought her here otherwise."

I already knew that. Did Badger? "What about her ethics?"

"You mean is she a black hat?"

I knew enough about hackers to know I probably didn't want to know the answer to that. "No. I mean does she value people, or just computers?"

Cory frowned over that one. "People, I think," he said after a moment. "But she's a loner, like me."

Which he wasn't. But he definitely identified with her. I just hoped his crush hadn't messed with his judgement.

"And she keeps her word," he said.

"Okay, that's good enough for me," I said. "Come on."

Badger was glaring at the door when we walked back inside. I grinned at her. "Decision made. I'm hiring you for this case, at your normal rate."

Two hundred an hour. Cory had told me, and after I'd quit choking and thought about it, I'd decided I'd be happy to pay. This time.

My accountant would kill me, but my gut was happy, so I knew I'd made the right decision.

She gave a quick nod, but waited to hear the rest of what I had to say. I definitely liked her.

"I think you need to know more about the case in order to do your job," I said. "So everything is bound by the confidentiality agreement you'll sign."

She nodded again, and Cory caught my eye.

"Want me to print it off for you?" he asked.

That's right, he knew where the agreements were. I nodded, and he gave me a grin.

"Wait," Badger said in a tone that had Cory freezing halfway to the computer. Oh, this wasn't good. If she wouldn't sign the agreement, I couldn't hire her.

"Is that the computer your assistant uses?" she demanded.

Oh. "Yes," I said.

"Then Cory can't use it," she said. "Not for anything. And especially not to print off any contract that has my name on it. In fact, you can't keep a record of my name in any digital form. If you intend to, then I won't work with you."

I could work with that.

"Cory, print a copy from my computer," I said calmly. "You know the password."

He nodded, looking a little sheepish as he passed me, heading into my office. I'd never told him my password.

"I haven't used it for any searches today. We'll complete the form by hand. And I'll only keep hard copies, and those in the office safe," I said to Badger. "All right?"

She nodded. "So what's so important?"

"It might not be," I said, though my gut disagreed. Strongly. "But when you asked about who might have had access to the missing woman's tablet, I realized I'd need to talk to her sister. And that you might have heard of her. Sonya Lang."

Badger's eyes widened.

I took that to mean she recognized the name. And thought there was a connection.

I'd begun to suspect as much. And really hoped I was wrong.

"Tell me," I said.

She shook her head. "Not yet. I could be wrong."

Her tone said she was hoping she was. Given the shock on her face, so was I.

What had this case landed me in the middle of? And how did Sonya fit in?

Now I really needed to know more about Sonya and her sister. But digging about online was clearly not an option.

"When?" I asked Badger. Not feeling very patient.

"When I'm done," she snapped at me.

Okay, then.

Since I needed her way more than she needed me right now, I backed off. "Do you need anything from me?"

"No," she said. "Except, don't go near her. Not until you hear from me. I'll call you."

Twenty minutes later I had her signed agreement, she had my check and a list of the websites Marie had been searching, and Badger and Cory were gone.

Leaving me staring at the whiteboards, wondering what I'd just got us involved in. And what I was going to do until I heard back from Badger.

Whenever that might be.

CHAPTER TWENTY

BY THE TIME I WOKE the following morning, it was nearly eleven and my head felt foggy. Good thing it was Sunday, and I didn't have anywhere I had to be.

As I opened the blinds on a cool, overcast day, I could feel the chill coming off the glass. Yesterday's sunshine had given way to heavy clouds and the trees across the street were flattening in the wind that felt like it came off the ocean.

There was no sign of Cat. I guess he'd decided it was no weather to be venturing out. Smart cat.

I shivered as I pulled on jeans, an extra sweater and a long scarf. I didn't feel much better than the weather looked—I hadn't had the heart to do much on the case after Badger and Cory left, so I'd come home and painted. Until about five a.m.—by which time I was too tired to see what I was painting.

Now I was half-afraid to look at what I'd done. The mood I'd been in, I was afraid I'd ended up with a grim canvas reminiscent of Anthea Swan at her bleakest.

I made French Roast coffee and a bagel thick with lox-flavored cream cheese. When I couldn't put it off any longer, I opened the door to the second bedroom, now my studio, and glanced towards the easel.

Then turned the overhead light on and moved closer to examine it.

It wasn't bad. In fact, it might be damned good. In an uncomfortable kind of way.

And it reflected pretty closely how I was feeling about this case. Confused. Angry. But determined, not bleak.

Okay, then. I had work to do.

By three p.m. I still hadn't heard from Badger. Or Cory. And I hadn't managed to do much more on the case than getting my notes in order. Somehow that had cleared my thinking. I was seeing the case through new eyes.

I just hoped Cassandra was in a mood to talk. Because I had a lot of questions.

———

I NEEDN'T HAVE WORRIED. When I walked into the quaint little tea shop Cassandra had chosen, and glanced around, I spotted her at a secluded table in a back corner. It wasn't hard. She was wearing a fitted turquoise suit over a blouse patterned with yellow irises. Her only concession to the weather was an umbrella with the same pattern of irises.

She fit the decor perfectly. And she'd chosen the perfect place for a quiet chat. It made a slightly nauseating picture. But at least it meant she was serious about this little chat.

Good. So was I.

She looked up and gave me a little wave. As I made my way to her table, I noted the flowered wallpaper, the mismatched not-quite-antique tables and chairs, the English china teacups and saucers, the three tier serving trays with paper doilies. The tea shop was comfortingly warm on a cold day, and smelled of fragrant tea, fresh-baked scones and vanilla.

It was everything Cassandra had told me it would be. I took a calming breath. Quaint anything makes me nervous. This had better be worth it.

Cassandra brushed back a strand of perfectly cut dark hair, then waved me to a comfortable armchair opposite her. "Barbara. Right on time, as usual.

I knew you would be, so I took the liberty of ordering for you. I hope you don't mind, but their tea for two is simply an experience not to be missed."

So much for my hope they'd have good coffee. Apparently I was going to enjoy a full afternoon tea. Oh goody.

Cassandra made up for it with her next words. "And I thought I'd get the ordering out of the way, to give us more time to talk."

I smiled at her as I sank into the comfortable chair, then glanced around us. There was no-one close enough to overhear. "Good choice," I said.

Then neither of us said anything more as three servers, all wearing short white aprons with unnecessarily large frills around the edges, clustered around our table. One bore a steaming teapot, an old-fashioned Brown Betty earthenware.

Another carried a three tiered serving plate, covered with what I had to admit looked a tempting variety of food: tiny sandwiches, small pastries and elaborate little cakes.

And the third brought an elaborate basket of condiment dishes, each with its own small spoon, fork or knife.

Finally they left us alone.

Cassandra poured the tea. "Do you take milk or sugar?"

I just shook my head, managing not to cringe. Bracing myself, I took a sip. Actually, it had more flavor than I'd expected. Not bad at all.

I tried a small triangle of crust-free sandwich. It appeared to be some kind of white cheese. On the white bread, it looked anemic.

I took a cautious bite. Hmm. Using old cheddar with fresh basil and a red-pepper spread with just a hint of heat was a nice twist. Also not bad at all. I reached for another sandwich and settled back to enjoy myself.

"So Barbara," Cassandra said, having arranged her own plate to her satisfaction. "What did you want to know?"

"Why don't you start by telling me what you know about Anna Lang?"

"The missing woman?" She leaned towards me. "Not a great deal, because of course she's such a young artist. Hardly established in her career at all. Which of course is why she's working at Zanthus."

Cassandra raised her cup, sipped a little tea. "Though I hear that she has the beginnings of an eye for new work. And I must say, I do enjoy her blog. She's rather opinionated, but really has some quite intelligent things to say, on occasion."

She paused to nibble on a small triangle of cucumber sandwich.

"I am surprised young Anna is still working at Zanthus, though. For Don James, you know," she said.

"Though I've heard a rumor that she's been looking elsewhere. And I think Ian Wong at the Omega is interested. But I don't think anything's been finalized yet."

She picked up her teacup, took another sip, then looked at me expectantly.

This is why I value Cassandra as a source. In less than fifteen minutes, she'd just told me everything I'd learned about Anna in four days of digging. I should simply have talked to Cassandra in the first place.

"Do you know anything about Anna's family life?"

"Her family life?" Cassandra repeated. "Let me think."

She took a tiny scone from the tray, adding clotted cream and a deep red jam from the condiments tray. "I know about a sister, I think it is, who works for some software firm."

She took a bite of her scone, closed her eyes as she savored the taste. Putting the scone down, she grimaced a little. "I should know more. There was something…"

She sipped her tea, then finished the scone, her attention turned inward and a tiny frown formed between her carefully groomed brows. "I have it. The company—and I believe it's a gaming company—went public and the sister has, or had, I'm not sure, a decent number of shares. She's worth a lot now, the sister I mean. You'd think with all that money, she might start an art collection, with Anna being in the business and all. But I heard she wasn't much interested in art."

Cassandra gave a little "what can you do" shrug that didn't even wrinkle her blouse.

I wondered if Sonya's sudden wealth—or her lack of interest in art—were an issue with her art obsessed sister. Maybe that was where Anna had got the money for her own collection?

I pictured the art I'd seen on Anna's carefully staged walls. No, those had mostly been early works, predating Sonya's supposed windfall. I'd have to look into that. After I had the all clear from Badger.

If I ever heard back from Badger. "Anything else?"

"No, I think that's it. It's hardly my area of interest you know, a gaming company."

She paused to nibble on a hummus and cilantro sandwich. "Although the graphics they use these days are really interesting. Even if it is graphic art, rather than fine art. I'm thinking of suggesting a course on it, one of these days. If nothing else, it would get our numbers up."

Cassandra, interested in graphic art? That was a side of her I'd not seen before. Though I'd seen an article recently about the declining enrollment in university level fine arts programs.

A talented commercial artist really didn't need a degree to find well-paying work these days. Or to create their own on-line business. Cassandra might be onto something. Inspiration came from all kinds of places.

Like Marie, with her love of tattoo designs and her appreciation for fine art.

"I know someone you might want to talk to," I said. Then realized what I'd done.

"A game designer?" she asked, eyes focused on me.

"Not exactly," I hedged.

What was I thinking? Introducing Cassandra, with her love of gossip, to Marie, who had no discretion at all and thought she knew everything? It had disaster written all over it.

"She designs tattoos. Intricate ones."

Cassandra looked taken aback for a moment. Then she leaned forward. "That could be interesting," she said. "Is this person any good?"

Marie was very good. "Yes. She's also studying at Emily Carr. Part time."

Now I'd done it. Emily Carr University of Art and Design didn't accept just anyone.

I could tell by the curl of Cassandra's lips that she was hooked. Though she just passed me her card and said, "Have her call me, then," in an off-hand voice.

I nodded and pocketed the card. I was going to regret this, I just knew it. But it could be good for Marie. Competitive though she was, Cassandra had mentored a few students in the past, and rather well. I'd checked.

And it might be good for Cassandra, too, if her interest in graphic and commercial art was real. Though I could just picture her reaction to Marie.

I couldn't decide if I'd rather see them meet, or be very, very far away. I stifled a grin at the thought. Far away it was.

"Now, you had more questions?" Cassandra said briskly, reaching for her teacup.

She didn't want to be the one owing me, did she? Fair enough.

"How is Anna regarded, in your opinion? Anyone have any trouble with her?"

"No, I haven't heard anything," she said. "And I would have heard. In fact, she's pretty universally liked, with a reputation for being on the bland side, if anything."

"Being too nice doesn't serve artists well," she added.

And just when did she get so cynical? But Cassandra had a point.

The art world—as in any career where there are too many

hopefuls with their eye on the starring roles that are available for too few—can be a vicious one. Talent is important, but that only gets you in the door. The rest is a combination of hard work, sheer drive, luck and an ability to recognize and exploit opportunities when they arise.

"What about Don James?"

"With regards to Anna, you mean?" she was quick to say, though I'd carefully not specified. "I haven't heard anything for certain, of course."

"But?"

"But there are a few rumors."

"Rumors?"

"Do you know him?" she asked, instead of answering.

"Yes. But not well." Not anymore, anyway. I wondered if I'd ever known him—or just thought I did.

"Then you probably know. Don's only been back in Vancouver for a little over a year, but the rumors about him and the ladies follow him. And he's not exactly subtle when he's interested in someone."

"You've heard that Don is interested in Anna?"

"Don is always interested in his sales associates. Who are often female," she said tartly. "Anna is just the latest."

"And no one's complained?"

"Not officially, anyway."

Which meant there was no shortage of gossip, and warnings from one gallery worker to another. "Is he violent? Reportedly, I mean."

"No, I've never heard that. Why? Did someone hurt Anna?"

"No, she's just missing. I'm trying to get a feel for what's going on at Zanthus."

"They're making good money these days, I can tell you that," she said. "Not surprising, given the artists they represent. And Don seems to have a knack for schmoozing the wealthiest of the buyers."

I'd seen that. Though it didn't match what Jeremy and his two coworkers had said.

If it hadn't been for the work Marie had done on Don's work history, I would have wondered how much of that had been sour grapes, getting even with a difficult boss, and how much was accurate.

Now I was wondering just how bad it really was. "So he's successful in his job? Don James, I mean?"

"Oh, I'd say so. I know the owners are pleased. He's brought in a few new buyers, from what I've heard. Collectors, the kind who don't count the cost if they want a piece of art."

That kind of collector was the lifeblood of a high end gallery like Zanthus. Which meant the owners would be very pleased with Don indeed.

And not likely to be questioning anything he did. Or didn't do. Not as long as the buyers, and the money, rolled in.

Which might be very bad news for Anna.

CHAPTER TWENTY-ONE

MONDAY MORNING I DIDN'T HAVE the heart to paint. I still hadn't heard from Badger or Cory, and it had been driving me crazy all night. I'd left Marie a voicemail at her desk, reminding her not to do any online searches, but I felt the need to reinforce it in person.

Ironically, Marie's no better at following directions than I am. Especially when it's for her own good.

Which I was never telling Andrea, who would laugh uproariously before telling me it served me right.

I needed espresso—the good stuff. And I never seem to make it as well as the baristas at Beans, my favorite local coffee shop. Consider it my reward for giving up this morning's painting time.

Traffic on Granville was already bad, so I double parked in the alley. Beans has a hard to find entrance back here—one they'd shared with me, because I'm often in a rush to get somewhere, and parking out front is impossible. There's a trick to it.

Then I punched in the code on their heavy back door—yup, I'm that much of a regular—and raced in.

My rushed entrance got me several greetings and a few quick

grins. Three minutes later I was on my way again, double espresso in hand. See why I love the place?

Not to mention their espresso is magic.

I fought my way through traffic and found a decent parking spot. The weather was warming up, and for once it wasn't raining. Glancing up at the office windows, I was relieved to see they were dark. I'd beaten Marie in, at least.

I took the stairs to work off some of the frustration from being stuck in traffic.

When I reached my floor, I could faintly hear the grinding of the ancient elevator as it descended to what sounded like the first floor. The hallway was deserted, and none of the offices showed lights. Wherever all those commuters were going, it wasn't here.

With a grimace, I juggled my overlarge bag and the heavy key ring, cursing the weight of my laptop while trying not to spill—or worse, drop—my coffee. I got the door unlocked and pushed open, holding it that way with my foot while feeling blindly along the wall for the light switch, when I sensed something wrong.

And froze.

I don't know what alerted me, but after listening hard for a long moment and hearing nothing, I flipped the switch. To see the chaos of a ransacked office.

The room divider was flattened, Marie's small desk had been overturned and the file cabinet gaped open. A scattering of papers lay across the floor, and a handful of empty file folders had been tossed carelessly on top of the printer.

My desk drawers had been flung every which way and my mid-century, burgundy leather swivel chair was lying sideways. For me, that chair represented everything I was as a P. I.

How dare they?!

I closed my eyes for a second. Took a deep breath. Then got to work.

Using the camera on my phone, I documented the mess, then called the police number and reported the break-in.

Filing a police report was a formality for the insurance company, more than anything. I could already tell there wasn't enough damage for the police to do much. But as the operator asked questions, I realized I'd probably heard the vandal, or vandals, leaving in the elevator.

In fact, if I hadn't taken the stairs, I'd have run into them.

The way I was feeling, I'd have welcomed the opportunity. Probably just as well I hadn't had it.

Swearing under my breath, I dug out a pair of thin plastic gloves, so I wouldn't compromise any fingerprint evidence they might have been stupid enough to leave.

Then I righted desks and chairs, put the drawers back in my desk and closed the filing cabinet drawers. I checked the safe, where I stored the most confidential information, and discovered with relief that it was untouched.

As far as I could tell, nothing had been stolen.

So why the break-in?

I looked again at the chaos around me. No-one was this mad at me. As far as I knew, anyway.

I mentally ran through all my recent cases. Nothing came to mind.

It wasn't until I went to right the awkward room divider that I discovered that the whiteboards had been wiped clean. Pulse thundering in my ears, I glanced at the door behind me. Stepped over there and locked it.

If this was related to Anna's case…

Then Badger was right. Our searches had come to someone's attention. And fast. But how had they tracked us here and acted this quickly?

And had they recognized our abstract diagram on the whiteboards for what it really was? Thinking about all the information we'd crammed onto those boards, I cringed. We'd used initials, but still.

If this had been Don James's doing—or one of his cohorts… Seeing their own information written there probably would've given them a pretty solid hint. Unfortunately.

So what were they looking for? My eyes went to the empty file folders and the scattering of papers across the office. I was glad I'd had Marie shred the printouts of her various searches after she created the electronic version.

Old habits sometimes paid off.

I just wished we'd erased the whiteboards.

At least I hadn't left the pages I'd found in Anna's collage up on the third whiteboard. In fact—I lifted my purse and heard the reassuring crinkling.

I wasn't worried about losing the information on the whiteboards—I'd taken a couple of photos of both boards for reference before I'd left on Saturday. We could recreate it from the electronic files—assuming they were still there. There might even be enough data in the photos alone for my purposes.

Had they taken anything? I glanced through the battered filing cabinet, then leafed quickly through the scattered papers. As far as I could tell, nothing was missing.

So what had they been looking for?

What worried me most was what our intruders had seen on those boards. And that they'd gone to the trouble of erasing them all. Which creeped me out.

Those boards must have meant something to our intruders. And with even a suspicion of what they were looking at, they might have been able to figure out exactly what we were working on, and how we'd put the information together.

That couldn't be good.

A quick rap on my door had me jumping, then striding to the door. I glanced at my watch.

Eight o'clock. That was a quick response time for a break-in that had to be low priority. It must be a slow morning down at the station.

I flung the door open. Wrong again.

I looked into Badger's startled eyes. At least she didn't have Cory with her this time.

"You weren't answering," she said accusingly, then her eyes looked over my shoulder at the papers everywhere. "Oh."

Pushing me gently to one side, she stepped into the room and closed the door behind her. Hands on her hips, she examined what was left of the mess, her eyes considering.

I watched as she noted the empty whiteboards. "You got a record of those?"

"Yes."

"Good." Her gaze went to the file cabinet, then into my office beyond. "That contract I signed."

"Safe. I checked."

"Good," she said again, but I could see the fine tension leave her shoulders. "So. You figure this is our conspirators?"

"You tell me," I said. "Though I can't imagine who else would erase the whiteboards."

"You didn't see them?"

"No. I think I just missed them."

"Lucky," she said.

"For whom? Them or me?"

She smiled at that, though her eyes were still cataloguing the mostly picked up office. "What did it look like before?"

I passed her the phone with the photos on it.

She looked at them for a long moment, enlarging several sections, then nodded briefly and handed the phone back. And wandered towards the window, picking her way through the papers.

I followed. I was starting to get annoyed with the way she seemed to have taken over.

It was only when I stood watching her stare at the floor in front of the windows that I noticed that all the blinds had been drawn. I hadn't left them like that.

"What do you see?" I asked.

She pointed to an indentation in the carpet. I was even more annoyed that I hadn't noticed it yet. "Tripod," she said.

"They recorded this?"

"Something."

Okay, it was time for her to start talking. "What did you find out about our quintet of bad guys?"

Apparently she still wasn't ready to answer. She prowled over to Marie's desk, stared at the computer. "This on the floor?"

I nodded. Two could play at that game.

"You have your laptop?"

"Yes."

"And the info she gathered yesterday?"

"On our network."

"Good," she said. "Where's the server?"

"You'd have to ask Cory. He says it's protected, so I didn't ask."

Just paid the bills he'd managed to run up. I'd complained at the time, though I know how expensive good security can be. Now, I wouldn't have minded if he'd charged me twice as much.

"Good," she said again.

"I'm glad you approve," I said dryly.

She grinned at me. "Time for a report?"

"Oh, yeah."

But I didn't get it then. There was a knock at the door. The police had arrived. Followed closely by a quickly hysterical Marie.

With Cory not far behind her.

The rest of the morning was hectic, and by the time I had a chance to catch my breath, it was lunchtime. I'd got nowhere with my case.

Not much further with the break-in. And I couldn't remember the last time I'd seen Badger.

This was not my day.

———

BY ONE I was still putting out fires. I'd already sent an overwrought Marie home. Without her help reassembling the files was taking forever.

Badger reappeared just after two. She looked around, grunted something, and locked the door behind her. My eyes followed the path hers had taken.

The place looked pretty close to normal. Or at least as normal as it ever got.

The obvious changes from last night were the whiteboards—still sans writing—now hanging on the walls, and the divider pushed against the far wall. I wasn't risking re-creating our thoughts on the case for our intruders. Or anyone else.

The invisible change was that after the police had left, I'd swept the entire office for bugs. Hadn't found any, but I had found a tiny camera tucked into a light fixture near the window.

Trained on the door, it would capture images of anyone who came in.

I'd pulled it down and stuck it in a glass of water. Put the glass in the back of the cabinet in the kitchen area, right next to the pipes—just in case it was capturing video and sound.

I considered showing the bug to Cory, but he was only fifteen. He'd got himself into enough trouble with his computer skills all by himself, without my introducing him to a world he might not have encountered yet.

I decided to wait for Badger to show up. Which she just had. Finally.

"You want that report now?" she was asking.

"Yes. But I'd like your opinion on something, first."

She followed me to the kitchen area without asking questions, though her eyebrows went up when I pulled out the glass from under the sink. I handed it to her.

She held the glass up to the light and stared at the contents for a moment. Then brought it closer to her eyes and squinted. After a silent moment, she looked at me. "I need to look at it closer."

"Fine by me."

She grabbed a couple of paper towels and laid them on the counter, then carefully emptied the water from the glass into the sink. At the last moment she dumped the mini camera onto the paper towels. Picking them up, she patted the camera dry, and held it closer, turning it this way and that.

"You're not worried about being seen?" I asked her.

"Given the model, I doubt it was transmitting, even before its bath," she said. "But it certainly isn't now. Good thinking, by the way."

"Thanks."

"Where was this?" she asked after a moment.

"Tucked into the light fixture, right above where you found the tripod marks."

"How'd you find it?"

"I swept for bugs. Didn't find any. But the marks on the carpet irritated me. I borrowed a ladder, got up and looked."

"Impressive."

It wasn't a compliment. I nearly told her it was all part of the job. But I was still inclined to like her—and Cory clearly thought highly of her—so I held back.

"Thanks."

She went back to examining the small device.

"What do you make of it?" I finally asked. "Just a camera, right? Unless I'm missing something?"

"No, I think it's just a camera. But a good one. I won't know if it was set to transmit somewhere until I take it apart, but I'm fairly sure this model has to be physically collected. It's the trade-off for the size."

"And it also foils security sweeps," I said.

"That too." She grinned at me. "After all, you are a P. I. They obviously knew that."

So she'd been pulling my leg earlier. Probably testing me, too.

I did like her, I decided. "Will it tell us anything?"

"Probably not. Especially after its bath. I don't suppose you have a bag of rice around?" She glanced at the coffee counter.

"Sorry."

"Too bad."

"So that really works?"

"Sometimes. I'll take this with me, try it later," she said, wrapping it in the paper towels and tucking it into a pocket in her battered messenger bag.

"Let me know if you find anything. Now about that report?"

"Sure."

I waved her to the guest chair opposite my desk. "You want coffee?"

"Nothing, thanks."

I filled my cup. As I sat down, she passed me a couple of printed pages.

"This is from my preliminary search. Most of the sites that your assistant visited yesterday were fine. Two of them were monitored."

"Is that how they found this office?" I asked.

"I assume so. I'll have to check her computer to be sure, but if you're working off of a network that Cory set up, then I'm surprised they found you so fast."

She looked at my laptop. "Did you do any searching on your laptop?"

"I looked at a couple of sites. But not for any of the stuff Marie was working on."

"Let me check your browser?"

"Sure," I said. I typed in my password, opened the browser, and slid it across the desk to her. Then watched as she leaned into the machine, fingers flying, and a focused look on her face.

She was entertaining to watch. Occasionally she'd grimace, or scowl. Or mutter something to herself.

After a bit she looked up.

"I think your computer might be the problem," she said.

What? "How?"

"That's the interesting thing. It isn't any of the sites that you've accessed yesterday that are the problem. It's these two," and she turned the laptop so I could see the screen. "These were in your cache from Thursday."

I read the URLs she'd highlighted on the screen. I didn't recognize either of them, but they did look familiar. I'd probably seen them before, but in what context? Then it hit me.

"Anna's blog." At her questioning look, I added. "That's the missing girl's. And the other one must belong to Don James. But that means we have bigger problems."

She gave me a skeptical look.

"I knew there was spyware on both. Cory told me," I said. "He thought it was largely passive, warned me what to avoid. If that's not the case, then his computer could be compromised too."

"Okay," she said slowly. "That's a rookie mistake—not like Cory at all. We must be missing something. I'll get in touch with him, see what I can do. But let me clean this up for you first. As long as you don't go near those blogs, you should be fine."

I nodded.

"But first," she continued. "What's the connection between Don and this girl?"

"She works for him," I said. "At the art gallery he manages."

"So it could be one of his group that set this up," she said. "But why are they watching her blog?"

"Wait," I said, flipping rapidly through my notes. "I told her sister—Sonya Lang— about this blog. She was upset by it. Said Anna had no reason to be using computers. And that—I found the page, and quoted it to her—"blogging is a waste of Anna's time.""

"Seems a bit extreme," Badger said. "Especially from her."

There was that edge again. "As someone who makes her living designing computer games, you mean?"

She nodded.

I had the feeling there was more she wasn't saying, but I let it go. For now. Badger was still an unknown quantity, and I needed her expertise. My questions for her could wait.

The questions I had for Sonya were a whole other matter. My client knew something. That much was now clear to me.

Her panic over her missing sister wasn't a result of work stress, or guilt at ignoring her sister. She was afraid for a reason.

And it was past time for her to share it with me.

———

PINNING SONYA DOWN was harder than it sounded. Xtreme Systems was located in a nicely landscaped industrial park in the suburbs. I'd never visited this particular complex before, and spent a few minutes checking it out.

All of the buildings were large, blocky and nondescript, with flat roofs and no decorative flourishes. All had small, discreet signage that was hard to read, often giving only the company name. Few of them had windows, though skylights and even solar panels seemed popular.

Xtreme Systems didn't stand out from the rest—a three story white-fronted concrete structure that sprawled over the equivalent of three city blocks. Their double front doors were glass, but heavily reinforced. Almost opaque, in fact, which suggested to me that this wasn't regular glass, but rather the latest in security glass. Probably wired. Overall the impact was intimidating.

Interesting. Clearly they didn't encourage visitors.

Swinging through the doors, I was confronted with a reception station staffed by two security guards, who had a bank of monitors on a sloping panel in front of them. I stole a quick glance. They appeared to be watching various interior and exterior entrances throughout the building.

On the left of the reception station was an "Employees Only" entrance with a solid door, blank except for the sign, secured by a keycard system. On the right was a "Visitors" entrance, also a solid door, also blank except for the sign. This entrance was also secured, but with what seemed to be a fingerprint sensor.

Worried about security much?

The more muscular of the two guards asked me to sign in, very politely. Then watched my every move, carefully comparing my ID to my face. Only then did they buzz through to, presumably, Sonya's assistant.

Fat lot of good that did.

First Sonya was unavailable. Tied up in meetings, I was told.

Then they couldn't find her. Finally I gave up. I left my card, and asked them to have her call me. Urgently.

So now what? I scrolled through my email as I walked back to the car. I seemed to be hitting dead ends in every direction.

Then I got a text from Nick, and my world stopped.

CHAPTER TWENTY-TWO

THE LOCAL RCMP HAD FOUND a woman's body floating in the Fraser, just off a pier in Steveston, south of downtown Vancouver. Her basic description matched Anna's.

Had I been so wrong?

Nick's words were brief, to the point. He'd known there was no cushioning this blow for me. I punched in his number with shaking fingers, but it went straight to voicemail.

Probably not much he could tell me yet anyway. They wouldn't release any details until they notified the family.

Sonya. Someone had to tell her. I just wished it wasn't me. I punched in her number. Voice mail.

I rang her assistant, insisted it was beyond urgent. Still nothing.

Heart pounding, I sat behind the wheel for a moment, trying to find my composure. I'd been so sure Anna had run, left town for a carefully planned hideaway.

But that was before my office had been ransacked this morning. Which obviously changed things.

If they'd been looking for Anna too, they'd obviously found her. If it was her.

The sinking feeling in my stomach aside, there were any

number of reasons it was unlikely to be Anna. And just as many reasons that it could be.

It was too soon to make assumptions.

I texted Nick, asking for details. He knew the bare outline of my case, but it was enough that he'd know the state I'd be in until I knew for sure. He'd send me what information he could, as soon as he could.

Meanwhile, I wasn't just going to sit around and wait. I started the car, and headed for Steveston.

———

I WASN'T THINKING CLEARLY, just driving south, aiming for the nearest route across the river to Richmond. Which happened to be the Knight Street Bridge. Meaning I hit the beginning of rush hour, merging into the snarled traffic fighting its way home.

With a muttered curse I turned off at the first exit I could—along with what seemed to be half of Richmond. The weather had continued to warm up as the day went on, and Richmond was drenched in sunshine. Which left me sitting in a line of traffic, in a hot car, fuming.

By the time I made it to the far corner that is Steveston, I was completely out of patience. Especially when I discovered First Street was completely blocked off.

Surely this was too far away to be related to the body at the pier?

Muttering under my breath, I made a detour. Then another. It was only when I saw the food trucks that I realized they must be filming in town today. Steveston is a favorite backdrop for a number of currently popular TV shows.

Why me?

I finally gave up and grabbed the first parking spot I could find, then hotfooted it down to the pier, arriving hot and sweaty. And even more worried than I'd been when I got Nick's text.

Some part of me was convinced that this was Sonya's sister.

And knowing I hadn't found her fast enough was the price I'd pay for my determination to show my paintings, despite the toll I knew it would take on me, and on my business.

A warm and sunny day had brought out the crowds. As I reached the pier, it looked normal at first glance. Fishing boats were moored here and there among the restored historic buildings and tourist signs. The souvenir shops were open, the patios of the seafood restaurants that lined the pier jammed with tourists and early diners, the tables laden with drinks.

Looking past them, I could see a knot of people clustered around the railings leading down to the dock itself.

Yellow police tape blocked off the weathered wooden stairs leading down to the dock. Both were almost hidden behind a cluster of bodies.

I headed there, wormed my way through the crowds until I was against the railing. Looked down.

The main dock floats, and it was low tide, so I was looking eight feet or so down, past pilings heavily covered with barnacles and still wet from the morning's high tide.

Police and emergency workers were busy on the far side of the dock, where the boats that had fresh caught salmon or shrimp to sell tied up on the weekends. Since it was a Monday, those berths were empty.

I spotted Nick, deeply involved in a conversation with two of the other RCMP officers. From his text, I hadn't been sure if he was involved in the case or not.

Clearly he was. And if it weren't a suspicious death, he wouldn't be there.

At first they seemed to be finishing up, the body already removed. Then I looked further down the dock. And saw a yellow tarp covering a body-sized lump lying nearly at the end of the dock.

From my vantage point, it was impossible to tell how tall the woman might have been. Or what color hair she had. Or how long she might have been in the river.

My eyes went to the dark oily water, then to the seagulls screeching overhead. I shuddered.

And wondered what I was doing here.

I was too far away to learn anything. And from the activity below me, it would be hours before I'd be able to talk to anyone there.

Assuming they'd even talk to me. There was nothing for me to do here.

I think I'd just needed to see it for myself.

And seeing it, I suddenly doubted it had anything to do with my case. Another irrational response.

But a comforting one.

CHAPTER TWENTY-THREE

AS I WALKED SLOWLY BACK to my car, my phone beeped at me. I skimmed Cory's text. Then registered what I was seeing and read it again, slowly.

He'd found a reservation for Anna on a flight out of Vancouver last Wednesday morning, and a flight manifest confirming she'd been on that flight. I didn't want to know where he'd found the information.

Clearly we were going to have to have another chat about using legal sources. But for now, I was too relieved to care.

If Anna had been on a flight to—he hadn't said where she'd gone—she couldn't be the body in the river.

Unless she'd come back?

I texted him back, asking where she'd gone, and where she'd gone from there? Held my breath.

"Basel. No other flights booked. No return," was the reply.

Basel? That made no sense at all. "Which airline?" I typed.

"Air Canada."

Huh. "Where is she staying?"

"No record."

Really? "Fake identity?"

"Maybe. Want me to get Badger to help?"

"No. Thanks."

If I decided to go that route, I'd ask Badger myself. Cory was in deep enough already. After the break-in—knowing how vulnerable fifteen could be—it spooked me.

"Just talk to her about server security." That seemed safe enough. I hoped.

He sent a sad emoticon and signed off. I guess I wasn't the cool aunt any more. Oh well.

I suddenly realized I was only twenty minutes from the airport. I sent a quick update to Nick, then started the car. I had places to go.

———

PARKING at the airport was a nightmare. Inside was worse. The international concourse was jammed with harried travelers. The Air Canada counters were swamped.

And I was glad I'd come.

Seems Air Canada has regular evening flights to Basel—who knew?—which were both popular and inclined to be overbooked. Everyone looked and sounded frantic, and the lines for the self-service check-in were even worse than for the regular check-in.

To make matters worse, they announced every few minutes that the flight was overbooked, and would anyone who was interested in taking a later flight, please speak with the attendants.

Judging my moment, I took my place in the long, long lineup. Two ahead of me was a frantic woman with an overstuffed suitcase and a toddler she was trying to calm down.

Behind her was a professionally dressed woman with a laptop bag and a wheeled carry-on. She was the one I'd had my eye on.

"Is it always this bad?" I asked the woman with the laptop bag. She looked like someone who'd done this route before.

She rolled her eyes and gave me a wry smile. "I'm afraid so. I take this flight way too often, and they never seem to expect as many travelers as they have."

"So they're always overbooked?"

"Pretty much."

"Do they make it worth your while to give up your seat?" I wondered if Anna might have done so, especially if she was short of cash.

"No. It just means you have to go through the same thing the next day."

"Oh. Does booking early help?" Anna hadn't booked early.

She glanced at the lineup ahead of us, the chaos around us. "Does it look like it?"

"How do you cope?"

"Never use the check-in machines. They slow everyone down."

She eyed me, with my purse and the carry-on I keep in the car, packed for emergencies. "And you've already got the big one nailed. No checked baggage—it slows you down, and it isn't worth it when they send your bag to Chad."

A quick smile. "Or wherever they're sending luggage this week."

"Ah, the voice of experience," I said, with an answering smile. Not that I planned to actually get on the plane.

But she didn't need to know that. "Thanks. How often do you take this flight, anyway?"

"About once a week." She sighed, glancing around her. "It would be cheaper to open an office there. But oh no. They'd rather just send me on the overnight flight."

Once a week?

"Think of the airline points," I said as we inched forward. The toddler ahead of us began to wail.

She rolled her eyes. "My company won't let us keep them," she said.

"Hardly seems fair," I said.

"Tell me about it. Especially today. I just got back on Saturday. And here I am. Again."

"Saturday? When did you fly out?"

"On the Wednesday."

She'd flown out the day Anna had? What were the odds?

I glanced around me. Even if they'd flown the same day, how likely was it that my new friend had seen her?

I pulled out Anna's photo anyway. "I don't believe it. My niece flew out that day," I said, showing her the photo. "I'm going out to meet her. Any chance you saw her?"

She glanced at the photo, started to shake her head, then stopped. Reached for the photo, took a closer look. "I didn't see her on Wednesday," she said slowly. "But I'm nearly positive that this woman was on the flight back on Saturday."

What? "The flight back? You mean back to Vancouver?"

She nodded. Then hesitated, an odd expression on her face. "Well, back to Canada, anyway. I didn't actually see her in Vancouver. In fact…"

"In fact?" I prompted when she took too long to finish the thought. The toddler ahead of us wailed louder.

"I'm not certain," she said, raising her voice a notch to be heard. "But my impression is that she got off in Toronto. She was sitting a few rows ahead of me, you see. And I didn't notice her after we changed planes in Toronto."

Another pause. "But I could have just missed her. It was late, and I was tired. Not really paying attention to the other passengers."

"Of course," I said. "But she was on the flight?"

"I think this woman was," she tapped the photo. "Or someone who looked very much like her. But as I said, I'm not sure."

"I have to call my sister," I said. "If she's not in Basel, then there's no point my going."

"If this is the same woman," my informant said. "She didn't board in Basel. I noticed her because she was already on the flight when it arrived in Basel, and I walked by her seat on the way to mine. So it probably isn't her."

"Where was your plane coming from, do you remember?" I asked urgently.

"Munich."

"Now I really need to call my sister."

Someone's sister, anyway. I made my way back through the throngs, leaving a very puzzled frequent flyer behind me.

———

BACK IN THE car I sent a text to Cory, asking for names of passengers from Basel to Vancouver last Saturday. "I'm looking for a young woman who had boarded in Munich and got off in Toronto."

Cory replied immediately. "No prob."

Which meant what? Sit and wait? Get going?

Apparently it meant five minutes or so. I hadn't even left the Pay'n Park when my phone pinged and I had to pull over.

"Greta James," his text said. "That help?"

No. It didn't.

"Any record of her leaving Toronto?" I sent back.

And coming back to Vancouver and getting herself killed.

But I didn't tell him that part. I'd keep it quiet for now.

It took Cory longer this time. Or maybe I was more impatient.

"No Greta James and no Anna Lang from Toronto to Vancouver," he sent back.

Well at least he was thorough.

I stared at the phone. James was a pretty common surname. So why couldn't I get a connection to Don James out of my head?

What was Anna up to?

If it was Anna.

I wondered what Mona Gruen looked like. And how she factored into this situation. If she did.

It was time to bring in the big guns.

I texted Badger, and got back on the road.

CHAPTER TWENTY-FOUR

BADGER AND CORY WERE WAITING for me when I got back to the office. It took me aback to see Cory there—I'd deliberately chosen to exclude him from this meeting. Apparently Badger had other ideas.

But they had two steaming pizza boxes and half a dozen cans of Coke sitting in front of them—on my desk, no less—and the whole room smelled like dinner. My stomach growled audibly, and Cory grinned at me.

"Hope you don't mind," he said. "I let us in. And I'll be billing you for the pizza."

I waved it off, since my stomach had betrayed me—but looked pointedly at him 'til he moved out of my swivel chair and into the guest chair beside Badger on the other side of the desk. "It looks like you two have news," I said as I dropped into my chair.

Cory glanced at Badger—for approval?—then nodded enthusiastically. "Yeah. The good news is that the bad guys didn't get into the office server."

"Cory did a decent job of setting that up," Badger said.

He beamed.

Good to know. "Then how did they get our location?" I asked.

Badger took over. "It started from your computer, as I suspected earlier. You checked out a couple of blogs last week. Don James's blog. And Anna Lang's."

"And?"

"Somebody hacked your service provider, looking for whoever owned that laptop."

"Me," I said. It was a creepy feeling.

"Nope, it's in your company name. And the company listing is public—address and all," my nephew added helpfully.

"It's advertising," I said.

Badger just gave me a look.

Obviously it was time to rethink some of my security measures. "So how did Marie's computer get compromised?"

"It wasn't," Badger said. "Just yours."

"Which was enough," Cory said with a grin.

Right. Like I needed this. "I thought you said two of the sites Marie visited were monitored."

"Sure. And they may have logged her computer IP address in case it shows up again. But they didn't go any further."

"So her computer isn't how they found this office."

"Probably not," Badger said.

"And it's clean? Her computer?"

"It's fine."

Okay, then. "So what exactly is the spyware on those blogs I visited doing?" I said. "And who is monitoring them?"

Cory sat forward in his seat, and exchanged a look with Badger. He didn't say anything, though, despite his air of suppressed glee.

"Two different parties," Badger said.

Cory grinned. Broadly.

What? "Two?"

He nodded.

She sat calmly.

"How…?"

Badger smiled. "I have my ways."

"She's magic," Cory added, hero-worship in his eyes.

I didn't want to know. "So who are they?"

Again the exchange of glances. This time Cory spoke, though I couldn't see the signal Badger had given him.

"Don James himself—or someone he gave access to—on Don's blog," Cory said. "And Sonya Lang on Anna's blog."

"What?" Sonya Lang had known all along about Anna's blog? Was she lying to me about everything?

No wonder she'd been willing to pay me such a high fee.

But what was she up to? And who was Anna really running from? Her sister?

Then I remembered the body in Steveston. And shuddered. Whatever Sonya's role in all this, someone was playing a very dangerous game. And we didn't yet know how Anna was mixed up in it.

I put the question aside for now. "So why would Don James have allowed a piece of spyware to run on his blog?" I asked. "What's it doing, anyway?"

"Watching visitors to the blog. Logging IP addresses. Like in your case," Badger said. "But Cory is right, there's something running underneath it."

"Like what?"

"Not sure yet, but it looks like a very sophisticated portal to me," Badger said.

"So it would take someone to another site entirely?" I asked.

"If they had the right log ins, I suspect so," she said.

And wasn't that interesting. "Any idea what kind of site?"

"Not yet. But I'm just getting started," she said, with a sly grin.

Cory had that hero-worshipping look on his face again.

"Look for some kind of black market commerce site," I said. "I suspect he's dealing stolen artwork, or something similar. And be careful."

Badger gave me the stink-eye. "I'm not an amateur."

Oops. "No. But neither is Don James. I suspect he's been doing this—or something like it—for years. Without being caught, or even suspected."

"I'm better," she said.

"Better is whoever stays alive—and out of jail—the longest."

Unexpectedly, that earned me a grin. "I hear you," she said.

Cory looked proud. Of her? Of me? It was hard to tell. But at least he wasn't arguing.

"What about Mona Gruen?" I asked them both. "Have you unearthed anything about her?"

"Who?" Cory said.

Badger's fingers were already flying on her phone. "Don James' associate," she said without looking up.

"Oh," he said.

"I need to see a photo of Mona," I said, following a hunch. "Can you find one?"

Badger glanced up at me, tapped a couple of keys, then turned her phone so I could see the screen. Cory crowded around to look over my shoulder.

I stared at the woman on the screen for a moment, then pulled the photo of Anna out of the case file and showed it to them.

"They look like sisters," Cory said.

"More like ten year old and recent photos of the same person." Badger nodded towards Anna's photo. "This is the missing woman?"

"Yes. Anna Lang. And now I'm wondering about the woman who flew to Basel on Wednesday as Anna Lang, then flew back to Toronto as Greta James," I glanced at Badger. "Cory told you?"

She nodded.

"So was that was Anna? Or Mona Gruen?"

"With a little makeup, it could have been either," Badger said.

"And Mona's background suggests she's more likely to have access to fake passports than Anna is," I said.

Though I had the uneasy feeling that I still knew too little about Anna to make that judgement.

"You want me to dig," Badger said.

"Yes," I said.

"Us," Cory said. "You want us to dig."

Badger just looked silently at him, but he stuck out his chin and refused to back down. After a moment she gave a small nod, and he grinned.

"I need to know where Greta James is now," I said. "And if she isn't Mona, then I need to know where Mona is now. And who she's working for. Whoever it is—I suspect they're local. I'm pretty sure Mona Gruen must be living here."

"Since Don is?" Badger said.

"Exactly. And it worries me that Anna looks so much like Mona. I'm beginning to wonder if Don had plans to use that likeness, if that's why he promoted her."

"He's setting her up?" Cory said.

"Possibly," I said, impressed that he'd drawn that conclusion so quickly.

Though it was also possible that Don was attracted to the younger version of the woman who was his conspirator—and probably long-time lover—and hoping to replace her with Anna.

If that was the case, I was guessing neither Anna—given her complaints about him—nor Mona were cooperating with his little fantasy.

Despite my words to Badger earlier, I still had trouble taking Don James seriously as a villain. He seemed more of a comedy act to me—I remembered the young Don too clearly—despite everything I'd learned so far.

That kind of thinking could get me in trouble.

And spell disaster for Anna.

————

BADGER HAD JUST LEFT, Cory in tow, when my cellphone buzzed. Nick's number. I pounced on it. "Have you news?" I asked.

"Very little," he said. "But our victim has a name—she had her passport with her for some reason. Waterlogged, but still readable. We're not releasing the name yet, though…"

My heart dropped into my stomach. "Greta James," I said.

"How did you know?" he demanded.

Damn. I hadn't wanted to be right. "It might intersect with one of my cases. How old is the victim?"

"Don't you know?"

"No, I don't. I suspect the name "Greta James" is an alias. But it could be one of two women. One of whom is missing."

He groaned. "Your current case, I assume?"

"Yes."

"Passport says our Greta is thirty. That narrow it down?"

"Nope. It's half-way between the two I know about. Can you tell by looking at her?"

"She's been in the water too long. And the crabs have been at her."

Ugh. I wouldn't be ordering fresh crab for awhile. Which was a shame, because nothing beats a fresh crab and corn chowder.

But not with Nick's words in my mind.

He guessed it, too. "Oops, crab chowder. Sorry, Barbara."

The man knows me too well. Which used to panic me. Now… not so much.

Before I could reply, I heard something in the background, then a muffled sound. Nick had covered the mic, was talking to someone. A moment later his voice came back.

"I've got to run. I'll let you know if we find something. And Barbara? I hope it isn't your case we found."

"Thanks, Nick. Me too." I dropped my phone in my purse.

Since both of us are all too aware how very not-private cellphones can be, our phone conversations are strictly professional. We keep the mushy stuff for situations we know are truly private.

Taking a deep breath, I texted Badger. "Greta James passport found with drowned woman's body. Police may be monitoring any records."

Especially given what I'd just told Nick.

"Thanks," she sent back.

"Need to know which one is Greta, soonest."

"Got it."

Okay, then. For a moment I considered asking for a timeline. Then I pictured Badger's likely reaction. Naw.

Now what? There was no point talking to Sonya until I knew if her sister was on her way to the coroner's office. If Anna was dead, my case was closed.

And if she wasn't? If it was Mona who had died? Then what?

I didn't have enough information yet to begin to answer that one. I needed to hear what Badger had dug up first.

Essentially, I was on hold until either Nick or Badger, with a little help from Cory, figured out who had died in the Fraser.

And it had been a hell of a day. Since I was waiting anyway, I figured I might as well go home and paint.

So I did.

CHAPTER TWENTY-FIVE

THE FOLLOWING MORNING, CAT WOKE me far too early, demanding food. After I'd fed both of us, I didn't even try to paint, just went straight to the office. Marie still beat me in.

I took one look at her haggard face and tired eyes. "Should you even be here?"

"What? I'm fine."

"You don't look fine."

"So I didn't sleep well. It isn't easy, working in a burgled office." She cocked her head to one side like a demented sparrow, gave me a long once over. "You don't look so good yourself."

"Thanks a lot."

"No, really. Are you okay?"

She thought that was helpful? I wasn't about to tell her about the dead body. Not until I knew for sure if it was or wasn't Anna Lang.

"I painted too late," I said instead.

It happened to be true—I'd quickly discovered I was too wrought up to sleep anyway, and art is good therapy. Even though I suspected Margaret Courtland would refuse the resulting painting for my show—too bleak.

But I felt better. Tired, but better.

Predictably, Marie beamed. "Oh, good. I'm glad you're painting, despite everything."

Uh huh.

"Did you hear any more about Anna? Or why someone broke in here?"

"We're still waiting for information," I told her.

Which was mostly true. I was still waiting to hear back from Badger. And hoping to hear from Nick.

I'd expected him to have found out least something more about Greta last night, but either he'd been caught up in something else, or my tip on Greta's fake name had sent him off on a hunt. I knew how long those could take.

The lack of calls had to mean the victim was Mona, the one with the shady and complicated history—not squeaky clean Anna. Right?

But when the phone finally rang, I pounced on it. "Barbara O'Grady."

"Barbara? I need your help. Can you come?"

It was Andrea.

I didn't hesitate. "I'll be right there. Home or office?"

"Office," she said.

"Don't move," I said, wondering what could have gone wrong now.

———

ANDREA'S ASSISTANT waved me straight in. I nodded my thanks, and opened the door to find a wan Andrea looking lost behind her cleared desk. Her ever present laptop was closed, and she seemed to be staring into space.

She turned her head towards the door as I walked in. "Barbara? I'm so glad you're here. I've lost another employee."

It was the last thing I'd expected to hear. "I'm so sorry," I said. "What happened?"

"The police don't know for sure," she said. "She drowned, apparently. They found her off the pier…"

"In Steveston," I said quietly. "Greta James worked for you?"

"She did," Andrea said on a gulp. "For the last six months. She was really efficient. But… Barbara, how do you know? Does this connect with one of your cases?"

"I'm afraid it does." I breathed a silent sigh of relief. If Greta James worked for Andrea, she couldn't possibly be Anna Lang, who had only been missing for a week.

"I think your employee may be the latest persona of Mona Gruen, who worked with Don James for more than a decade."

"OMG." Andrea said. "That can't be good. Barb? I hired a … what?"

"A con artist, at the very least," I said. "Possibly a sophisticated thief. But I'm just starting to put the pieces together now. I'm still waiting for information to come in."

And why hadn't Nick called me back, if the police had already been in touch with Andrea?

I was relieved to see Andrea's color was back. She was sitting straighter, too.

"I don't mean to sound callous," she said. "But I'm hoping you're right. It's still awful and all, Greta, I mean Mona is still—I mean she was still—an efficient employee. But if she is—or rather was—a criminal of some sort…" She stopped dead and stared at me.

"Was she working on something criminal—was that why she was working for me?" she asked.

"I think so."

"Then I don't care if it is callous—I won't mourn her. Though I am sad for her—that she's dead. But knowing what I know about Don, I'm glad Mona can't cause any more trouble."

A more convoluted piece of logic I'd seldom heard—my best friend was really stressed. But she was right. Mona had most likely been bad news.

I was just glad it wasn't Anna.

Though I still had to find Anna.

Just as soon as I figured out what was going on between the sisters.

And what Don James was really up to.

"Greta James," Andrea said thoughtfully. "You don't think she and Don were married?"

"I doubt it," I said. "Given that the name was an alias. Though they did work together for a dozen or more years, from what I've uncovered so far."

"So they could have been a couple?"

"Probably were," I said. "But what really interests me is why she'd take a temporary assignment, and under a false name."

And why now?

As Mona Gruen, Marie had been able to track her career pretty easily. And I didn't recall any obvious gaps in her work history that might suggest she'd been working under an alias.

Which didn't mean there weren't any gaps.

"Hang on a sec," I said to Andrea, and sent a quick text to Badger to ask her to check, and to see if she could find any employment records for Greta James.

I looked up to find her staring at me. "Well?" she said.

"When did you last see Greta James?" I asked her.

"She took a week off," Andrea said. "So it would have been—last Wednesday," she said, flipping through her online calendar.

The same day Anna Lang disappeared.

"Barbara?" Andrea said, a note I didn't like in her voice. "What's going on?"

"I'm not sure yet," I said. But the underlying pattern for this case was starting to emerge. Finally.

"What were Greta James's work skills?" I asked Andrea. "And which assignments was she sent on?"

———

HALF AN HOUR LATER, I sat waiting for yet another left turn through snarled downtown traffic. It probably should have surprised me that Greta James had been working as a temporary office assistant for Xtreme Systems. And in Sonya Lang's section, no less.

It didn't. But why not?

Somehow this whole mess—which had started with Anna Lang's disappearance—tied together. I couldn't yet see how. But I now suspected that Sonya Lang was at the center of it.

It was time for my too-busy client to come clean.

And now that I knew that Anna, while still missing, at least hadn't just been pulled from the Fraser, there was nothing stopping me from having a 'gloves off' talk with her sister.

Well, nothing except Sonya herself.

She hadn't got back to me after yesterday's visit. And I'd left three urgent messages for her since I left Andrea's office.

Still nothing. Which meant she was avoiding me.

Why? She'd hired me to find her sister. What could be more important to her than that?

Or she said she'd hired me to find her sister.

As the white SUV ahead of me finally began to move, a question floated up from my subconscious. Why had Sonya really hired me, anyway? And what had she hoped I'd do?

I stewed on that one all the way back to my office. By the time I got there, I was steaming. But I had a few strategies in mind.

None of which my client was likely to be too happy about. Still, the contract she'd signed gave me the flexibility to take whatever actions I deemed best in solving a particular case. A flexibility I was about to take full advantage of.

Looking for Anna had gotten me nowhere. It was time to look at Sonya.

But first I texted Nick, suggesting he might find Mona Gruen of interest in his current case. Multi-tasking at its best. I knew he'd find a way to share whatever he found. Eventually.

Then I pulled up the few facts Marie had been able to uncover on Sonya. It was pretty skimpy.

Before I started digging, I texted Badger. I needed to be sure my laptop was secure. Moments later, I got a green light from her.

I started digging.

I may not be at Badger's level—or even my nephew's—but when I need to, I know how to research. I took the criteria I'd given Marie, and went deeper. Marie had only looked at Sonya's career.

I was more interested in her life, and especially her family life.

Sonya and Anna Lang. Who were they? Where had they come from? And how had they ended up in the situation—whatever it was—that I'd been hired to solve?

Though I suspected that Sonya didn't see the terms of my hire in the way I did. But she'd signed the contract. I wondered if she'd even bothered to read it first.

Not my issue.

CHAPTER TWENTY-SIX

TWO HOURS LATER, I HAD some basic facts about the sisters, but I'd run into block after block when I tried to go deeper. The records either didn't exist, or they'd been well hidden. Or erased.

In fact, neither sister seemed to have much history at all before their move to Canada. What was that about?

I'd just started to dig into their parents' background—which did appear to be solid—when I got a text from Badger, asking if I was at the office. An affirmative answer got me a "we'll be right there."

Good. "They" suggested Cory would be coming with her, and I had a few assignments for him. I was going to need more help here than I'd anticipated.

I glanced at the clock. Just after eleven a.m. Why wasn't Cory in class? Maybe he had a study period?

At this rate, I needed to get a copy of his class schedule, or we'd both be dealing with my sister.

Spare me.

"GRETA JAMES WAS WORKING for your friend Andrea," Cory announced before he and Badger were fully through the door. Good thing there weren't any clients in the office. Though Marie's eyes had gone wide, and she mouthed "Greta James?" at me.

I hadn't exactly brought Marie up to speed on what was going on. I probably should have, given that she worked here, if only temporarily. But I was still having a hard time taking her seriously.

And now was not a good time to update her. Or to tell my nephew and Badger—especially Badger—that I already knew Greta was working for Andrea. Oops. Should have sent them the info as soon as Andrea told me.

Apparently I was too used to being a one-woman show. Not smart—not when I was counting on the two of them. And Marie, too—in her way.

"But the real news is that she was doing temp work in Sonya Lang's unit at Xtreme. Though she worked on another floor, not directly for Sonya," Badger said, closing the door behind her. She glanced over at Marie. "And who is this?"

I'd forgotten she hadn't met Marie. "My assistant," I said, a little surprised at how easily the words came out.

"On the office side," I quickly added, seeing the affronted look on Cody's face. "Cody is the technical side."

Marie and Cody glared at each other, then Cody grinned at me, while Marie gave me a "told you so" look. I concentrated on Badger, ignoring both of them.

Was that a hint of amusement I saw on her face? I was remembering all the things I liked about being a one-woman show.

"What was Mona doing at Xtreme?" I asked. Hoping I hadn't put my foot in it. With their level of security, Badger probably hadn't uncovered that info yet. I needn't have worried.

"Mostly data entry," Badger said. "But given her varied background, she probably has skills that gave her access to a lot more than they intended. Even with their level of security," she added, with an expressionless glance at me.

For a super-techie, she was pretty good at reading people. I wondered what her story was.

"So what are they up to?" I said, half thinking out loud. I looked directly at Badger. "Why Xtreme Systems? How do they connect with whatever caper Don and company have planned?"

I glanced at Marie's confused face. "Greta James is the alias that Mona Gruen seems to be using in Vancouver."

Marie's expression cleared, and she started to smile.

Then she put it together that I'd left her out of the loop, and glared at me. I couldn't blame her. Either she was working for me or she wasn't.

The reality was that I owed them all more information than I'd given them.

So I filled them in on what I knew of the body found in the Fraser yesterday, and what Andrea had told me this morning about Greta James. Which earned me glares from all three of them.

"You know now," I said, to forestall the inevitable complaints.

"Well, at least we know it's Mona Gruen who died," Cory said. "And where she is now."

He'd put that together pretty fast. I was impressed. "Because Greta James was working full-time at Xtreme Systems while Anna Lang was working full-time at Zanthus."

"That too," he said, though it was clear from his momentary frown that he hadn't put that bit together.

"But when I couldn't find any trace of Greta James flying back to Vancouver from Toronto, I looked for Mona Gruen. And I found her. Greta James flew from Berlin to Munich. Then a day later, she flew from Munich to Toronto. Then Mona Gruen flew from Toronto to Vancouver later that same day."

Okay, then. "Good, then we we've confirmed that the body in the Fraser was Mona," I said. "Not Anna. So let's put this thing together."

"But that means that Anna never left Vancouver, right?" Marie said.

"Well, her passport did," Cory said.

"What?" Marie said, her tone edging on a screech.

"Anna's passport was used on the first flight, the one from Vancouver to Basel," he said. "Anna herself didn't leave Vancouver."

"Unless she has an alias too," Badger said.

Marie ignored her, turning to me. "So where is she? Where's Anna? She's our job, not all these others."

I was still wondering why only Greta James' passport had been found with Mona's body, if she was traveling with two other aliases.

But Marie was right. "We haven't found any sign of Anna since she left Zanthus on Tuesday night."

"She hasn't used her credit cards anywhere," Cory said. "She hasn't left town by plane, train or bus."

"Not under her own name," Badger said again.

I gave her a nod of recognition. "Exactly. So either she's safely hidden somewhere, possibly under another identity…"

Though given everything I'd learned about Anna so far, the latter seemed like a long shot.

"Or she's been kidnapped. Or worse." Marie's face was bleak.

There was nothing for it but brutal honesty. "Yes. Our only lead seems to be Don James and his gang of thieves. So we follow that, and hope it leads us to Anna."

"Alive," Marie said.

"Yes."

She gave a slightly desperate grin. "It worked before. For my sister." It was a statement of faith.

I wish I felt the same confidence. But I knew just how lucky we'd been that we'd found Celeste in time when she'd been kidnapped. I couldn't count on the same kind of luck again.

"It did. So, we'll focus on Don James and his gang." I glanced at the faces around me.

"We still don't know what Mona Gruen was up to. What did she hope to learn—or do—working for Xtreme Systems as Greta James? Why go to Basel, Munich and Berlin? And come back via

Toronto? Why the sudden trip? And what was her body doing in Steveston?"

"The airport's in Richmond," Cory said, leaning forward. "So is Steveston. Mona's flight came in on the seventeenth, and her body was found the following day. Maybe someone met her flight."

"Her killer?" Marie said. "That makes sense."

"Presumably someone she knew, in that case," I said. "It wouldn't be easy to abduct a stranger from that airport. It's too busy."

"But why take her to Steveston, then?" Cory said thoughtfully.

"Maybe she was taken further upriver and the body dumped," Badger said. "You said she was found floating against the wharf?"

I nodded, momentarily wondering about river currents, and exactly where a body would need to be dumped to end up against that wharf. But I knew the RCMP would bring in experts to figure that out. We didn't need to waste our energy on it.

"But who killed her? And why?" Marie asked.

"Exactly," I said. "We all know pieces of this. What does it tell us?"

"Let's put it up on a white board," Marie said. "See where the blanks are."

"Good idea," I said. "Only this time, we scan the result, then erase the white board."

I was trying to lighten the mood, but Marie flinched a bit. So much for that.

I tried again. "Cory, you order the pizza. We probably need Cokes all round, and any appies that strike your fancy."

That worked better. Even Badger smiled.

———

BY THE TIME we had everything up on the whiteboard, the pizza had arrived, and everyone grabbed a couple of slices and something to drink. I made a pot of dark French Roast, but I was the only one drinking it. Everyone else had a Coke. I had to wonder at their taste. Food in hand, we gathered our chairs around the wall with the whiteboards on them.

The short break helped. There was a new energy in the room as we looked at everything we knew Don and Mona had done since they arrived in Vancouver. Which was a good thing, because there was much less there than I'd hoped.

We knew where Don was working. We knew where Mona had worked for the last six months. We knew when Anna vanished, and the broad outlines of Mona's recent travels. That was it.

"We need to figure out what Don and company are up to," I said. "For now, we can probably assume it's illegal, and complex. We also need to know why Don chose Vancouver as his base."

"It's his hometown?" Cory said.

"That could be part of it, but there has to be more. Why did he come back now? And why here?" I paused, glanced at the intent faces around me. "What's here that he needs?" I asked.

"A port city?" Marie offered. "And an international airport. He seems to operate internationally. Maybe he's expanding."

"Asia as well as Europe?" What had the Zanthus Gallery's sales associates said? "And maybe the Americas. He's met recently with supposed art buyers from Hong Kong as well as South America."

"Where in South America?" Cory asked.

"Possibly Colombia," I said.

Cory and Marie exchanged glances. "Cocaine? Or emeralds," he asked her. She gave a half-shrug.

I glanced over at Badger. "Did the links on Don's blog get you anywhere?"

She gave me a bland look. "At least one of their team is really good with computers. Not as good as I am, though."

She had confidence, I'd give her that. "Oh?"

"Hmmm."

I let the silence stretch, unwilling to play games now.

"Just tell her, already," Marie said impatiently.

Cory frowned at Marie, but Badger just nodded. I wondered if we'd passed some kind of test, because Badger walked over to the whiteboard, and began drawing layer after layer of a complex organization.

I watched her, trying to figure out what I was looking at. Finally I got tired of guessing. "What is that?"

"Don James's blog links to a portal," Badger said, without stopping drawing. "For those with the right passwords—mostly clients. A few contract hires. Depending on what code is entered along with the password, the client, let's say, is taken to one of these levels."

I stared at what looked like an insanely complex organizational chart. "How does it work?"

"Very smoothly," she said. "This,"—and she pointed at the various levels of the chart—"is all linked, but only if you're really good at peeling back the layers. For most of their clients, it would seem like they're dealing with several different agencies."

"And they're not?" I asked, fascinated.

"No. They're dealing with the tentacles of one over-reaching organization. But this organization doesn't really exist, except as a way to connect the tentacles."

"It's a shell game," Marie said flatly.

"Of a sort," Badger agreed. "One played out in cyberspace, with multiple simultaneous games. And multiple shells in each."

My eyes were crossing as I tried to imagine it. "And they're establishing new tentacles from Vancouver?"

"And extending the reach of older, existing ones," Cory said. "Badger showed me earlier," he added a little defensively when I looked over at him.

"And it's still just the five of them that Marie identified?" I asked.

"I don't think so," Badger said. "They're the active players, but there's too much money at stake. And they're playing at too high a level for anything I could find out about them.

Look at Don James's resume—he's a player, but not a senior one. No, they have to have a silent partner, someone capable of this level of strategy. Maybe more than one."

"Why didn't you say something earlier?"

She gave me a look. "You didn't ask," was all she said.

Ouch. She knew I'd been holding back information. So she did too.

Note to self. Don't mess with Badger.

I glanced at the intent faces around me. Made another mental note. Always include the team.

"What about the other three members of Don's team? The ones we know about?" Marie was saying. "Do we know where they are now? Are they working locally too?"

"Two of them sort of are. I can't find the fifth," Cory said. "One is based in Seattle, and the other is in Richmond."

"Near the airport?" Marie asked, and he nodded. "Our killer then?"

It was a possible explanation for why she'd ended up in Steveston. But…

"It's too close," I said. "I doubt any of this team are stupid enough to leave a body in their own back yard. So to speak."

"What about the third man?" Marie asked.

"He seems to have changed identities again," Cory said. "I've been digging, but I couldn't find any trace of him here. Or anywhere else."

"I think he might be their computer guy," Badger said. "Somebody is really good with computers, and none of the other four have that level of knowledge. So I've taken Cory off that search, and I'm looking now. But whoever he is, he's good, and he's gone deep. It may take some time."

I nodded, staring at the lines she'd made on the whiteboard and thinking hard. "What do all of the different tentacles have in common?"

"Nothing. On the surface," Badger said.

"And under that?"

"It's all buying and selling. They seem to function as middlemen. Very expensive ones, from the little I could see of the commissions and expenses they tack on."

"But buying and selling what?"

"Don't know. It's all coded, and I haven't broken that code. Yet. But small, easily portable items. Really expensive ones."

"Like emeralds?" Marie said.

"Or cocaine," Cody added.

"Emeralds, possibly," Badger said. "I couldn't find any drug connections."

I was thinking through Don's CV. Art. Investing. Security.

"Expensive art," I said. "And maybe antiquities. Easily portable, and high end. In markets with avid collectors willing to pay top dollar."

Badger nodded. "Something like that, I think."

"So Don's using the Zanthus Gallery as a cover," I said.

"Or a way to make connections," Marie added.

Evidently she'd learned a few things about how the art world operated, growing up with Anthea Snow, despite her aunt's reclusive habits.

"Yes," I said. "They'd be dealing in stolen goods, most likely. Or items that couldn't be sold on the open market."

"Money laundering?" Cory asked.

"Something like that," Badger said. "It would explain the complexity of their supply channels."

"What do you mean?" I asked her.

"I wasn't quite sure what I was seeing before," Badger said. "But that would make sense. It looks like items travel a relatively short distance in any one tentacle. Then they disappear. Probably handed off to another tentacle, but there's no record of that. Making it impossible to track. For a normal person."

She glanced at me, grinned and grabbed a green marker. All of us watched fixedly as she added green lines, some solid, some with dashes, some dotted, connecting some of the "tentacles" she'd drawn before.

"These are the connections I've found so far. A tentacle with a solid line, for example, is only visible for those parties who use solid lines," Badger said.

Which sounded like gibberish, but as I looked at what she'd drawn, I saw that no more than two levels of the organization were ever connected by a solid line. The next level up or down might have a dotted line, or a dashed one, but not a solid one.

She muttered something to herself, put down the marker and grabbed her laptop. Typed rapidly for a moment. Then sat back with a look of satisfaction.

"Unless you're inside their organization," she said. "Then you can see the entire journey an item takes. But that's hidden so many layers deep, I can't imagine more than one or two people in the organization have that access."

And since I had a feeling there were few if any hackers with Badger's capabilities, the chances of it being broken from outside were slim.

"It must have taken years to set this up," Badger said, half to herself, her fingers still flying over the keys. "Gradually adding layers, and building in more complexity with each one.

She hit a sequence of keys and shut her laptop with a snap.

"They've had at least a dozen years to set it up," I said. "Maybe longer, depending on when Don met up with the silent partner. So what do we do with this information?"

"Get them arrested," Marie said, surprising me.

Where had this belief in the law come from? She certainly hadn't relied on them when it came to finding her missing sister, choosing to hire me instead.

"Except that none of this information can be used in a court of law," Badger said calmly.

"Then what good is it?" she spit back.

What was this? Last time I'd checked, it was Cory whom Marie was competitive with. Now she couldn't stand Badger either?

"It keeps us from chasing our tails in circles," I said flatly. "At least now we have a direction, as well as confirmation that we were right to suspect Don James of criminal involvement, as well as possibly having a role in Anna's disappearance."

"Yeah, but now what?" Marie said.

"Now it's up to us to expose him and his circle of thieves for what they are," I said.

———

CORY LOOKED from me to Badger's complex diagram and back again. "But how do we expose these guys, Aunt B.? This organization of theirs isn't a simple thing. I mean, it took Badger"—the hero worship in his tone unmistakable—"to understand it. How're we ever going to explain it to some cops?"

"Don't ever assume they're stupid," I said sharply. "Any more than we can assume Don and his partner and their people are stupid…"

"Especially not his partner," Badger put in.

I nodded. "That's why we need more information. If we can't use this, we need to use what we now know to find information we can use. And a way to present it to the police that they can use."

"So we do their jobs for them?" Marie asked.

"We do our jobs, and let them do theirs," I said. "That's how being a P. I. works."

Which shut Marie up, at least for the moment. "Now if you're finished arguing…"

But apparently Marie wasn't finished. Nor was she ready to let go of Anna.

"So where does Anna Lang come into this?" Marie asked. "If it's this complex, Don James isn't going to let some random employee in on it."

It hadn't been that long since Marie's sister was kidnapped. She seemed to have transferred her emotions from that experience to this case. So I cut her some slack. Besides, she was asking good questions.

"From the little Anna seems to have confided in her sister, she saw or overheard something at Zanthus that made her suspicious," I said. "And at some point she decided to run."

"Marie's right, that doesn't make sense," Cory said, earning him a surprised look from Marie. "If Don James has been building this thing for so long, he's not going to make stupid mistakes."

"But something made Anna run," Marie argued. Apparently she didn't like siding with Cory.

"Yes, it did. And something also sent Mona Gruen on a quick trip to Europe," I said thoughtfully. "The day after Anna vanished. Using Anna's passport. Or a very good fake. I wonder when she got that. And how long she'd had it?"

Marie and Cory exchanged glances, and Marie made a note, then nodded at me. They'd check into it.

Don't tell me they'd actually figured out how to work together?

Badger watched the interaction with her patented straight face. "And when Mona got back, someone killed her," she said. "She'd been working with this team for more than a decade. What happened to trigger both those things? And why now?"

"We need to know if quick trips to Europe were the norm for Mona," I said. "And if there's any footage from the airport of her meeting someone. We also need to find Don's silent partner."

Badger nodded, and made a few notes.

"Marie… You need to work with Cory to find out everything you can on Anna's background. I want to know everything: who she went to school with, everyone she's ever worked with. And I particularly want to know who she met with in the last month."

Marie looked skeptical. "Everything?"

"I know. I took a look, and didn't find much. That's why I want you and Cory working together. You have good instincts,"—she looked pleased—"And Cory's good at digging deep."

Cory did that "don't care" teenage thing, but his eyes gleamed. And both of them nodded. Maybe this really was working.

"But Cory goes back to school after lunch. You can pick up again after school," I said, ignoring his crestfallen look.

"And you both need to be careful. We're dealing with dangerous people. If you find anything that makes you the least nervous, or you think you might have triggered something, call Badger."

I glanced over at her, raised an eyebrow, and she nodded. Good.

"Meanwhile, I'll dig deeper into Anna's last few days in town. See if I can find the trigger that made her run," I said.

"I also intend to talk to our client. If Sonya was tracking Anna's website, she may know something."

Sonya obviously knew more than she'd told me. And I really wanted to know what would cause her to put spyware on her sister's computer.

"There's pop in the fridge," I said. "And we'll all meet back here around six, talk over takeout. That okay with everyone?"

A series of nods.

"Indian food?" Cory said.

"Sure. Order anything you want."

Judging by Cory's grin, that would cost me. But if we could break this case, it would be worth it.

CHAPTER TWENTY-SEVEN

AFTER BADGER LEFT, CODY AND Marie settled down at her desk to work on their part of the assignment. I retreated to my "office"—first moving the partition back between her desk and mine. Which wasn't much help, since the two of them started to bicker within minutes. It sounded like friendly bickering, for a change, but it was still hard to concentrate.

And I needed to think about the meeting we'd just had. The longer I looked at the lines Badger had drawn on the whiteboard, the more I felt like I was missing something.

But what? I'd rerun everything I'd uncovered, everything the team had told me. Nothing.

So what was niggling at me?

I glanced around the office. Everything was back in place from the break-in. Which we hadn't even talked about. What were they looking for? And what were they likely to do next?

Still, that wasn't the source of the niggle. This was something about Anna.

Something more about Anna and Sonya, maybe? I pushed and prodded at that thought like you do at an inflamed tooth, but still nothing. Whatever it was, my mind was in no hurry to give it up.

A particularly loud argument from the two on the other side of the partition decided me. I couldn't stay here. I needed to be doing something. Maybe then the missing bit of information would come to me.

I grabbed my laptop and stuffed it in my oversize purse. "I'll be out for a few hours," I called out as I passed them, heading out the door.

That got me an absent nod from Marie, no acknowledgement at all from Cory, who was bent over his own laptop.

Not knowing where I was going, I got in my car and drove. Over the Granville Bridge linking downtown and the west side. Cutting across to Oak Street, then over the Oak Street Bridge and into Richmond. Apparently I was going to Steveston.

Trusting my gut on this one, I focused on the road, the traffic and the weather rather than trying to think through a case that was resisting logical thought.

Not even two p.m. yet but traffic was already starting to build towards its rush hour volumes. It was sunny, fairly warm, with pale blue skies and a few wispy clouds. The roads were clear, seemingly giving some drivers permission to cut in and out without signaling.

I rolled my eyes and stayed in the fast lane.

Across Steveston Highway and down Three Road. Through row on row of the upscale townhouses and condominiums that had sprung up in the last ten years. I snagged a parking spot and hoofed it down to the walkway that ran along the river.

Why was I wasting time like this? Anna was still missing, Mona Gruen was dead, and we were so close to breaking what was going on. And here I was, staring at the river. Which was broad as it spread out towards the ocean, deceptively still, and a muddy brown. Despite all the new buildings, it still smelled of river water and river grass.

As I walked towards the wharf beneath which Mona had been found, I watched the river traffic. It was busy, with huge barges being pulled upriver on the far side of Shady Island, a man-made breakwater which bisected the river and protected the sprawl of the town. On the near side of the island the occasional fishing trawler or sightseeing boat motored by.

I could see why Mona's body had been found so quickly. And unless she'd been dumped right off the pier itself, her body must have gone into the water after dark. Someone would have seen something, otherwise.

Still baffled by what I was doing here, I bought a double espresso at a coffee and gelato place and drank it as I walked down along the wharf. It was a weekday, so no boats were tied up selling fish, and the wharf felt strangely empty. Like my brain.

I strolled back. Grabbing a latte from the same café, I strode along the board sidewalks that fronted the deliberately quaint shops and boutiques. As I glanced in the window of a home decor store with mass-produced artwork displayed for sale, it struck me that there were no art galleries in Steveston. No antique stores, either, not anymore. They'd all disappeared a decade ago.

So why had Mona Gruen ended up here?

And what were she and Don James really up to?

I walked a few steps further, and stopped dead. The fellow behind me muttered something as he walked around me, and I got a few strange looks. I ignored them. That niggling thought had just broken through.

The shadow box Anna had had on her walls. The lists of numbers. What if they corresponded to the tentacles that Badger had found?

I found an empty bench facing the harbor and sat down. Took a moment to enjoy the sun on my face, the sparkle of it on the water.

Then I might as well have been back in the office. I'd loaded up the photos I'd taken from Anna's collage on my phone, and slowly went through them, looking for a connection to what Badger had found. I couldn't see it.

That didn't mean it wasn't there.

I texted Badger a brief explanation and the photos.

Sat back and savored the latte and the location the way it deserved. Then ran through all my notes on Anna.

I ended up creating a timeline for her on a napkin, looking for holes in my knowledge as well as anything that might be significant, given what I now knew. Wishing I had her calendar.

I'd bet Sonya had it. Probably without Anna's knowledge.

And I was tired of her games.

———

SONYA LANG'S expression was unforgettable when I strode into her meeting room three-quarters of an hour later. She looked first stunned, then furious. The young programmers she was meeting with looked ready to climb under the table.

In other circumstances I might have laughed. But I was too angry to be amused.

"How did you get in here?" she all but snarled.

"I'm sorry, Miss Lang," her assistant bleated from the doorway, providing the answer. "I couldn't stop her. She…"

A wave of Sonya's hand cut the explanation short. "We'll finish this later," she said to her staff, her eyes still on me. They scrambled towards the door.

In seconds the room was empty except for the two of us, the door firmly shut.

"I assume you have an explanation?" she said, her tone icy.

"And I'm hoping you have one," I said.

"Me? Have you forgotten that I am the client?"

"No. Have you forgotten that you hired me to find your sister?"

"Not at all. Have you found her?"

This was getting ridiculous. I didn't answer, just walked closer, until we were less than a foot apart. "No. Did you expect me to?"

For a moment she was speechless. Whether it was at my effrontery, or because she couldn't come up with a good enough lie, I wasn't sure.

It didn't last, though. "Of course I did. That is why I hired you."

"Really? Because there seems to be rather a lot about your sister that you didn't tell me. Perhaps you forgot?"

"I...you..." She stopped, drew in a breath, gathered her armor around her in a remarkable display of control. "This is clearly not working. You may consider yourself fired."

I nodded. I'd expected that. "And based on the contract you signed with my firm, you may expect me to continue looking for your sister until the retainer you gave me is used up. Which means I have some questions for you."

She stared at me silently for a moment, but her mouth had gone hard.

"Oh, I think not," she said at last. "In fact, you will be hearing from my attorney."

"First you might like to explain to him—or her—is why you'd hacked into your sister's blog and were monitoring her activities," I said. "That's illegal, you know."

She flushed. "How..." Then she got herself under control again. "That is slander."

"Only if it isn't true."

"I'll sue."

"Feel free." I knew a very good lawyer I could call on. Claire Chan would make mincemeat of Sonya.

Something in my face must have told her how little I feared her threats. She seemed to fold in on herself, until that perfectly cut suit seemed to hang on her.

"Or you could just help me find your sister by telling me what I need to know," I said after another moment of silence. "She's in danger, you know."

"Anna? In danger? Physical danger?"

So she hadn't known. "Yes."

"But how?"

"I'll tell you. After you answer my questions."

She straightened and glared at me, looking ready to argue the point. I met her gaze steadily, and she looked away. "Very well. What is it you need to know?"

"Why did you hire me?"

"I am worried about my sister."

She had a funny way of showing it. "But you didn't know she was in danger?"

"I thought she was going to get herself hurt. But she wouldn't listen to me. I am her sister—her elder—she needed to listen."

Whoa. "Get hurt how?"

"She—Anna has always been a dreamer. She wanted a career in the arts. It is a very tough world, and especially for a woman. These galleries—they chew you up. Anna would hear none of this."

"You didn't choose an easy career either. Especially for a woman. And you've thrived."

She gave a wry smile. "I paid a price. Only I know how dearly I paid. Anna—she wouldn't listen. She thought for her it would be different. She wouldn't even listen when I told her blogging could be a dangerous on an unsecured website."

True, but it was hard to see what a hacker could gain on a small, limited interest site like Anna's. "Why did you hack her blog?"

"To prove to her what she would not believe any other way," Sonya said, as if it were the most reasonable thing in the world. "She thought herself so safe. I would show her exactly how unsafe what she was doing could be."

I couldn't even find words, so I didn't bother to try. "Anna's disappearance—do you know where your sister is?"

"No! How should I? That is why I hired you to find her."

"Who is she running from?"

At this she flushed, pale skin turning an unlovely red. "From me," she said. "This is why I hired you—she cannot win this argument by refusing to talk. Or running away."

Which is what I'd begun to suspect. Until Badger had dug into Don James world. "Are you sure?" I asked.

"Yes, I…" She stopped, stared at me. "Why do you ask me this? What have you learned? Is she truly in danger?"

"Yes, I think she is. I think she has information about criminal activity at the gallery where she works that has put her in danger."

Sonya sat down hard. "That is real?" she said.

Finally. Someone that Anna had talked to. Even if it had been her sister. "What did she tell you?"

She shrugged, a fleetingly bitter expression on her face. "What didn't she? It started with some nonsense about her boss making advances. As if she hadn't expected it, wearing those tight sweaters of hers."

I had to bite my tongue on that one. No wonder Anna and Sonya were having problems. "Was that all?"

"No, it was just the beginning. She tried to tell me about stolen antiquities she'd found at her gallery, and things she'd overheard about a major buyer. She wanted my help to learn more about what they were up to, so we could stop them."

Anna had learned more than I'd thought. "Your help?"

"She wanted to trace an email she'd managed to obtain."

"And what did you do?"

"What do you expect me to do, when she made up such stupid lies?" She let out a bitter little laugh. "I told her not to steal the plots from one of our games if she wanted my attention. Did she think me a fool? I was so angry."

What? From a game? "Were the details that close?"

She rolled her eyes and listed them.

They were. And some of them were also close enough to our speculations about Don James' activities that a chill went down my spine.

"Which game?" I asked her.

"Super Thieves, Inc.," she answered.

Whoa. I wasn't a gamer, but even I'd heard of that one. It was one of Xtreme's top sellers. And even with only a sketchy sense of what it was about, I could see the similarities with this case.

It was enough for me to wonder if both of us were being conned. And by Anna.

Had Anna known Sonya would hire an investigator if she vanished? Was everything I'd uncovered so far—scant though it was—part of an elaborate game?

Mona Gruen's death was no game.

Nor was the elaborate scheme Badger had uncovered.

But they might have nothing to do with Anna's disappearance. It was an unsettling realization.

"Was Anna a gamer?" I asked.

Sonya shook her head. "Not at all. She had no interest in what I did. But she expected me to be interested in her work."

"Then how would she know the intricacies of your games? Even the best-selling ones."

Sonya stared at me. "I… hadn't thought. Anna has never been interested in gaming. But there are enough articles written about Super Thieves. And Anna is a good researcher. If she wanted my attention, she could easily learn what she needed to tell me this story."

"And if the situation she described at the gallery was real? Then what would you say?"

Sonya's face had gradually tightened as we talked. "I'd say my sister was in a lot of trouble," she said, her expression bleak.

That's what I'd been afraid of. I opened my notebook.

"I'll need every detail you can remember of what Anna told you, no matter how preposterous it sounded."

"You think it's real?"

"I think I need to know everything she told you."

"I see." A pause. "Then I'll set up a spreadsheet for you. I think more clearly that way. And I can keyboard faster than you can write."

"I'll wait. And I'll also need a copy of her calendar for the last two months, if you have it."

Sonya didn't even bother to look embarrassed, just nodded and opened her laptop.

———

I WAS STILL REELING from the list Sonya had handed me when I got back to my office. Which seemed strangely quiet as I opened the door. For a moment I was afraid Marie had abandoned her post again, but no.

There they were, Marie and Cody, heads bent over his laptop.

If they were working together, I wasn't going to interrupt them and risk breaking the mood. They were concentrating so hard they barely noticed me. I got a half nod from Marie, and a glance from Cody.

Okay then. I put a pot of coffee on, and pulled out Sonya's list. I could sort of see why she hadn't believed her sister. It did read like something out of a bad heist film. Or an on-line game.

I'd used my phone to do a little research of my own while Sonya was typing, and she'd been right. It was possible to get a decent sense of the plot twists in just about any game through some of the gaming sites. Comparing what I'd found out about Super Thieves, Inc. against Sonya's list, it was nearly point by point.

No wonder she hadn't believed Anna.

Next I considered our list of everything we knew about Don James and his operation. Compared that to what Anna had told Sonya. It all fit.

There were a lot of holes, but the pieces I had fit together.

Which raised some interesting questions. And the only place I was going to find answers was at the Zanthus Gallery itself.

Which was probably a stupid move. I'd be walking right into the middle of a plot that had already killed one of its own members. And after the break-in, Don had to know I was looking at him. Just like I knew he didn't think I'd find anything.

He thought he was smarter than I was. And maybe he was—though I doubted it, remembering the younger Don.

But all criminals slip up. Eventually.

And I wanted to be there when he did. He'd had the nerve to break into my place. I wouldn't let that go unchallenged.

Essentially, I was daring him to act. And he was doing the same to me. And yes, I knew exactly how dangerous that was. I just didn't care.

Which wasn't quite true. It was a calculated move on my part. I was pretty sure Don was too arrogant to be able to resist taunting me. Showing me his setup, knowing I wouldn't be able to catch him, would be irresistible.

Killing me outright wouldn't be nearly as satisfying.

I hoped.

I glanced at my watch. Nearly four. I had a couple of hours before the team met to pool what we'd discovered. And Don had offered me a tour of the gallery.

Now would be a perfect time to take him up on it.

CHAPTER TWENTY-EIGHT

THE ZANTHUS GALLERY WAS AS gleamingly immaculate as ever. Aside from one sales associate at the counter—it was Drew, I noted —it was also deserted. I hadn't phoned ahead. If Don wasn't there, I was hoping I could talk my way behind the scenes anyway.

He was there. And apparently happy to see me, coming forward with a broad smile and an outstretched hand. I studied his face as he walked towards me, wondering if he'd heard the news about Mona Gruen's death yet.

There was no sign of grief, or even sadness in his eyes. If he'd heard, he was much better at subterfuge than I'd ever have expected. Or much crueler.

If he didn't yet know about her death, then why didn't he? What relationship existed between Don and Mona and the killer?

"Barbara," he said, leaning forward for a little continental cheek kissing that came too close to a hug for my taste. Especially with everything I'd learned about this man.

"I'm sorry for the lack of notice, but I had a little time free, and I hoped you might be able to give me that tour?" I said, deftly extricating myself, and determinedly not noticing the look of sympathy Drew sent me. "I'm dying to see what you've made of the place."

I winced a little at my phrasing, hoping it wouldn't prove prescient. Apparently I wasn't quite as comfortable confronting him on my own as I'd thought. Don didn't seem to notice.

"But of course," he said, laying on a faux French accent, taking my hand and leering outrageously at me.

So maybe he had noticed.

"What would you like to see?"

"You've really turned Zanthus around. Now that I'm getting back into showing my work…"

"And congratulations on that little coup," he broke in with another grin.

Had he recently bleached his teeth? If so, he needed a new dentist. A subtler one. His smile glared whitely at me under the lights.

"Thank you. But I've ignored the way business practices in the art world have changed for too long," I said. "I'd love to see some of the things you've done behind the scenes that have been part of your success."

"And I would be happy to show you," he said, taking my arm and leading me down the corridor that ran past his office.

As he reached past me to open the door into the back area, I glanced at his half-familiar face. I couldn't read his expression.

He didn't look flattered, but he didn't look worried, either. He looked—thoughtful? Now what had I given him to think about?

Uh oh. Maybe this wasn't such a good idea.

———

THE BACK ROOMS at the Zanthus Gallery were fairly typical—a warren of storage for upcoming shows and packaging and shipping areas. Everything was brightly lit and neatly labeled and stored. I stopped and stared.

"How did you get it so organized?" I asked. From earlier days, I was used to seeing artworks stacked haphazardly back here, grouped by whichever show they were intended for. Things were organized, in their fashion, but nothing like this.

"It took a little time, but the space itself was well designed. It was just a matter of implementing a system, and insisting that it was followed."

I still couldn't believe what I was seeing. Nor could I believe that the very disorganized Don I remembered could have changed this much. No way he'd set up this system.

I wondered who had done it for him, thought briefly of the dead woman. If Mona had been the brains behind this, she would be a real loss to Don. Again I wondered why she'd had to die.

And if he'd killed her.

For the first time I wondered if Don was capable of that degree of ruthlessness. It wasn't a happy thought.

"It's really impressive," I said, falling back on the mundane to cover up my sudden fear. "This must have improved your efficiency tremendously when you're setting up a show. And when you're taking it down, too. Especially when it comes to shipping out the sold pieces."

"You're right, it did," he said. "I always appreciated that quick brain of yours, Barbara."

Now why did that comment make me so uncomfortable?

"I'm proud of what we've achieved, but even Zanthus still has flaws," he continued. "Let me show you our basement."

And he led the way down a set of uneven stairs off to one side that I'd barely noticed, pulling the chain on an overhead bulb as he did so.

I followed him down into a dimly lit basement. Which was a crazy risk to take. But I wanted to know what he was planning on showing me.

And at least someone knew I was here. Drew had watched us as I followed Don into the backroom.

He'd notice if I didn't come out again.

———

THE BASEMENT LOOKED like it had served as a storeroom for years, rarely visited, even more rarely cleared out. It was clean, I'd say that much—or at least there was no sign of cobwebs. And the lighting was too poor to see any dust.

The place was full of cheap metal shelving on both sides of an uneven central aisle, with random stacks of boxes jammed everywhere else. The shelves ran floor to ceiling, looming out of the shadows with barely two feet of walkway between each.

The floor was concrete, and I was relieved to see that at least they'd bolted the shelving to the floor. The thought of all those loaded shelves toppling over like dominoes while I stood helpless was the stuff of nightmares.

Every shelf was full, mostly with plastic wrapped canvases or lumpy objects. Between the poor light and the lack of labels—or any obvious identification system—it was impossible to make out what anything was.

"How do you find anything?" I asked.

He shrugged. "We don't. Most of this stuff has been here for decades. Some of it I moved down when I took over, because I couldn't figure out what else to do with it. Dreadful stuff. You would not believe how bad some of it is."

He gave a mock shudder, then waved an arm that took in the whole space. "I fear most of my predecessors were pack rats," he said in a loud whisper. And grinned at me.

Nothing to see here. Move along.

Aloud I said, "Well, this certainly proves what a difference you made upstairs. I can't believe this is how things were organized before you took over."

I wondered why he'd shown me the basement. This would be a great place to hide almost anything. If you didn't know where something was, it could take days of searching to find it. If not weeks.

If he was trying to convince me that Zanthus was an open book, he'd failed. And he had to know that.

So why bother?

Unless he was mocking me? Knowing I suspected him, but certain I couldn't prove anything. Was this an elaborate game to him?

Maybe he considered me no threat—just a washed up artist trying to make a half-assed living as an investigator. Easily misled. The thought stung.

But it did remind me I couldn't assume anything. I still knew too little about what was going on here.

And it was past time to get out of this basement.

I started to tell Don so, and everything went black.

———

I FROZE.

I couldn't see a thing, and there wasn't even a hint of light coming from anywhere. The power must've gone out.

Or we were too deep underground.

I put out a hand, but the shelving unit wasn't where I'd thought it was, and I was afraid to step in any direction in case I misjudged my direction and tripped over the boxes stacked everywhere.

I heard Don breathing somewhere in the dark behind me, but he didn't say a word. And the odd acoustics of the crowded basement, with its low ceilings and odd angles, made it impossible to tell exactly where he was.

I had no idea if he'd created this situation. Or what his intentions were.

He had to know I was investigating him. That I was a threat to him and his little crime empire.

I had never felt so helpless.

I heard a soft shuffling sound, and his breathing grew faster. Harsher.

I tensed.

Choked back the fear. I couldn't afford it now.

Braced for whatever might be coming.

Nothing happened.

We stood in absolute darkness forever.

———

IT WAS PROBABLY LESS than thirty seconds before the lights came on and I could breathe again.

I spun to see Don standing with one hand on the light switch and a shit eating grin on his face. "It's pretty dark down here without the lights, isn't it?" he said.

He'd done it on purpose.

The idiot was toying with me. This was his version of a threat.

The low-life scum.

I gave him a deliberately weak smile. Two could play at this game.

He was going to regret this.

CHAPTER TWENTY-NINE

I GOT BACK TO THE office just before six, still fuming over the stunt Don had pulled, and plotting revenge. I was the last to arrive, so everyone took a seat from a variety of chairs around a long folding table I didn't recognize. It was enough to distract me for a moment.

Where exactly had that table had come from? How had Marie managed to get it in here in the three hours I'd been gone? And what it was going to cost me?

The new table was certainly handy, though, even if she'd had to push most of the furniture out of the way to make room. For one thing, there were paper plates and a variety of takeout containers in the middle of the table, and the room smelled of good curry, basmati rice and naan bread. For another, there was room for four laptops, even with all of us facing the whiteboards.

Compared to that, the feeling that if I breathed too hard, something would fall over was irrelevant. I was going to have to do something about the space in here if we kept having meetings like this, though.

I glanced around. Cory was discussing something with Badger

in low tones, a frown between his thick brows. He looked more angry than frustrated.

Unlike Marie, who was alternating between scowling at the two of them and the open file in front of her. Whatever was in it, she wasn't happy about it. Or about being excluded from Cory's conversation, if I was any judge.

I turned my attention to the whiteboard—which hadn't been updated since I last saw it. It was time to change that.

———

"WHO WANTS TO START?" I said.

"We do," Marie said, with a defiant look at Badger.

Who looked amused.

Whoa. What was going on here?

Marie didn't wait for me to figure it out. "We know who Anna met with," she said.

"Yeah. After Aunt B. sent us her calendar," Cory said, earning himself a poisonous look.

"So?" Marie countered. "We found out who they all are. And how they're connected." And glared at Cory.

"Go on," I said, figuring a little encouragement might help at this point. Given that I had very little patience for whatever games were going on. Or why they were going on.

"But we're missing a few more pieces, I think," Cory said.

Which explained Marie's earlier look of frustration.

"That's why we're here tonight, instead of doing whatever you'd prefer doing on a Tuesday night," I said. "To pool our information. I have a feeling that when we put it all together…"

I looked at Badger in silent appeal.

She met my look for a moment, then nodded. "I don't have answers either, but I think I have a few more pieces."

Badger checked them off on her fingers. "First, Mona Gruen wasn't in the habit of making short trips to Europe. Last

Wednesday appears to be the only time she's done so since she moved to Vancouver.

"Under any name," she added, with a slight smile towards Marie, who'd been about to interrupt and now sat back sullenly.

"So something was urgent enough to send her on that trip, possibly the same something that got her killed," Badger said. "But I found nothing to indicate what that might have been."

"Second, I've found more traces of Don James's silent partner, but no name. And nothing concrete enough to find me one. Yet. Whoever he is, he's very good."

Cory looked surprised. That seemed to amuse Badger, because her smile widened slightly. It was the most expressive I'd seen her since I met her.

I was just glad that both Marie and Cody seemed to amuse her. I don't think I could have handled Badger at odds with the others. The very thought of it made me nervous.

"However, third," and Badger folded down a third finger, leaving only her middle finger extended, and no indication on her face that she'd done so on purpose—though I had no doubt that she had—"Barbara also sent me some coded data she'd found at the missing woman's apartment."

It surprised me to hear the beautifully written documents from Anna's collage described as coded data—they'd hardly looked like what I considered data.

Antiqued and presented as they'd been, they'd been transformed into art, as far from their origin as it was possible to be. Then framed and hung on a wall, hiding in plain sight.

Which was a brilliant move on Anna's part.

"And that data, fitting in with what we already knew," and here Badger got up and strode over to the white boards, and proceeded to add dates and destinations to a number of the channels she'd drawn earlier.

Cory gasped.

I stared at what Badger had written, and then I saw it too. "She had information on the various shipments. The channels you found, these tell you when they were used."

Badger nodded. "Yes. But not what they were used for. Or by whom. Some of the information may be there, but I haven't broken the code. Yet," Badger added as she sat down.

I heard the determination in her voice, and had no doubt she would do so before we were done. Nodding, I handed out copies of the notes Sonya had given me, as well as my comments.

"These might help," I said.

———

"SUPER THIEVES!" Cory said. "This is related to Super Thieves? I love that game."

Of course he did. "Just read the list," I said.

For a moment there was silence in the crowded room, as all four of us looked from my notes to the various scribbles on the whiteboards. Cory was the first one to speak.

"I don't get it," he said. "How could what Anna told Sonya match Super Thieves so well? Especially when it's Xtreme's own game. Was she pulling her leg? Or just trying to piss her off?"

"I think that's what Sonya thought," I said. "With Anna's disappearance being that final step too far."

I glanced over at Marie, who was frowning.

"That's why she hired me... us. Sonya was pissed off, and she was going put a stop to her little sister's games. She wasn't going to waste any more of her own time on them."

Marie's frown turned to a scowl. "You mean that whole sob story she told me—that was a lie? But that's not possible! She was upset, really upset. You can't fake that."

"Yes and no," I said. "Sonya really was that upset, she wasn't faking. And she was extremely upset that Anna was missing. But she was furious with Anna, not worried about her safety. She lied about that."

"So she went from being angry that Anna was playing her, to playing us to get even with Anna?" Cory said. "That sucks."

Judging by their expressions, for once he and Marie were in agreement.

"She played me," Marie said, wearing a look I'd never seen before as she turned to me. "She can't get away with it. Using us like that."

"Don't worry," I said. "She decided to fix this problem of hers by throwing money at it. Only the problem is a lot bigger than she thought, and it's going to take one hell of a lot of fixing. You can help me prepare her final bill."

Marie started to protest, then paused, biting back the words. Her eyes brightened. "Okay," was all she said.

I'd hate to be Sonya when she got that final bill, because it looked like Marie and I were thinking exactly the same thing in our ideas of an appropriate revenge for our client's actions.

And wasn't that a scary thought.

"Can we get back to how this helps us find Anna," Badger said, her voice sharp.

"Tell us what you're thinking," I said, putting the ball firmly back in her court.

Her expression didn't change, but I suspected she was amused. "Is there any possibility that Sonya Lang is right, that Anna is a gamer?" she asked.

"No way," Cory said. "All she had was an underpowered tablet. The only game on it was Angry Birds. The first version."

He snorted. "She couldn't have played Super Thieves if she'd wanted to. She hadn't even accessed any games online. Ever."

Badger looked at him. "She never wiped her browsing history?"

"Nope."

They shared a look of horror, which amused me, even as I made a mental note to wipe my own browsing history more frequently.

I didn't want to be on the receiving end of a look like that from my fifteen-year-old nephew.

"There's only one conclusion to be drawn here." Badger tapped a long finger against Sonya's list. "These can't be coincidences. If Anna is not a gamer, then someone else is."

Cory straightened from his usual teenage slouch. "Someone involved in this case has to be a gamer," he said excitedly. "A good one. Cause they know the twists and turns of Super Thieves really, really well."

Badger nodded. "And whoever it is has to be calling the shots at Zanthus."

"Not Don James?" I said, thinking about it. It made sense, given the Don James I remembered. Who'd probably never really existed.

"Nope. His computer was useless too. And there were no games at all on it."

"The missing fifth player?" I suggested. "Meaning he or she might have more say in all of this than we'd suspected."

"Or the silent partner," Badger said. "The silent partner and the fifth player may not be one and the same."

"I only found signs of the fifth player in Europe," Marie said. "Nothing here."

If the silent partner—whoever he or she was—was based here, then perhaps the fifth player had only been needed abroad.

Maybe that was why Marie couldn't find him. They'd left him behind. If that were the case—I wondered uneasily if he was still alive.

But could Don James' silent partner be an extremely good computer gamer?

Why not? A serious gamer would have the mind for creating that octopus of companies that Badger had dug out. But what kind of gamer could have funded something this big?

Something didn't sit right.

"Why this game?" I said slowly.

"It's big. Everyone plays," my nephew said.

"Yes, but there are other games, as big or bigger, right?" I said.

He nodded. "Sure, but..."

I held up a hand. "And are any of the others a better fit for the kind of organization Badger found hidden behind Don James's blog?"

"Yes. Several are," Badger said.

So she was a gamer, too. It fit.

"And are any of those produced by Sonya's company?"

"No," Cory said. "Super Thieves is their biggest hit. But…"

I kept going. "Then it doesn't make logical sense that they'd use Super Thieves. Not unless whoever this is…"

"Oh, just call him Mr. X," Marie said.

"Or Ms. X," Cory put in.

I was glad to see he wasn't growing up gender-biased, but this wasn't helping. "We'll call him or her Moneybags," I said.

Cory grinned. So did Badger. Marie just looked annoyed.

"So why did Moneybags,"—and didn't I feel like an idiot saying that—"choose this particular program? Unless he or she is somehow connected to Xtreme Systems. And connected in a way that gives him or her a reason to know that particular program well enough to borrow some of the ideas," I said slowly.

Badger was nodding. "Borrow them and twist them for a completely unrelated use. That fits."

Good to know. It still felt like a reach to me. "Tell me why."

"Moneybags"—and her lips curled ironically as she said it—"has to understand Super Thieves on an almost instinctive level to use it this way."

"Which means…?" I said.

"Super-user?" Cory asked her.

She smiled a little. "Programmer. Working for Xtreme Systems."

Right under Sonya's nose. It made a warped kind of sense. And explained so much.

"If Moneybags is a programmer, he or she could still be either our fifth man or the silent partner."

"Programmers are well paid," Cory said.

And wasn't it interesting that he knew that. I wondered if this signaled his future career plans—and if my sister knew about them.

"But not well enough to be the secret partner behind a scheme this big," he finished.

He made a good point, except for one little detail. "Not unless Moneybags was at Xtreme Systems from the early days, and had a lot of cheap stock options," I said, recalling what Andrea had told me. "Then they'd have more than enough to fund anything they wanted."

"So we need to find out which programmers work on this game now, and how long they've been there," Marie said. "And if any of them made a lot of money in the IPO."

"Well put," I said. "That's it exactly."

"I'll see what I can find out online," Marie offered, surprising me. She must have enjoyed her earlier research more than I'd realized. "If I'm allowed, that is," sending an angry look at Badger.

I held back my grin as I shook my head. "It's still too dangerous," I said. "I wouldn't even attempt to find out anything online. Badger is the only one who's probably safe to get anywhere near Moneybags."

I raised an eyebrow at her, and she nodded.

"And I'll hide behind layers of fake identities," she said, with a conspiratorial smile at Marie.

Who blinked, and smiled back. Before she turned her face blank and gave a short nod.

Okay then. "So, does the information you and Cory gathered on who Anna met with mean any more now?" I asked Marie.

"No," she said. "But it might to Badger, once she starts looking at the programmers at Xtreme Systems. I'll send you the list."

"Thanks."

"We still need to figure out what sent Anna running," I said. "I suspect whatever it was is also what sent Mona to Europe. Marie, can you and Cory see what you can find? Without doing anything that might alert Moneybags?"

They both nodded. Cory looked at Badger. "The airline records should be safe enough, and things like cameras in the airports and bus terminals, stuff like that?"

She nodded. "And use your knowledge of Super Thieves to see if you can see any patterns in the stuff Anna told her sister. Especially what happened when, and what she put in her diary."

"I… I mean we can do that," he said. He looked at me. "What'll you be doing Aunt Barbara?"

What I should have been doing all along. "I'm going to find out more about Mona's death."

And I intended to talk to Don James again.

CHAPTER THIRTY

I WOKE EARLY THE FOLLOWING morning, feeling groggy. I'd been up half the night, trying and failing to figure out how all the pieces connected on this case. Of course I hadn't slept well after that, kept waking from confused dreams with my heart pounding and my mouth dry.

And Cat draped across my middle, which didn't help matters any.

I knew the signs—well, the non-Cat signs, anyway. I'd reached this stage in cases before. It was time to focus—hard. And the rest of my life needed to be put on hold until the case was done.

I still had all those paintings to finish. And three I hadn't even started. But it didn't matter. The case needed to take over.

But first I had to clear my head. And the only thing that might do that was to go for a run. Followed by a very hot shower. And coffee. Lots of coffee.

I threw on my running gear and headed down towards Granville Island. It was misty and cool this morning, only just light at not quite five-thirty, and traffic was already heavy down Granville Street towards downtown. I wondered, as I always do, about the people in each car, and what drew them into their cars so very early in the morning. Where did they have to be, and why?

I didn't feel like breathing fumes, so I detoured a few blocks to a quieter street. The soft chill of the air cleared my head, as did the steady monotony of my steps. Stride after stride—my body was working, and my mind cleared. It often works that way for me.

I'd left a message for Nick last night, and hadn't yet heard back. He must be as caught up in his latest case as I was in mine. It was why we suited so well.

And it was the threat that could end our relationship, too, if we weren't careful.

I hadn't expected the thought to hurt so much.

I breathed deeper and quickened my pace, focusing on my steps. Stride. Stride. Stride.

From somewhere came the distant blare of a horn and the sickening crunch of metal. Probably just a fender bender. Someone had tried to drive into work too early, and without enough coffee. Still I listened for the whoop of an ambulance, relaxing a bit when it didn't come.

My mind clearer, I shifted to the case. To Mona Gruen. And to Moneybags, the nameless, faceless plotter in the center of whatever this was that we'd uncovered.

My brain worried at how we were going to expose them for a moment, then flitted back to the nagging worry that had been with me since I'd left the others late last night.

I'd overlooked something. Something important. And I couldn't figure out what.

Were there clues in Mona's death I wasn't seeing?

If there were, I had no idea how to find them. I needed more information.

I crossed the hidden overpass onto Granville Island and stopped on a leafy side path. After catching my breath, I called Nick again. Still no answer. Which wasn't surprising—so why did I feel a trickle of worry for him?

I left a message for him to call asap.

Then I thought about Mona's sad ending. Maybe I'd get further if I knew more about what she'd been doing before she was murdered.

I called Cory. Who did answer. And I could hear Marie's voice in the background. Wait, what were they doing in the office so early?

Never mind. "Where did Mona Gruen go in Europe. Exactly?" I asked him.

There was a mercifully brief pause. "How much detail do you want?" he asked cautiously.

"As much as you can give me," I said.

There was another pause and I could hear the clicking of keys. "I've just sent it."

"Got it," I said, checking my email. The attachment he'd sent looked like it ran several pages. "Thanks."

We disconnected, and I began to read. He'd tracked her by her spending, and Mona had been busy. In each of the three cities, Basel, Berlin and Munich, all her activity had been in a central area. She hadn't left the downtown core in any of the three cities.

What was she up to?

I scrolled back through the document again. I needed to visualize this. Opening the maps app, I checked the various locations, looking for some kind of pattern. Nothing.

The screen was too small to see much, though. I zoomed in on each place she'd stopped. It would be all too easy to get lost in the detailed views, looking from street to street and building to building for whatever it was that connected them.

I didn't have that kind of time.

And I was getting decidedly chilly. Running gear is not meant for standing around in.

I called Cory back, asked him to use a program he'd been working on to create an annotated map for me, the same kind we'd used to find Marie's sister last month.

"I need it showing everywhere we have a record Mona went from the time she arrived in Basel, and anything else we knew connected to this case. I'm particularly interested in the number of museums and art galleries in her general vicinity. Then email it to me.

"Sure, Aunt B," he said readily. "How urgent is this?"

"Immediate," I said, going off an uneasy feeling that had been growing for the last few hours. "Send it to me as soon as you can."

I glanced at my watch. Nearly eight. "Then off to school. Where does your mother think you are, anyway?"

"Sure thing," he said, and I could hear the rapid clicking of keys. "And I stayed over at Jeff's last night, so she doesn't need to know I got in late and left early. It's all good."

Not if Susanna figured it out, it wasn't. And I swear she has a sixth sense about stuff like this.

"We'll figure out a better solution in future," I said. "Oh, and send a copy to Badger, too," I added.

It probably wouldn't help her, but you never know. We couldn't afford to overlook anything.

Not now.

———

I RAN ON, until I could see the inlet. The mist was rising thickly off the water, and I couldn't see downtown at all, except for the tops of a couple of our tallest skyscrapers, popping up out of the feature-less whiteness.

My steps echoed hollowly against the cracked concrete, and the image of Anna's face popped into my mind, just as she'd looked in the photo Sonya had given me when she hired me.

Only this Anna's huge brown eyes met mine in desperation. She was asking, pleading for something. Help? To be found?

My steps slowed and stopped. I stood still, staring out at nothing while my mind raced.

Of course. Anna. I still wasn't really focused on Anna.

In all the discussion of the case yesterday, none of it had been about actually finding Anna, and getting her back. Instead, we'd focused on why she was gone, what had been happening around her, and solving that. As though that would somehow magically get her back.

It probably would, to be fair—but it would take some time.

Did Anna have that kind of time?

I ran through everything I'd learned about Anna's disappearance. It still seemed that she'd chosen to vanish, had indeed prepared rather carefully to do so. But I needed to question all my assumptions about why.

Maybe it was just an over-reaction to Don's expression in that basement, or to my gradual realization of just how much money was at stake in this game of thieves. But something told me I needed to find Anna.

And fast.

I cut my run short and headed home. It was time to get to work.

CHAPTER THIRTY-ONE

AS SOON AS I GOT to the office, I called the VPD's missing persons department, asked for Officer Yip. She hadn't been my biggest fan when it was Marie's sister who was missing, but by the end of that case she'd come around. Let's hope that carried over now, when I really needed her cooperation.

"Cathy Yip."

"It's Barbara O'Grady. You have a missing persons file on Anna Lang?"

I heard a sigh over the line, but her voice was neutral. "Let me guess, you've been hired to look into it too?"

"I'm afraid so. And I'm hoping to share information."

"Okay."

She'd agreed? I hadn't expected that. "Good. I can be there in"—I glanced at my watch—"twenty minutes. Does that work for you?" I wasn't risking annoying her and losing her cooperation.

"It's fine. I'll see you then."

Right on time, I was seated in front of one of four battered metal desks in a room that could easily fit at most two desks. It felt hard to breathe, though lack of oxygen wasn't the problem. I wondered how anyone got anything done there, especially when the phone on the desk beside us rang, and we were suddenly trying to hear each other over that competing conversation.

Officer Yip glanced through the depressingly thin file that lay on the desk between us, removed the top page, and closed it again. "I'm overdue for a coffee," she said. "Follow me."

I don't know why I'd expected her to offer me the usual burnt motor oil that passes for coffee at the police station. But to my surprise we ended up at the same run-down coffee shop that Jerry and I often frequent, the one with great coffee.

She drank it black, too. My opinion of her went up. A lot.

Good coffee is important. Too few people seem to realize that, despite the fact that Vancouver—like Seattle— is a coffee city.

I liked her even better when she grabbed us a quiet table at the back and passed me the page she'd taken from the file. She didn't say a word until I looked up from reading it. And reading it again.

"You haven't found any trace of her either," I said.

"To be honest, we didn't take it too seriously at first," she said, surprising me again with her openness.

Apparently we really were going to share information. "I'm not sure you were meant to," I told her. "I suspect her sister had doubts of her own."

Actually, I knew she did. But Sonya Lang was still my client, lies or not.

Officer Yip was nodding. "That explains it. In any case, when Anna Lang didn't show up after three days, and the few enquiries we made dead ended, we sent out alerts."

"And?"

"And nothing."

"Nothing at all?"

"No. She really does seem to have vanished."

"But there's no sign of foul play?"

"Nothing we found. You?"

"Also nothing. Except she seems to have set it up so there will be little fallout when she does return."

"How do you mean?"

"She prepaid next month's rent. None of her friends seem worried."

"Just her sister. And her coworkers," she said thoughtfully.

It sounded like we'd found similar information, despite our parallel searches. Now might be a good time to see what her resources could unearth about Mona Gruen.

I pulled out the photos of Mona and Anna, and filled her in on Mona's sudden journey and death.

When I was done, Officer Yip was looking at me quizzically. "I'm afraid I don't understand the connection between these two women."

Not surprising. "I'm not sure I do either. And it may be coincidental, but the day after Anna disappeared, Mona travelled to Basel —which was not a routine journey for her.

And on that leg of her journey, she used Anna's passport. Whether it was a fake, or she stole the real one, I don't yet know. But two days later Mona was back home. Where she was murdered."

"This Gruen travelled as Anna Lang?"

"Yes."

"Who had vanished the day before."

"Yes."

"It's pretty hard not to see the connection to Anna's disappearance."

"Exactly." I was pretty sure Mona had travelled on a fake passport, but there was no need to tell Officer Yip that. At least the information would get her looking in the right direction.

Which could only help Anna. Wherever she was.

"Have you found any other connections?"

She had to ask that. "Beyond the passport? Nothing substantial. Mostly the timing, and their similar appearance. And some assumptions at this point."

The assumptions rested on both women's connections to Don James, but it was too soon to tell her that. Not until we could explain how we knew—without using the term "hacker".

"Do you have anything that suggests these two women knew each other?"

That one hurt.

"Not yet," I told her. In fact it was quite likely that they didn't know each other, given that the only person they had in common was Don. As far as I knew, anyway.

"So why did you come to me?"

"Frankly, I was hoping you'd found something that would lead to a connection."

"Huh." Officer Yip finished her coffee and set the empty cup down carefully before meeting my eyes.

"I don't understand your methods, but you've proved to me that they work," she said. "At least some of the time. I'm willing to do a little digging into this Mona Gruen, see where the case is at. And whether I can find any connection between her and our missing woman. I'll let you know."

It was more than I'd hoped for. "Thank you. And I'll update you if I find anything further."

There wasn't anything more to say, so we went our separate ways.

———

AS I WALKED BACK to my car, my cell phone rang.

It was Nick.

"Hey stranger," I said as I clicked open the locks and slid into the driver's seat.

"I know, I know. It's been busy."

"Yeah." We both understood that code. Only too well. And his terseness meant he was somewhere he could be overheard. "Anything you can tell me on your Steveston body?"

"You were right about her identity."

"Mona Gruen?"

"Yeah. But keep that to yourself for now, will you? I'm only telling you because you already knew. And we haven't notified next of kin yet."

That was odd. "Oh?"

"Can't find them."

"Oh."

"Yeah."

Translation? "Mona Gruen" was likely another false identity. I wondered who she'd been, before. Then I had a thought.

"Have you been able to trace her back more than ten years?" I asked him. Mona had hooked up with Don James about twelve years ago, from everything we'd been able to find.

"No. But how…?"

"Just a hunch, for now. I'll fill you in when I have more." Meaning when we knew for sure.

And had figured out how to present the facts, and to which authority. "It's nothing that will help you find her next of kin, though."

Just her murderer. Maybe.

"Fine," he said, though I could hear the struggle not to keep questioning me in his voice. "Dinner soon?"

"Yes. Definitely." When both of our cases allowed the time. Whenever that might be. "I'll be looking forward to it, Nick. I miss you."

"Me too," was all he said. But I heard everything he couldn't say just then in his tone.

"Don't be a stranger," he added. Which meant both that he'd try to stay in touch, and that he really needed any information I could give him on Mona Gruen. They must not be getting anywhere.

"Sure. I'll call you soon. Promise," I said, and ended the call.

Then sat staring out through the windshield at a featureless parking lot, wondering about my chances of finding Anna Lang alive. I really hated the way this case was shaping up.

Almost as much as I hated having to talk to Nick in code all the time, instead of live and personal.

I just missed him.

Maybe living together would work. We'd still be working insane schedules most of the time, but at least we'd see each other every day. Even if it was only a kiss goodbye or a quick hug.

Though knowing us, it wouldn't be only a kiss. Or quick.

Unless the tension of trying to live like that tore us apart. But maybe that was just my fear speaking.

———

I'D BEEN BACK in my office for an hour when the phone rang. "Barbara O'Grady," I answered absently, my mind still on the timeline I'd been drawing up for the week before Anna Lang went missing.

"Barbara? It's Cathy Yip in Missing Persons."

My attention snapped to the call. Her voice sounded—what was it? Controlled, but with a hint of excitement? Which for her was like jumping up and down and whooping.

"Officer Yip. You found something?"

"Maybe. I'm not sure yet. But please, call me Cathy."

We were making progress. "Cathy, then. What have you found?

"They officially have a name for the drowned woman—and you were right that it's Mona Gruen. And I think I found a connection between her and our missing woman."

She had? How? I hadn't been able to find a thing. And I'd looked hard. "You did?"

"Yes. Anna helped out a friend of hers who was teaching an extension class in Art History at Vancouver University. The drowned woman, Mona Gruen, was taking that class."

However had she dug that out? I was impressed. "When was this?"

"Last fall."

"That must have been interesting, given how alike they look," I said.

"It left me wondering if they'd had any interaction beyond that.

I'm about to go and talk to the people at VU, see if they know anything. Care to join me?"

Oh, yeah. "Thanks. Where do you want to meet?"

"Can you pick me up? I'd rather not sign out a squad car, and I didn't drive today."

"I'll be there in ten."

I sent a quick text to Marie, asking her to find out if Mona had taken other extension courses anywhere else, and I was out the door. I spent the drive over wondering if Mona had talked to Don about Anna.

———

WE GOT NOWHERE AT VU. Mona hadn't taken any other courses there, and they had no information on Anna Lang—who apparently hadn't been paid for the course she'd assisted on. It must have been a favor for her friend. Whose name Officer Yip wouldn't tell me. Though this person was hardly likely to be a confidential informant.

Fine. I had my own sources.

After I'd dropped Cathy Yip off, I got a text from Marie, who had uncovered two other courses Mona had taken, at two different universities. One was another art history survey course. The other was on pre-Colombian South American art.

And Don had met with a couple of "buyers" who were South American. Now wasn't that interesting?

"Find out more about pre-Colombian art. And the current market for it," I texted back.

Finally it felt like we were getting somewhere. "And see if Cory can find even a hint of communication between Mona and Anna."

CHAPTER THIRTY-TWO

BACK AT THE OFFICE, I shot a quick look at Marie, her head bent over something on her computer. I couldn't quite make out what she was doing, but no way was I interrupting her. Especially if whatever she was doing resulted in more information on what kind of con Don and Mona had been running.

Which Anna had found herself in the middle of.

I still had trouble believing that Don had been careless enough to let her catch even a hint of what he was up to. Much less get her hands on an email, as Sonya had said.

It didn't seem to fit the pattern of Don James' actions over the last dozen years. To the extent we'd uncovered them, anyway. Maybe we'd missed something?

What if he'd done it on purpose? Maybe even told Anna some of it because he'd been trying to recruit her?

Sitting behind my own desk, I stared at my closed laptop and thought about what I knew so far of Anna, of Don and the shadowy Moneybags.

Was that even possible?

And why would Don bring Anna in, anyway? It was very high risk, for seemingly little reward. And it was unlikely he'd gone unsuspected this long, had been able to build the crime network that Badger had found for us, without having a clear head for which risks were worth taking. And which were not.

Unless lust had clouded his judgement? Anna was a younger, prettier version of Mona. She was also an artist, which Mona, it seemed, was not. That might have appealed to Don.

But would it be enough to overcome his self-preservation instinct? Was he really that stupid? Or self-sabotaging?

Maybe.

Or maybe frustration was pushing me into seeing connections where they didn't exist.

I picked up a pen and started to sketch the creamy, hand-thrown pottery mug full of pens and pencils that sat on my desk. The distraction was enough to jump my brain out of its rut.

What if Anna had something Don wanted?

But what? From everything I'd learned about her, she didn't stand out.

Except for her ability to spot potential big name artists early in their career. And I knew someone with a similar gift.

Kathleen Marshall was making another fortune for herself in her gallery, Journeys, by providing avid collectors with pivotal works of key artists, often work done early in their careers. It was an interesting premise, but it required someone with the right kind of eye to pull it off.

An eye quite a bit like Anna's.

But Kathleen was legitimate. And Don was not. He was a con artist and a thief. At best.

What could such a man make of Anna's gift?

They could make some money by buying up the good stuff early, but then they'd have to hold it for years. And they'd still only have one piece to sell.

I had a gut feeling I was onto something, but I couldn't see it. I needed help.

I picked up the phone and called Journeys.

———

FIFTEEN MINUTES later I was seated at the round table in Kathleen Marshall's office at the back of Journeys. Through the door I could see the grey carpet and white walls of her main showroom. The luminous colors of her current exhibit seemed to leap off the walls. Over the white noise of the air conditioner, I could just hear the low buzz of one of her associates talking to a serious customer.

You could always tell the serious ones by the focused intensity of the conversation, even when you couldn't hear the words.

Seconds later Kathleen came in, carrying two mugs of coffee. The fragrance of really good coffee focused my attention immediately. She put one mug in front of me and closed her door behind her.

"Now, how can I help, Barbara?" she asked as she sat opposite me.

"You really should ask what I need before you offer to help," I told her with a smile. I took a deep, satisfying swallow of coffee.

She smiled back, shaking her head. "With what I owe you? No, I never need to ask. Besides, I trust you."

She did? I wasn't sure how I'd earned that trust, despite the fact I'd once helped her gain her freedom.

She'd been my client, after all. And for quite a while on that case, I'd thought she had serious psychological issues. Apparently she didn't hold it against me.

Good to know.

"I have a hypothetical situation I'd like to get your opinion on," I said.

She cocked her head a little to one side, and appraised me with intelligent eyes. "Fine. Go ahead."

I'd never doubted Kathleen's intelligence, no matter what else I might have thought of her. She undoubtedly knew it was about my current case, probably knew Anna Lang was missing. I'm sure the jungle drums had been busy. The local art world is a small one, and prone to gossip.

Which might actually be helpful in this case.

"On the one hand you have an art thief—one who has been in business quite a while and works with an international clientele. On the other, you have a young artist who has a marked ability to predict the eventual success of new or upcoming artists. Why would the thief be interested in working with someone like that?"

Kathleen stared at me for a moment, then smoothed back her hair, a gesture I'd seen her make to buy herself time. "This artist, she has shown in galleries? Or worked in one?" she asked.

"Worked in one," I said.

Kathleen gave a slight nod. She'd made the connection to Anna, I was sure of it.

"And the thief? He or she is also familiar with galleries?"

"The thief knows most of the aspects of the art world, has worked in a number of them."

Again the slight nod. This time I had no idea what connections she'd made. "But this thief would have access to, or knowledge of, art collectors around the world whose collections are—shall we say shady?"

Shady was a good word.

"Very definitely," I said. It was the only thing that made sense of the complex structure Badger had uncovered.

Some avid collectors didn't care where the work of art they coveted came from, or if they'd ever be able to show it to others. It was enough that they owned it, could view it any time they liked. For others, very valuable art was a kind of underground currency, one that appreciated in value, and could be used as collateral against illegal loans or debts, or traded for something else of equal value.

"Interesting," Kathleen said after a long pause. "I don't think I've ever heard of this particular scenario. But I can see why you came to me."

She smiled slightly. "Given that I've built my gallery on the exponentially increasing value on certain early works by successful artists. Works that mark a turning point in their careers—usually a turning point in their style or vision."

I nodded. That was exactly why I'd come to see her. "But only some of those works are truly important, right? They all go up in value eventually, but only one or two of the early works skyrocket in price. And only sometimes. How would someone guess which ones ahead of time?"

"Mostly they wouldn't. That's exactly the problem."

"So why would our thief care? Surely it would cost too much to buy and store all of an artist's early works in the hope that one of them would eventually take off?"

"Probably," Kathleen said. "But think about this. If our thief is also a forger—or has access to a good one—having more than one copy to sell of certain works could certainly be worth someone's while."

Forgery.

It added another dimension to the ring of art thieves I was now convinced they were.

It also made sense.

I'd been wondering how Don and his gang had been stealing masterworks of art from European museums and collectors for the last dozen years, without being caught...

But if they'd replaced at least some of those paintings with exceptional fakes—then those particular thefts might have gone undiscovered. Making it appear the gang had gone underground for a time.

And making them even harder to track.

The 1990 thefts at the Gardner Museum in Boston—the most expensive private theft in history—are still talked about. Not just because of which works were taken, including a Vermeer painting —one of only 35 known to exist—two Rembrandt paintings and a Manet. But also because of the blank spaces the museum has left on the wall where these masterpieces once hung.

Every visitor to the museum continues to be reminded of exactly what has been lost.

In this case, the opposite could be true. No-one talks about an unacknowledged theft. No-one investigates it, either.

It was possible international police had no idea just how widely this Don and his gang of thieves operated.

And maybe forgery was the missing fifth man's role? I'd have to take another look at the information Marie had unearthed on him.

But if Kathleen were right about why Don was interested in Anna—and she might well be—why had the idea even occurred to him? Unless they were already forging more than one copy of a stolen masterpiece.

What were the implications of that?

If Don and company were into forgery as well as theft—and selling into the very shady end of the market—multiple forged copies could increase their opportunity for profit exponentially. As well as the risk.

They couldn't afford to get caught.

These would be some dangerous people they had as clients. Even more dangerous if they found out they'd been cheated.

Which could explain the complex, layered company structure that Badger had uncovered. A structure that made it very difficult for any customer to know who they were really dealing with, or to track any particular sale back to its source.

Smart. In a daring, winner-takes-all kind of way. Just the kind of thing a computer game designer might come up with.

Though my superficial knowledge of Super Thieves, Inc. didn't include any mention of forgery. I'd have to check with Cory on that one. Maybe the computer geek wasn't the one that came up with the forgery angle?

Might that make it a weak link in their system?

"How would it work, if they were trying to sell more than one forged copy of a supposedly unique work?" I asked Kathleen, my mind racing.

"The young artist you talked about, the one with the feel for what will eventually sell big, would identify the potential artistic successes. The thief would buy up their early works—painting, sculpture, it wouldn't matter. Though paintings are easier to hide and transport."

I pictured it in my mind. Don could collect these artists openly, possibly through Zanthus—with its focus on emerging artists, it was a perfect fit—and store them until the value rose.

I wondered again what was hidden in that grimy basement of his. Or maybe that was a red herring, and they had a warehouse somewhere with a slowly growing collection of forgeries.

"Once this thief owned the paintings, he'd forge multiple copies of key pieces, is that it?" I said. "And he'd need somewhere to store those frauds."

"That's it," she said. "He could even wait to make the copies until he knew which works became the most valuable over time.

The original pieces could then be stolen—ideally while they were on loan to a high profile gallery in a big name city. Or maybe the works would be sold, and then stolen, so that it wasn't too obvious.

Leaving the thief free to sell those now valuable works as many times as he could get away with."

The shady side of the art world depended on secrecy. They could probably get away with quite a bit.

Except this complex picture only worked if Anna cooperated. What if she hadn't?

CHAPTER THIRTY-THREE

I LEFT KATHLEEN WITH HASTY thanks, and headed home. There were too many facts and details spinning in my head. I needed to finish the run I'd abandoned this morning.

I changed into running gear and headed straight for the walking path along Burrard Inlet. I kept my breathing deep and easy, ignoring the rush and groan of traffic along the way. As my feet pounded the pavement, I mentally ran through the facts I had on this case.

From everything I'd learned about Anna, cooperating with Don James was the last thing she'd intended to do. So what had she done instead?

I almost knew. There was something about Anna that I'd heard or seen—I'd nearly had it when Kathleen mentioned fraud. Then it vanished again.

If Don and his little gang were trading in both stolen and fraudulent art, and Anna knew about it—what had she done with that knowledge?

She'd tried to tell her sister, who ignored her. She tried to tell her best friend, who was condescending about her needing to "learn the rules". She hadn't told anyone else that I'd been able to find.

She did talk to Ian Wong about a new job at the Omega, but didn't commit to it. She didn't talk to the police. Or the owners of the Zanthus Gallery.

Instead, after months of silence, she firmed up Ian's offer of a new job, made arrangements that would cover her trail, and disappeared.

Picking up the pace, focusing on lengthening my stride, I'd just turned onto Granville Island and the trail that runs along the south shore of the Inlet when it hit me. We'd been looking at what Anna had been doing the week she'd vanished.

But what had she been up to in the time between when Don must first have approached her, and the week she vanished? She'd been promoted eight months ago. He'd probably talked to her not too long after that. And from everything I'd learned of her and her passion for art and for artists, she wouldn't just ignore art fraud on that scale. She'd have to do something.

But everything we'd found so far said Anna had done nothing.

It didn't fit.

What if she was running some scheme of her own designed to expose all of them?

Then either her disappearance was part of that scheme, or they'd figured out what she was up to. And she'd been killed to keep her quiet.

I shivered, thinking of Don's expression when he showed me that basement. Anna's body could have been behind one of those shelves, and I'd never have known.

I needed to get back into that basement.

But before I did something terminally stupid, I needed to put myself in Anna's shoes. She's just learned exactly who she was working for.

What did she do with that information?

———

I RAN along the Inlet as far as the Cambie Street Bridge, going flat out for the last half mile, then headed towards home. My breathing was still a little off, but I had the beginnings of a plan. Until my cell phone rang.

I slowed to a walk, glanced at the screen. "Yeah?"

"Barbara?" Marie said. "Is that you? Are you okay?"

"I'm fine," I said. "What's up?"

"There was a really big theft of pre-Columbian ceramic carvings and things from a museum in Mexico City a few months ago," Marie said. "Valued in the multi-millions. No sign of the thieves, and the pieces haven't surfaced anywhere."

"Nice work," I said.

Wondering just how many diverse types of art Don's complex structure could handle at the same time. And how hard it would be to create an exact copy—or copies—of a very old carving.

I'd have to ask Badger exactly how much money was flowing through their systems every year. And if there was any sign of more than the five conspirators we'd identified so far. Six if you included Moneybags.

The logistics alone for the various things they'd been involved in had to be crushing if there was only the six of them.

"And Cory's found a couple of emails between Anna and someone he thinks is Mona," Marie added.

"He thinks it's Mona?" I repeated.

"Well, she's using the Greta James identity, just like she did at the VU course."

Which made sense, if that was the name she'd met Anna under. And there was no link between Xtreme Systems, where "Greta James" worked, and stolen Mexican artifacts. She'd likely have thought it safe to use the same persona for both.

Though if we were right, and Moneybags did work at Xtreme Systems, having any kind of link between "Greta James" who also worked there—even temporarily—and pre-Columbian artifacts was short-sighted. At best.

There might be more than one reason Mona Gruen had been murdered.

"So what did these emails say?" I asked.

"They were arranging a meeting," she said.

"Between Mona and Anna?"

"Yeah."

"Just the two of them?"

"Uh huh. At a place called the Burrow Inn."

I knew it. The Burrow Inn is a popular local pub, located on a quieter stretch of Main Street. "When were they supposed to meet?"

"That night. When she disappeared," Marie said.

"Email them to me," I said. "I'll be back in the office within the hour. I'll need both of you there."

"But…"

"Both of you," I said, my tone final.

"Fine," she said.

I ignored the sullen note in her voice and opened the emails she'd sent.

CHAPTER THIRTY-FOUR

THE BURROW INN WAS HARDLY the cozy, slightly kitschy place suggested by its name. It might have started out as a faux English pub, but somewhere along the way it had morphed into an artsy hipster bar.

Long, battle scarred wooden tables were matched with handmade benches polished to a gleam, and stamped cardboard coasters. Artisan ales with names like "Main Street Amber" rubbed shoulders with small batch local vodkas and whiskeys. Short haircuts and full beards were everywhere, and the place buzzed with intense conversations.

At four-thirty in the afternoon, it wasn't completely full yet, but if I was lucky the same people who'd been working last Tuesday night would be on shift now. Anna and Mona were both attractive women. Together, looking like mirror images, they'd be unforgettable. Someone would remember them.

I hoped.

The bartender was clean shaven and friendly, running quickly through what was on tap. I ordered coffee—which came dark and fragrant. And delicious.

"Good beans," I commented.

He smiled. "Yeah. Designated drivers deserve a good time too, y'know."

He had a point. And with a customer-centric perspective like that, I could see why the place was so busy. Especially if the beer was as good as the coffee. And I suspected it would be.

"I'm looking to talk to whoever was behind the bar a week ago. Last Tuesday evening, to be specific. Around eight."

The smile vanished and he gave me a neutral look. "That would be me. How can I help you?"

I quickly ran through my usual approaches, decided he'd respond best to something straightforward, and pulled out the photos of Anna and Mona. Placed them on the bar between us.

"I'm a P. I.," I said. "Hired to find this woman,"—handing him Anna's photo. "She went missing sometime that night or the following morning."

"She was here that night?"

"She was supposed to meet this woman," I said, handing him Mona's photo. "At eight-fifteen."

He held the photos under one of the pendant lights over the bar and looked from one to the other, scrutinizing their features carefully. "I think I might remember them," he said. "What time did she leave the bar?"

"I'm not sure."

He gave me a quick glance. "Are you implying that she"—and he held out Anna's photo—"might not have left here? That something happened to her here?"

He paid attention to nuances. Good. I needed that ability in a witness. "Not at all. I just don't know what time she left."

"Why don't you ask her?" he said, pointing at Mona's photos. Wary still.

"She left town the next day. I haven't been able to talk to her since," I said. Absolutely true, if a little misleading. But he was already wary. I suspected he might clam up if I told him Mona was dead.

Besides, I wasn't sure the police had released that information yet. Not if they couldn't find her next of kin.

He gave me a speculative look. "So you don't even know if they were actually here that night," he said.

Where was he going with this? "True. It's why any information you have would be very helpful."

A slow nod. "Okay."

He laid the photos side by side on the bar. "Tuesday night, you said? I do remember them—in person, they look even more alike. Sisters?"

And wasn't that an interesting thought. Sonya looked very little like Anna. "No relation."

As far as I knew. But then I knew little about Anna's background. And even less about Mona's. Something else to follow up.

"Huh." He glanced down at the photos again, then checked along the bar to make sure no-one needed a refill. No-one did.

"I didn't see them arrive," he said. "It must have been later than this, after eight, and we were busy. Really busy. It was quarter after nine when this one"—and he tapped Mona's photo—"made her way up to the bar and ordered a couple of white wines. I could see the other one standing just behind her, looking wary."

"Wary?"

He nodded. "That's the word for it. Wary. As if she didn't really want to be there, and wasn't sure quite what to expect."

He paused, looked hard at Anna's photo.

"And that's odd," he said more slowly. "Because I think she's a regular. She's usually here with a group, so she didn't stand out the same way."

So it was Anna who'd picked the location. Smart of her to have picked somewhere she was known. "Did you notice them again after that?"

"Yeah. They ordered more wine at least once. Appetizers too, I think. Whoever served them might remember."

"Who was that?"

"They grabbed a table in the back, so that would have been—

Ruby, I think." He looked around. "She's over there. Red hair. Arm sleeves."

I followed his look.

He wasn't kidding about the red hair—and not your normal red, either. Ruby red. The color matched the densely inked rose tattoo climbing her left arm. The ink work was beautiful—Marie would approve. "Think she'll talk to me?"

A shrug. "It's Ruby. Depends if she likes you." The look he gave me suggested my chances weren't good.

"I don't give up easily," I said, watching Ruby move between her tables for a moment. She was good. I'd bet her tips were too. "I have a couple more questions, though."

"Fire when ready," he said, with not a hint of a grin.

Okay, then. "When did you last see them?"

"They weren't here for last call, that I'm sure of. So, around ten maybe?"

"You can't get any closer than that?"

He looked from me to the photos and back. "No, sorry. That's the best I can do. Talk to Ruby."

"Any idea if they left together?"

"Sorry, no. Try…"

"Ruby. Thanks, I will."

"Any time," he said, passing the photos back to me.

I pulled out my card, handed it to him. "If you do think of anything…?"

He glanced at it. "I'll call you, Barbara."

He wasn't flirting. More like committing my name to memory. I wondered if he did that often, and how many of his regulars he knew by name. I held up Anna's photo. "Any chance you know her name?"

He looked puzzled, but answered readily enough. "The others called her Andie, I think."

Or maybe Annie. "Thanks," I said, as I tucked the photos away in my bag and stuck a twenty in the tip jar for him.

He grinned at me. "Anytime."

I started to turn away, stopped and turned back. "One more thing. Was there anything unusual that happened that night?" I asked him. "Any kind of problem or disruption here?"

"Last Tuesday? Nothing I know about."

I wondered about his choice of phrasing, but thanked him for his time. Finishing my coffee, I went looking for Ruby.

RUBY SEEMED to have a sixth sense for people moving into her section. She was standing watching me walk towards her before I was half-way there, an assessing look on her narrow face. I wondered what she was seeing, and just how good she was at reading people.

"I'm Barbara O'Grady," I told her when I was close enough. "I'm trying to find a woman, one of your regulars, who was here last Tuesday night. Do you have time for a few questions?"

Apparently I'd passed whatever test she was using, because Ruby gestured towards the back. "I'm due for a break, and I could use a smoke."

I followed her into an alley full of garbage bins behind the bar, and was bemused to find myself looking across broken pavement into someone's well-kept back garden.

Ruby was lighting a cigarette with the practiced motions of a long time smoker, but she apparently had no trouble following my thoughts.

"It's why we close at eleven on a weeknight," she said. "Neighborhood pub, you know."

"Right." So Anna couldn't have been here after eleven on Tuesday night. I should have realized that already, but I'd been preoccupied with less mundane issues.

"Who're you looking for?" Ruby asked.

I showed her the two photos, tapping Anna's. "This is the woman I'm looking for."

"Uh huh." Ruby tilted it towards her, squinted a bit. "I might recognize her. Might not, though. Why're you looking for her?"

"She hasn't been seen since that night, and her sister is worried."

Ruby looked skeptical. Of me? Or of a family that cared?

I wondered what her story was. She had that defiant look of a girl who'd started looking after herself early, had been fighting her own battles for a long time.

"And what do you want from me?" she asked.

"The bartender says she's a regular," I said. "You recognize her?"

"Yeah, I've seen her around," she said, having apparently decided in my favor.

"Was she here a week ago Tuesday? Probably around eight?"

She glanced around the alley, gave me a wry look. Waited a beat. "Oh, inside, you mean? Yeah, I saw her."

I grinned at her performance. "Both of them?"

Ruby exhaled a drift of smoke. "Yeah. It was more like eight-fifteen, though. I was just back from my break. Saw her come in."

"The two of them," I gestured towards the photos she still held, "came in together?"

"Nah. I saw this one,"—she waved Anna's photo at me—"look around, spot the other. Looked a little shocked when she saw her."

Shocked. "Oh?"

"Yeah. Judging by these photos, there's ten years at least between them. Maybe more. Your second lady's good at makeup."

Now how did she know that? "Oh?" I said again.

She grinned at me. "Yes, oh," she said. "Reason your girl looked confused? The other one was dressed and made up to look the same age as her. With the low lighting inside, they could've been twins."

Whoa. That would have taken some skill. My guess was Mona was in her mid-thirties. And it was clear from the email exchange that Mona had talked to Anna after the seminar at VU, so Anna already knew what she really looked like.

Which meant that Mona must have made herself look exactly like Anna for a reason. But what reason?

Maybe Mona had made herself look younger at the class she'd attended, too? No, the surprised look Ruby had described suggested otherwise.

"Hello?" Ruby said.

I felt like an idiot. "Um. You said "my girl" was a regular. You got a name for her?"

"Annie is what I heard," she said. "But I'm guessing it's a nickname. Not one she's fond of, either."

"What makes you think that?"

"I don't think she knew the people she hung with all that well. Kept a bit of a reserve with them. And a couple times, I saw her kinda wince when they called her that."

Ruby must collect huge tips. A server who could read other people that well usually did.

Time for the key question. Which I'm sure Ruby had been anticipating. "So last Tuesday night. Did you see them leave?"

"Yeah. They left together."

Jackpot. And not what I'd been hoping to hear. I now had a pretty good idea what had happened to Anna. "Any idea of the time?"

"Just before eleven."

I could see the scenario playing out in my head. And it raised even more questions.

If Anna had left with Mona, why had Mona flown to Europe the following day? Where had she left Anna?

Alive?

Or dead?

And was she using Anna's actual passport to leave the country?

But Ruby couldn't help me with any of those questions. "Which door did they use?" I asked her.

"This one," Ruby said, pointing to the one we'd just come out.

"Any cameras out here?"

"What do you think?"

I glanced around the quiet area. No cameras. There went any possibility of tracking them from here.

Ruby was watching me, a smug look on her face.

"I don't suppose you've seen Anna—I mean Annie—since?"

"Sure, the next night," she said, as if she'd just been waiting for me to ask.

She probably had. That explained the smugness. "That would be Wednesday night?" I said, scrambling to catch up.

A nod.

"What time?"

"Early. Before five."

"Did she meet anyone here?"

"No."

"Did you see anyone with her?"

"No."

"Did you see anyone talk to her?"

"No."

This was getting me nowhere.

I ran my mind back over the timeline I'd constructed for Anna. She'd left her apartment early—it had been deserted when Sonya got there. But where had she been until five?

Wait. The missing luggage.

"Did she have luggage with her?"

"A big shoulder bag. And a small carry-on type thing. And an umbrella, a big one," Ruby said. "She didn't seem scared. Nervous, but not scared."

Finally, a break. Anna must have come here to help hide her trail. Maybe she took a cab? "What time did she leave?"

"I don't know. I took a smoke break, and she wasn't there when I came back into the bar."

"What time was that?"

"Sometime after six."

I needed to know exactly when. Maybe we could find out which cab company, where she'd gone from here. "Are there cameras in the bar?"

"Sure. Talk to the manager."

"Thanks. I'll do that." Immediately.

———

IT TOOK A LOT OF TALKING, but eventually I convinced the Burrow Inn manager to let me see their videos for both the Tuesday and Wednesday night of the previous week. Not that it did me any good.

I could see both Anna and Mona clearly on the Tuesday night's tapes. And Ruby was right, Mona did look like Anna's twin. I froze the video on their faces, looking back and forth from the photos I held to the faces on the screen.

Mona had to be really practiced at disguises. It was the only explanation. And it added another layer of complexity to the role she played on Don's team.

What I couldn't figure out was why she'd exposed her abilities so clearly to Anna. Unless she wanted Anna's help with some scam they were planning?

Which made no sense. Unless Mona didn't know Anna worked for Don.

Maybe he hadn't mentioned Anna to Mona, hadn't told her he was trying to recruit his assistant manager? That would suggest a major breach in his team. If indeed that's what Don had been up to.

I needed more information.

And I wasn't going to get it from the videos.

On the Tuesday, once Anna and Mona grabbed a table, they sat talking with their heads towards each other. Probably for privacy, but it also meant the camera didn't see much. Just the intensity of the conversation—whatever it had been—which was evident from the tense lines of their bodies as they leaned towards each other.

On the Wednesday, it was worse. I could see Anna's face clearly when she arrived, but for the rest of the evening, I just caught glimpses.

After awhile it was clear that she knew exactly where each of the three security cameras was, and how to avoid them. When she left, at ten minutes after six, I just caught a glimpse of her in profile going out the front door.

Even that didn't help. It turned out no cab company in town had picked anyone up at that time from that location. None of them had even taken a call from that location in the entire time Anna had been on screen. And none of the businesses on that block had cameras that faced the street.

Even Badger couldn't track someone with that little to go on.

And since Anna had gone out the front door and not the back, I couldn't even hope for a nosy neighbor. I'd send Cory and Marie out tomorrow to talk to the neighbors about what they might have seen of Anna and Mona on the Tuesday night.

I wasn't expecting much, though. Not the way my luck was holding.

Except for the knowledge that Anna had been alive and well as late as six p.m. on the Wednesday night—and I couldn't yet see how that could help us find her—my visit to the Burrow Inn had been a complete waste of time.

CHAPTER THIRTY-FIVE

I WAS STILL FUMING WHEN I got back to the office. Marie and Cory were still huddled around her screen. And still arguing.

"Let's meet in half an hour," I said as I walked by them. "See if Badger can join us. And order in food."

And I left them to it. Probably cowardly of me, but I had enough anger of my own right now—I didn't need theirs.

I plopped down in my own chair, and scowled at the rain now dripping down the window. It only needed that.

I pulled a few sheets of printer paper out of the drawer and began to sketch. The bartender's face. Ruby's face. Anna and Mona sitting across from each other, deep in conversation.

What had they been talking about?

As I sketched, I calmed down and my brain re-engaged. The day hadn't been a complete waste, after all. My conversation with Kathleen about the possibilities of forgery in Don's little empire was a gem.

If I was going to bring Don down—and I was coldly determined to do so—the forgery angle might just give me the leverage I needed.

My mind went to Marie's earlier information about the heist in pre-Columbian art from Mexico City. If you combined that with the meetings Don had been having lately, and Mona's interest in pre-Colombian art?

Had Don and his crew been responsible for that robbery? Or was I trying to fit together a series of coincidences?

I don't believe in coincidence.

Would Don and his crew have the ability to pull something like that off? As far as I knew, none of them had any experience in Mexico.

But if they'd contracted others to pull off the actual heist, that might not matter. Though it would cut into their profit. Substantially.

Unless they planned on so much profit it wouldn't matter.

How difficult would it be to fake a Mayan sculpture, anyway? Because why stop at theft if you could sell the same priceless object more than once?

That would be a pretty dangerous game, though. Especially given the nature of Don's likely clientele—at best they'd be obsessed collectors, ones with a lot of money and questionable ethics, who didn't mind dealing in stolen items if it was something they wanted badly enough.

At worst they'd be the crime lords of one stripe or another who had come to view major works of art as a new kind of currency. Not people you wanted to cross. Or fool.

But was Don stupid enough—or arrogant enough—to try to play that game? I remembered the smug look on his face after his little stunt in the basement. Yup. He was.

I doubted his silent partner was, though. Which might be enough to keep Don from playing dangerous games.

Or it might not be, depending on his motivation. He was motivated by greed, obviously. But what was he doing with the money?

I did a quick online search. He wasn't investing in real estate— he'd only bought one property, the penthouse apartment he lived in, which was walking distance from Zanthus. Though these days that was probably several million dollars worth of nice. I wondered how big his mortgage was.

Owning that property outright would be hard to explain, even on his salary.

No, I was betting on a nice, safe Swiss bank account, or whatever the current, red-tape free equivalent of that was. For a man like Don, growing up as poor as he had, having very large amounts of money stashed away in a secure account probably gave him a feeling of invulnerability.

Which, given the people he was dealing with, was as dangerous as it was false.

Of course, I didn't have more than a gut feeling about the Mexican theft. And maybe you couldn't fake a ceramic sculpture. I did a little more digging online, then made a series of calls.

I dug up connections going back to my art student days, who were suddenly more than helpful. I'm not sure if it was our slightly dusty shared history, or the unexpected legitimacy that my upcoming show at the Courtland seemed to give me. Or maybe just the subject I wanted to talk about.

But I was stunned by how quickly I found answers, and how easily I was referred to the next source. Turns out faking small, very old ceramics and ceramic sculptural pieces is a hot topic right now.

A lot of the techniques I was told about related to aging a fake piece of pottery or carving, choosing the right mix of clay or kind of stone, then creating an appropriate level of weathering and wear. But what had people excited—or apprehensive—was the potential embodied in 3D printing technology.

No-one was quite sure where it was going, but they were all sure it was a game changer. And that it could be bad. Really bad.

I ended up Skyping with a member of Interpol's art crime team. Adrien Keller. He had a lot to say on the topic.

"Scan an object, your printer can create an exact replica," Keller told me. "Sure, if it uses plastic, it's really obvious it's a fake. But we've done our own testing in the lab here, and if the plastic is just the right weight, we've been able to put a coating of specially blended clay over it, and with a bit of aging, it takes an expert to detect the difference."

Which is similar to what forgers have been doing in paintings since at least the nineteenth century. Choose the right base—a canvas of the appropriate age—use period appropriate paints, copy the artist's technique, and—if you're good enough— voila. An unknown Monet. Or Vermeer. Or whatever.

Since this has been going on for generations, some experts suspect that as many as a third of the paintings currently hanging in museums around the world are very good fakes. Think about that, sometime.

For the curator of a big museum, or a serious collector, it's the stuff of nightmares.

"That has to be a major concern," I said, thinking about how easy this new technique would make it for forgers.

He gave a wry laugh.

"We haven't found this kind of fraudulent copy out there, not yet. Though I suspect it's just a matter of time," he said.

"But that's just the beginning of what this technology can do. Specialists are starting to use an individual's own stem cells and a specialized 3D printer to create a viable replacement organ."

"Like a liver? Or a spleen?"

"Exactly like that."

Wow.

"We're hearing rumors now that the potential uses of 3D printers are being expanded faster than anyone can keep up with."

"Let me guess," I said. "Using the right materials, a forger could recreate any three dimensional object?"

"That's what I hear," he said. "In essence, it could be similar to something like a manufactured stone countertop, which can be made to look like marble or granite or whatever. Only it's far more precise.

I don't know how exact some of this stuff is right now," he said. "Or how long it might take to develop specialized printers and techniques that are good enough to fool a museum's experts. Maybe that's isn't possible, given today's tools for scientific analysis."

"If the forgers—or whoever is backing them—are determined enough, and willing to throw enough money at it, I wouldn't bet against them," I said slowly.

"No. We aren't," he said. "I just hope it takes them a long time to get a workable version. Gives us a chance to find a way to recognize them for frauds."

"That would be good," I said, and we both laughed. What else could we do?

"Let me know if you come across anything interesting," he said. "Or if you ever have a big art fraud case you want to tell us about."

He laughed again, clearly not expecting that to happen.

I thanked him, and disconnected the call.

I had a feeling he'd be hearing from me before too long.

———

I STARTED SKETCHING AGAIN, and my thoughts turned back to Anna, and the last few months of her life. I was stuck, running over the same ground yet again, hoping to find something I'd missed.

If she had found out even some of what Don had been up to, what had she been planning in the seven months or so since then?

She'd started by talking to some of the people around her. That hadn't gone so well. If I assumed Plan A had been to enlist her sister's help, that hadn't lasted long—Sonya had shut her down. When had that been?

I checked my notes. Nearly six months ago.

And the conversations with her friend James had ceased around the same time. I'd found no hint that she'd talked to anyone else after that.

So what was Anna's Plan B? Was her disappearance part of that plan? From her careful preparation, I assumed it was.

But what was she hoping to accomplish? I still didn't know. And nothing I'd learned so far gave me so much as a hint.

What had Anna been up to?

And had she been found out?

CHAPTER THIRTY-SIX

BY THE TIME I GAVE up on Anna's Plan B, Cory and Marie had set up the room for our meeting. Chinese takeout containers covered half of our meeting table, and the smell of black bean sauce and shrimp fried-rice filled the room. My stomach growled, and I was just about to suggest we eat when Badger walked in.

I could tell she had news. Her face didn't give anything away, but the other two felt it too, and quit bickering, ceding her the floor.

I think it was the nervous energy pouring off of her.

Badger didn't even glance at the food or sit down, just grabbed a can of Coke, cracked it open and drained half of it in what looked like one swallow. Then she marched to the whiteboard and began scribbling.

The board was three-quarters covered with her tiny clear lettering when she stepped aside so we could read it and turned to face us.

"Mona Gruen was in Europe to transfer money," she said.

What she'd listed on the board were the names of several banks and banking institutions—sometimes one, sometimes two or even three—in each of the cities Mona had visited on her sudden flight to Europe.

"That's what got her killed?" Marie asked.

"How much money?" Cory asked at the same time.

From her spot at the whiteboard Badger grinned, then sobered. "A lot of money. Several million dollars, at least. That's just what I've been able to trace."

"Whose money?" I asked.

"Most of it was in her name," Badger said. "Or in what I assume is her name."

"It's another alias?" Cory asked.

"No, this seems to be her real name," Badger said. "Mona Acker."

"Acker?" Marie said. "Acker? But that was Anna's mother's maiden name."

Coincidence? Not likely. The bartender had said Anna and Mona had looked like twins. I'd wondered then if they were related, somehow.

"And where did the money go?" I asked.

"Wire transfers. All over the place," she said. "But they ended up in an offshore account registered to one Anika Acker."

Anika Acker?

"But why would she do that?" Marie asked.

"Another alias?" Cory suggested.

Badger looked smug. "Maybe. But I was able to access camera footage, from a number of banks."

An impressive feat. "Go on," I said.

"In all the cases I could access, the Mona who withdrew the money looked as unlike herself as possible. But when she opened the new account, she looked like a young version of her real self."

"Or just like Anna Lang does now," I said slowly. My mind still turning over that name. Anika Acker.

"You mean Mona Gruen gave all her money to Anna Lang?" Cory asked.

"Yeah, I think so," Badger said.

"Except I don't think all of it was her money," I said. "That could be what got her killed."

Badger was nodding. "Though it may have been her share of the money Mona withdrew. But to do so in three days?"

She shook her head. "This much activity? In these amounts and all at once? It's likely to attract the kind of official attention the gang can't afford."

"And she paid for it," I said.

"Probably."

"But why would she do that?" Cory asked. "Give everything to someone she just met? I don't get it."

"They have to be related, somehow. Anna and Mona," I said, and explained everything I'd learned at the Burrow Inn.

"But how?" Cory asked.

"I suspect her sister can tell me," I said. "And it's time she did."

I'd get answers if I had to wring them out of her. I was sick of her lies.

And they might just be the death of Anna.

———

"SO WHERE IS ANNA NOW?" Marie asked."

"Good question. She may be impossible to find," I said. "From what Badger has uncovered, and given what we know of Anna's actions, I think we have to assume Mona told Anna they were related. Then gave her access to enough money to vanish permanently. And probably told her to run."

There was a small island of silence while we all contemplated how Anna might have reacted to Mona's words. I wondered what else Mona had told her.

And how Anna had felt about it all.

I knew she'd been alive after that conversation, and as late as the following afternoon. And given everything I'd learned about Anna so far, she'd be smart about how she reacted, despite the likely emotional impact of whatever Mona had said to her.

What I didn't know is what options Mona had opened up for Anna. If Anna had left the country, gone far enough, and fast enough—could she stay ahead of Don James and whatever he—or his silent partner—had planned for her?

"Can you check for any recent travel under the name Anika Acker?" I said, turning to Cory. "I think we have to assume she now has papers in that name."

Cory glanced at Badger, then nodded. "Sure."

"I can trace the money," Badger said. "I think. But it'll take awhile."

"Time we don't have," I said bluntly. "Maybe later. For now, we have to assume that Don knows the connection between Mona and Anna, whatever it is. Especially since Mona opened an account in the name of Anika Acker."

I drew in a deep breath. This was the hard part. "Don needs to find Anna soon, if he hasn't already. Once he—or his partner—found out what Mona had done with the banks, they can't afford to have Anna out there. Not when Mona might have told her everything."

Cory grimaced, and Marie looked pale. Badger just nodded, and mixed a little rice into her pork and tofu and scooped up a mouthful. She was really good with chopsticks, which surprised me, somehow. I don't know why.

Badger struck me as someone who'd be good at anything she decided to take seriously. I wondered again what her story was.

"Anyone have anything else on Anna?" I asked. Looking at the faces around the table.

Cory shrugged and reached for another heaping serving of chow mein. I don't know where he put it. Even with running, I can't eat like that.

Neither Badger nor Marie had anything to add. Okay, then.

"We're getting nowhere looking for Anna," I said. "So we need to focus on Don James and his gang. And I do have some new information on that."

I filled them in on what I'd learned from Kathleen about the possibility of forgeries, as well as my conversations with my various sources including Interpol on the subject.

"Using 3-D printing to forge centuries old statues?" Cory said in an admiring tone. "That is sick."

Teenagers. "Also really hard to detect," I said.

Badger had put down her chopsticks, and was listening with a tiny frown between her brows, her face unreadable. Now she looked up.

"And the faster the technology changes, the more they can do. If these guys have access to a good hacker, they could probably modify something that's already out there to fit what they needed."

That made a scary kind of sense.

"Like Moneybags?" Cory asked. "As a gamer, he'd probably be into the possibilities of 3D printing."

"Maybe," Badger said. "And maybe he came up with the idea. But from what I've found so far, Moneybags is all about the money and the systems. He could've hired someone for a 3D project, though. I can check what rumors are out there. But it might take a while."

More time we didn't have. "See if anything pops," I said.

She smirked at me. Right. She'd do it her way.

"So that article I found about the theft in Mexico definitely fits in?" Marie said, looking defiantly pleased with herself.

"My gut says it does," I said. "But we need something more concrete than that. If we can find a connection, maybe that theft could be our key to getting these guys arrested on international art theft as well as murder charges. Badger, can you see if any of the channels you've found suggest that connection?"

"Yeah. I'll look," she said. No smirk this time. "It would explain a lot about the complexity of their systems. If they're selling frauds, and worse, multiple frauds, into the underground art market, they can't afford to be traced."

"Is that why they got rid of Mona so fast?" Cory said. "So a pissed off bad guy couldn't track her back to them?"

"That kind of money buys a lot of resources," Badger said.

"But does any of this get us closer to them?" I said.

"I think I found three guys who could possibly be Moneybags," my nephew said. "All three are programmers, all three work or have worked on that game, and all three made out like bandits from the IPO."

He flashed three photos with accompanying point form bios up on the blank second whiteboard, using it as a screen.

"Are any of them still working on Super Thieves, Inc.?" I asked instinctively. "This would need to be someone who lives and breathes that game."

Cory nodded. "This guy," he said and highlighted the middle photo.

Kevin Chadwell. Thirty-three. Brown hair and eyes, wearing heavy dark glasses that overpowered his narrow face. He had a nice enough face, if you stopped to notice, but overall he was nondescript. Most wouldn't stop.

He didn't look like a killer. And maybe he wasn't. The third and fourth men seemed like the team's heavies. But Kevin Chadwell hired killers. And set them after their targets.

He looked like the last person anyone would have expected to be Moneybags. Which made it even more likely that this was our moneyman.

"How much did he make?" Marie wanted to know. "From the IPO, I mean."

"Between ten and fifteen million," Badger said. "He was one of the first hires, and he's been amassing options and shares all along. And it looks like Super Thieves was originally his idea."

It all fit. "With that kind of money, why is he still working there?" I asked.

"No one's sure," Cory said. "But he gets to set his own hours, works remotely most of the time."

"So if he's working remotely, he could be anywhere?" I said. "Anywhere in the world, I mean."

"If he's good, oh, yeah," Badger said. "And no-one would know it, either."

"It's a pretty sick setup he's got—I'd stay too," Cory said.

"And it's his program," Badger said softly.

"Yeah. That too," Cory agreed.

I got that. I felt the same way about my paintings. While I was working on them, anyway.

And I guess with a game, it was never done. Computers kept improving, you could add more bells and whistles, new capabilities….

"Does he report to Sonya?" I asked.

"Technically, I guess so," Cory said. "But from what I found out, he doesn't really report to anyone. The stuff he comes up with for Super Thieves makes him golden."

Everything pointed to Kevin Chadwell as our money man. He had the chops, the money, the ability to travel, and the invisibility to pull it off. Didn't mean he was our man, though. We needed more than indications and gut feel.

"So now what?" Marie demanded. Seemed she was getting impatient. "You just get this guy arrested?"

"Maybe," I said. "In the long run. We need a little more proof first. Seeing as how we're going to be handing him and his cohort off to someone else for the actual arrest. And they're not going to do anything on our say so."

Marie looked like she wanted to argue. I was in no mood to listen. Luckily, she managed to restrain herself.

"Badger, can you"—I glanced at my nephew's eager face—"and Cory find any way to link this guy to the system you uncovered?"

"We can try."

"Good. I'll talk to Sonya again. See if there's a thread we can unravel on her end that will help us find Anna. Now that we know there's some kind of relationship between Anna and Mona. Marie…"

"I'll hold down the fort here," she said. "You need a communications hub."

I shook my head. "Not alone, this late," I said. "They've already burgled us once. Clear off the whiteboards, pack up. You're with me."

She started to say something, bit it back. Nodded.

Her face wore an odd expression. I guess she was trying for her usual nonchalance. And missing by a mile. Instead she looked constipated.

"So let's get going," I said, biting back a sudden urge to laugh.

CHAPTER THIRTY-SEVEN

ON MY WAY OUT OF town, I changed my mind about bringing Marie with me. No point giving our difficult client a reason not to talk to me. Instead I dropped her off at the Urban Grind, the coffee shop the three sales associates from the Zanthus Gallery favored.

"Stay alert, stay safe, and above all don't leave until I come back for you," I told her. "If any of these three,"—and I showed her the photos from the gallery's website—"are here, see if you can get them talking."

"About what?" Marie asked. She wasn't happy about the change in plans and was making sure I knew it.

"Anything to do with Zanthus, or Don James. You're an artist. Find some common ground with them, and get them talking. It's not hard."

As long as she didn't get carried away, anyway. Who knows, she might even uncover something useful.

Marie was looking happier by the minute, giving me a broad grin as she hopped out of my battered Civic and disappeared inside. As I drove across town towards Sonya's office complex, I wondered about that grin. And hoped I hadn't made another huge mistake.

I'd finally got Sonya to agree to a meeting at her office. She wasn't happy about meeting with me at all, much less this late, and made a point of finishing typing an email before turning to where I sat in one of her uncomfortable guest chairs. Clearly, lingering visits were not to be encouraged.

"Do you recognize her?" I slapped the photo of Anna and Mona Gruen on the desk in front of her.

She grabbed it up, and that mask of cool slipped. Something desperate looked out at me. "Who is she? And where did you get this?"

It had still been a long shot, one I hadn't expected to pay off. Ever since the bartender at the Burrow Inn had mentioned that these two looked like sisters, the thought had been niggling at me. What if Anna and Mona were related?

And the team meeting, with the revelation of Mona's real last name, had solidified that thought. I just wasn't sure where Sonya— who looked very little like either Mona or Anna—fit in.

In other words, I had a few questions for my reluctant client.

Sonya clearly recognized Mona. And it wasn't as a temporary employee—not surprising given they worked on separate floors. Here, Mona was just a necessary cog in the machine that Sonya was in charge of.

"She's using the name Mona Gruen," I said, answering her first question. "And she met with Anna the night Anna disappeared."

Sonya went pale, then looked closely at the photo. "But that can't be right. This woman is the same age as Anna. Mona is nearly twenty years older. It must be a daughter. A cousin."

I was surprised to hear her estimation of Mona's age. "Mona was expertly made up that night," I said. "She looks younger here than she is."

Much younger, apparently. She kept herself in very good shape. If this Mona and the woman Sonya remembered were the same woman.

"But..." Sonya was staring at the photo. She looked shell-shocked. "How is this possible? How did she even find Anna? Why is she here?"

Here? Where did she expect Mona to be? "Who is Mona Gruen and what relation is she to Anna?"

"I—I—" She stuttered to a halt. Glared at me, as if this was somehow my fault. "I can't tell you that. It isn't my secret."

"Whose secret is it?"

Sonya looked miserable. "It's a family secret. That's all I can tell you."

This was all kinds of messed up. "Your sister is missing and in real danger. Mona Gruen was one of the last people to see Anna before she vanished. I don't think you can afford to keep that secret any longer."

"But—Anna doesn't even know."

I was guessing she did now. "Mona Gruen was murdered two days after this photo was taken. You're risking your sister's life. You have to know that."

Sonya drew in a deep breath. "Anna's adopted." She blew out a breath

I'd already guessed as much. "And she doesn't know?

"No, she doesn't." Sonya shrugged a little. "It wasn't my decision. But they wouldn't listen to me."

"Your parents?"

"Yes."

"Even as an adult they didn't tell her?"

"No. The circumstances—they just couldn't bring themselves to tell her."

"Anna is illegitimate?" I guessed.

Sonya nodded.

"And?" I prompted. There had to be more.

There was. Sonya leaned towards me, and the words came pouring out in a low, clear voice.

"Mona is Anna's mother."

I'd been half expecting that since Sonya's comment on Mona's age. "Go on."

"Mona is my mother's grand-niece, so my second cousin, once removed. She was fifteen when she got in with some criminal types, a really bad element. The family tried to help her but she liked the risk, the high life. Her parents disowned her."

Sonya gave a choked half laugh. "They call it tough love, you know. I suppose that's what I was trying to do with Anna. I was afraid she'd turn out like her mother."

She stared into space for a bit. "I remember it as an odd time. The entire situation caused much turmoil in the family, as you can imagine. I was nearly nine, and I remember it vividly. Every one spoke of it in whispers, at every family gathering. Then Mona got pregnant."

Sonya shook her head. "The family didn't find out until it was too late to do anything about the pregnancy. Mona showed up one day, she must have been eight months along, tear stained and defiant. My parents took her in. What could they do? Or so they reasoned."

She paused. "That was the end of my childhood."

I'd known there was tension between Sonya and Anna, but I hadn't expected this.

"There were tears, there was defiance, there were scenes," Sonya said. "And at the end of the day, Mona vanished, leaving my parents holding a squalling newborn child. My mother's much older sister, Mona's grandmother, had passed on, as had Mona's mother. So the baby had no one. My mother refused to be parted from her. My father never forgave her for it."

She took a deep breath. "So I had a sister. And my life had become hell."

After a pause that went on too long, I asked her "Did you see Mona again after that?"

Again that wry laugh. "Until I was twelve or so, she'd come around, looking for money. Then things began to go right for her, and she vanished. My father kept tabs on her though. He called her a swindler, and a thief. Said she'd come to a bad end one day."

She glanced over at me. "As you say she has."

"Yes."

She grimaced, said nothing.

"Did you know Mona lived here now?" I asked.

"In Vancouver?"

I nodded.

"No."

"And Anna never mentioned her?"

"No."

Anna probably hadn't known Mona existed, until that chance meeting at the art history course. I wondered how Mona had felt, seeing a woman who could only be her long-lost daughter. And after so long.

But when had Mona found out about Don's interest in Anna? Maybe that meeting wasn't chance after all...

I really wished there was some way of knowing what Mona and Anna had talked about. Had Mona told Anna that she was adopted? And who was Anna's father anyway?

Given Don and Mona's long association—could it be Don himself?

I shuddered at the thought. Then did the math. Not possible, given that Mona had to be a few years older than Don himself. When Anna was born, Don was thirteen or so. And too poor for trips to Germany.

I asked Sonya who Anna's father was, but she didn't know. Apparently Mona had refused to tell them, and even her father was unable to find out.

It probably didn't matter. Unless it was Don.

"But how does this help you find my sister?" Sonya asked.

"It might not." I gave my client a hard look. "But I haven't got much else at the moment."

Thanks to you hung unspoken in the air between us. That was pretty much it for our conversation.

No wonder Sonya had been so conflicted about her sister. And so ready to think the worst of her. It sounded like a harsh situation for both of them to grow up in.

Poor Sonya, having to keep that secret.

And poor Anna, growing up with all those unspoken tensions and suspicions.

Living a lie that was never acknowledged.

———

STILL DIGESTING the information Sonya had given me, I drove in a kind of stupor to the coffee shop where I'd left Marie. I lucked into a parking spot right outside, and celebrated by ordering a double espresso to go. The way this case was going, I'd need it.

Coffee in hand, I headed towards a table near the back, where Marie was ensconced with two of the three sales associates from Zanthus. It looked like she'd taken my words to heart—that was a first. They were so deep in conversation, she didn't even notice me.

I stood about ten feet back from their table, waiting to catch Marie's eye. It took a while. Finally she noticed me, and made her excuses. I headed out to the car before she'd finished. I didn't want them making the connection between Marie and me. Just in case.

"So, what did you find out?" I asked as she pulled open the door and climbed inside.

"Geez, rude much?" she said, slamming the door behind her.

"You didn't tell them you were working with me, right?"

"Of course not. What do you take me for? An idiot?"

"So we don't want them to see us together."

"Oh," she said. "Sorry."

It wasn't the most gracious apology I'd ever heard, but I think it was the first I'd ever heard from Marie. "No issues. Were they helpful, though?"

"They really liked Anna," Marie said. "And they really don't like Don James."

"Did you get any sense as to why they don't like him?"

"You mean aside from the fact he's a real jerk?" she said, with a half grin.

"Yes, aside from that." I glanced over at her and returned the grin, then pulled smoothly out into traffic. Luckily there wasn't much of it. "And?"

She bristled again. "What do you mean, and?"

"And I'm assuming there's more? You wouldn't have stopped there."

She flashed me a look I only caught out of the corner of my eye. Was she laughing? Nah, couldn't be.

"No, I didn't," she said. "He—Don—is the reason behind her disappearance. And not just that he was so nasty he made her run, either."

This was like pulling teeth. I was beginning to suspect she was doing it on purpose. It had almost worked, too. I'd give her points for that.

"Go on," I said noncommittally. This time I caught her grin.

"Sharla thinks he killed her. Anna. And stashed the body in some basement under the gallery."

I felt a chill along my spine just at the memory. "Is she serious?"

"Oh yeah. Very serious. And Ramon thinks Anna left before Don could hurt her."

"So they both believe Anna was in real danger from Don."

"Yeah."

"They got any proof of that, either of them?" I asked.

"Nah, they're too scared of Don James to go looking," she said with relish.

They were scared of Don? Don James?

Despite my episode in the basement with him, I wasn't afraid of him. Angry, but not afraid.

And it hadn't really sunk in just how dangerous the man might be.

"Don? Never," some part of me was saying. The part of me that still remembered the skinny kid with big eyes and bigger ideas. There had to be some trace of that kid left in the man he'd become.

"Though I think Ramon had a crush on Anna," Marie was saying. "If he thought Anna was down there, he'd be digging up that basement right now."

My focus snapped to what she was saying. "Ramon? A crush on Anna?"

"Yeah."

Now wasn't that interesting.

"It doesn't get us anywhere, though," she said. "But they did overhear something interesting."

"Oh?"

"Yeah. Ramon heard Don talking to someone on the phone, assuring them that Anna wouldn't be a problem, that everything would be fine."

"When was this?"

"Just before she vanished."

He hadn't mentioned that to me. "Did he tell the police?"

She gave me a scornful look. "You think he trusts them? Have you seen his work?"

"His work?" What did that have to do with anything? "No, I haven't."

"He's Ruiz," she said. Then waited.

At my look of non-comprehension, apparently visible even in the dim interior of the car, she clicked her tongue.

"Call yourself an artist. Ruiz paints. He's still underground, but he's got a following. His work is going to break one of these days, and break big."

Still nothing.

Marie sighed. "Ruiz's work is all about oppression. Political, military, whatever. He doesn't trust any organized force, not even here."

Ah. Yes, that made sense. I flashed on the image of the small, but powerful painting of a devastated village I'd seen over Anna's desk. If that was a Ruiz, then Marie was right about his potential.

I hadn't seen it in him when I met him, though. I wondered if I hadn't been paying attention, or if he'd been hiding it. Probably the latter, since I hadn't picked up more concern for Anna from him than from the others.

But Marie seemed sure.

I made a quick decision. "I want to talk to him. Ramon, I mean." The man, not the artist.

"And Drew?"

"No, just Ramon. At least for now. Can you get hold of him?"

In answer she drew out her smartphone. Her fingers flew for a few moments. What seemed like seconds later, I had my answer.

"He says yes, for Anna. And he'll meet me back at the Urban Grind in twenty minutes. Can we do that?"

I made a right turn and retraced our route.

CHAPTER THIRTY-EIGHT

WE TOOK RAMON RUIZ BACK to the office. Partly for privacy, but mostly because I had an outrageous idea brewing in the back of my mind. What I had in mind would need the whole team, plus Ramon.

If it worked.

I had Marie text Cory and Badger while we were *en route*, so everyone was there when we arrived with Ramon.

I introduced him to everyone, then got us all sitting around the table, facing the now empty whiteboard. Cory got coffee for me, and soda or water for everyone else without even being asked.

Poor Ramon looked confused. "Why am I here?" he asked.

"I'll get to that," I said. "How long have you worked with Anna?" I asked him.

"Eighteen months."

Since before Don had joined Zanthus. That's what I'd thought. "And you know her well?"

"Not well," he said in careful tones. "We work together."

I needed him to open up. "Well enough that you have seen a change in her since Don James was hired as the new manager?"

He gave me an unreadable look. "It would take an idiot not to notice that."

And he was definitely not an idiot. "I need you to tell us exactly what you've seen. Even the smallest detail could be critical."

"This will help find Anna?" he asked.

"Yes," I said.

Hoping I was right. And that we'd find her alive. Which was far from a certainty when she'd been missing for this long.

But since it seemed that whatever Don James and his secretive partner were up to, Mona had been trying to help Anna, our maybe odds were better than I'd first thought.

"Then I will do it. Tell me what I can do," he said in soft tones.

"I need you to tell us everything you've seen or suspected between Anna and Don."

Ramon's jaw tightened. And he started to talk.

———

RAMON STARTED OFF SIMPLY.

"Anna was up to something in these last six months or," he told us. "Planning it. I don't know what. But now and again I'd see her looking sideways at Don, when he was occupied with something else. And there would be a look in her eyes…"

His eyes gleamed. "I would not want to be Don when her plan was complete."

So I'd been right. "What was she up to?"

"I have no idea. Unfortunately," he said.

"Any idea why she was so upset with him?" Marie asked.

I wouldn't have been that blunt—okay, maybe I would have—but it was a good question. I waited to see what he'd say.

"I can only guess," he said. "Since I did not see most of their interactions, only the results of them."

This was a man attuned to nuances. And especially the games played for power.

I pictured the Ruiz painting hanging on Anna's wall. Which told me by its presence what she'd thought of the painter. I wondered what she'd thought of the man. "Go on."

"He was—predatory in his actions towards her," Ramon said. "It was subtle, too subtle to be called harassment, but it was there. Standing a little too close, pushing her on things that did not require it.

There was a proprietary edge to his actions, also. As if he owned her. It was painful to watch. Though someone who was not looking might not have noticed."

Ramon had noticed. Or Ruiz had. Was it the man who cared who had noticed? Or the artist shaped by the political cauldron he'd grown up in? How closely were man and artist integrated here?

"And Anna?" Badger asked, surprising me. I'd noticed she tended to play the observer except when her technical expertise was required.

"Anna was calm, always professional," he said. "She used it to create little distances, to let his attention slide off of her." He took a sip of water.

"But it was a brittle calm, hard won. And under it..." Ramon hesitated, glanced around the table, as if debating what to tell us.

Then that firm jaw thrust forward. "Under it was the determination to get even. I think she was determined to win free. And to make him pay."

His knowledge and understanding of Anna would probably freak her out if she knew about it. Especially if she hadn't realized he was interested in her.

"But how?" Cory burst out, asking the question we were all wondering.

"Again, I know nothing for sure," Ramon said. "But I watched her. And I watched her watch him.

Every time he went down into the basement. Every time he met with certain clients," Ramon said. "And I saw her behind his desk a few times when he was out."

"She was his assistant manager. She could have had a reason to be there," Marie said.

Interesting reasoning. I slanted her a glance. What had she been up to when I'd been out?

"Her body language—though she controlled it very well—said she did not have such a reason," Ramon said calmly.

I didn't doubt that he knew what he was talking about.

"You think she planned to expose Don," I said.

"Yes," he said.

"But for what?" Marie demanded.

Not subtle. Apparently her patience had run out. We were going to have to have another chat about the role of an assistant in this office.

"I cannot know," he said. "I saw only the determination, and that only in the smallest of clues."

"But you suspect," I said. "Will you share those thoughts with us?"

A nod. "You must know they are suspicions—and fears—only. These are not things I am used to speaking aloud. But for Anna..." he flattened his hands, spread them wide.

"Don was cultivating certain clients, and not for the work the gallery sells." He met my eyes. "This the three of us told you nearly a week ago."

I nodded acknowledgement of both the facts and the subtle rebuke. It wasn't quite as simple as it seemed to him.

"Do you have the names of these clients?" Badger asked.

Ramon nodded. "I will give them to you. I have noted, also, that Don spent too much time in the basement for a man in his position. Most especially when he thought himself unobserved."

He paused, glanced at each of us. "His actions make sense only if he is dealing in illegal things," he said, each word dropping clearly into the silence.

"Drugs?" Cory leaned forward, expression intent.

"I think not. Maybe stolen artwork. Or even forgeries. Things of high value, easily hidden. And easily explained. Things you might expect to find at a place like Zanthus. Does this make sense?" he asked.

"It does," I said. "And there are a few things you need to know." Which earned me curious looks from the rest of the team.

I drew in a deep breath. It was time to gamble.

So I told Ramon—who was also Ruiz, the artist of chaos—everything we'd learned so far. And he shifted, right in front of me.

His spine straightened, his soft dark eyes turned hard and focused, and his jaw muscles hardened even further. He looked like a warrior now, not an artist.

I'd hoped for something along these lines, but this was more than I'd anticipated. I caught surprised looks from Badger and Cory. Marie looked annoyingly smug.

Figured.

"How does this fit in with what you already know?" I asked him.

"It will be mostly guesses," he said.

"Go for it," I said.

"Anna had grown very fond of that basement," he said. "Whenever Don went out of the galleries, she would disappear down there. Sometimes for a few minutes, one day it was over half an hour she was gone."

"Didn't the others notice?" Marie asked.

Ramon shook his head. "No, she was clever about slipping away unnoticed."

"But you noticed," Cory said.

Ramon gave a quiet smile. "Yes," he said.

"Do you know what she was doing down there?" I asked.

"No. My guess would be she was searching through the bins and boxes down there. But if she was, she managed to hide it well. If she got dusty, or dirty, she managed to clean herself up before even I saw her."

"Do you know anything for sure?" Marie challenged him.

He gave her a patient look that silenced her. "Only that in the last day or two before Anna vanished, she'd come back upstairs with a look on her face I hadn't seen before."

"What look?" I asked.

"Quiet satisfaction," Ramon said. "But it was more than that. There was a kind of focused determination that I have only seen in some of our rebel commanders when they faced a battle against overwhelming odds."

"She found something," I said.

"I think so," he said. "And whatever it was, it was enough to set her plan, whatever that was, in motion."

"That's a lot of whatevers," Marie piped up. "What do you really think?"

I felt like kicking her under the table. Even if she was right.

Ramon just gave her another smile. He seemed to be amused by her.

"Whatever she found, she didn't bring upstairs with her," Ramon said. "But she could have re-hidden it so Don couldn't find it. Or deliver it to his clients."

He paused, glanced around the table, meeting each of our eyes in turn. "Who he plans to meet with tomorrow night."

"How do you know?" Badger asked.

"I overheard a phone call. He thought everyone had left for the day."

The suspicion on Marie's face was faint but real. I shared it. It was pretty key information.

And awfully convenient that he'd happened to overhear it. Had my gamble backfired, after all?

Was this an opportunity?

Or a trap?

But we couldn't overlook what might be a break for us.

Cory didn't share our concerns. "Way cool," he said. "You were spying on him."

Oh great. My impressionable nephew had another hero. One I wasn't sure we could trust. And I'd been the one to tell Ramon everything.

Wait a minute.

"Thursday?" I said. "This Thursday?"

He nodded.

Now Marie had caught on. "Artwalk Thursday? Don James is having a hush-hush meeting on Artwalk Thursday?"

From May to October, the third Thursday of every month was Artwalk Thursday at all the galleries along South Granville. They stayed open late, they served cheese and crackers and champagne—or at least prosecco—and they had the artists on hand.

Everyone loved it. The galleries made money. The patrons got to stroll from gallery to gallery, sipping champagne and talking art. And the artists love the free food and drink.

Well, it was good cover, I guess. I was reminded again not to underestimate Don James.

Just get even with him. That would do.

"How hard would it be for Don to slip away tomorrow night?" I asked Ramon. "Unobserved."

"Not hard at all," Ramon said. "And even if he was seen, no-one would think anything of it. Just a couple of art lovers. People who never go to galleries, or buy anything, come out for this."

Smart. Very smart. "Did Anna know this meeting was going to happen during Artwalk?" I asked.

"It is possible. Don seems to have been planning this for a while," he said.

Then he stared at me. "And she would plan to use such a meeting to set up a trap for him."

That's what I'd wondered. "You're sure? She would use something like this in her planning?"

"I'm sure. That's exactly what she'd do."

I nodded. "It would create a perfect opportunity for her," I said.

Cory was the one who got it. "So you think she plans to be there? In person?" he said.

"But that would mean she's here," Ramon said. "In Vancouver? Anna is still here?"

Something in his voice put my fears about him to rest. There was a desperate caring, and under it the kind of fear for a loved one that can't be faked.

"I think she must be, if she knew about the meeting," I said. "No matter how good her plan is, I can't imagine anything she could set up that would work if she weren't."

"We have to protect her," he said. "She doesn't know who she's playing with. These men are dangerous."

From everything I'd learned so far, I suspected Anna was well aware of that. But that might not be enough to save her.

Still it was obvious, to me at least, that we had to act. And now.

"This is our chance. We have to do this," I said.

CHAPTER THIRTY-NINE

THE FOLLOWING MORNING ALL OF us, including Ramon, were back in the office at seven a.m., gathered around our makeshift meeting table.

I don't know about the others, but I'd barely slept.

After the others had left last night, Badger managed to decipher a couple more channels in Chadwell's system, confirming that Don and his gang had been the ones behind the Mexican heist.

Then I'd spent a few hours on the phone with various law enforcement agencies. Including Nick. And my buddy Jerry at the VPD. Plus Adrien Keller of Interpol.

Who'd all been very interested in what I had to say.

Still too wired to sleep, I'd gone home and painted until I couldn't keep my eyes open another second.

This morning I had a head full of impossible plans. Ironically, I also had another nearly finished painting. Who knew all I'd need to get ready for a show was a really awful case?

I glanced over at Marie, who looked as haggard as I felt. That, and a determined assistant who was also an artist, apparently.

"We're doing this," I said. "Is everyone in?"

They all nodded. "What's the plan?" Cory asked.

"You're going to school," I said.

He groaned, but didn't argue. I didn't like the stubborn twist of his mouth, though.

"The rest of us have until eight o'clock this evening to finalize the details. And everything needs to be idiot proof, because Anna is likely to be there. Somewhere. We can't afford to put her more in danger than she already is."

"What kind of details?" Marie demanded.

Apparently lack of sleep didn't agree with her.

I walked to the whiteboard. "This is our chance. If Don is meeting with his buyers, it's a huge opportunity to trap him."

And if we were really lucky, maybe Anna's plan, whatever it was, would tie in with ours. Instead of jeopardizing it.

I wasn't counting on that kind of luck, though.

"How?" Marie snapped.

I ignored her. "If Anna is in hiding somewhere, waiting to spring a trap on Don and company, this meeting could well be her target, as Ramon believes."

He nodded.

"It's also our chance to find her and get her out of this mess before she gets herself killed," I said. "If Don and company are holding her somewhere, it's our best chance to get them to talk."

I didn't mention the last option, that if they'd already killed her, we might at least find her body.

"And we're doing all this before we get ourselves killed, too, are we?" Marie asked.

I needed more coffee—a lot more coffee—if I had to deal with my would-be assistant in this mood.

"Yes," I said, giving her a look that shut her up.

"Third, and most important," I said. "This may be our best chance to hand all of them over to the authorities."

"We do all the work and then just hand everyone over to the cops?" Cory burst out. "What's fair about that?"

Marie mumbled something. It didn't sound complimentary.

The troops were pretty restless this morning. Was it the stress of the situation? Or maybe I should just feed them.

How did I end up with a team, all of a sudden? I liked it better when it was just me and my computer.

I glanced at Badger, rolled my eyes. She gave me a slight smile. Okay, maybe not.

No way I'd have figured all this out without their help. Even Marie's.

"Quiet," I said. "I'm going to put on a pot of coffee. Cory, you and Marie are going to order in breakfast. Try to agree. Then we'll put our heads together, and we'll figure this thing out."

I turned towards Ramon. He looked as fiercely determined as he had last night. Good. He was going to need every ounce of that.

"Thanks to Ramon, here, we have a chance we didn't have this time yesterday. And we're going to take it. And we're going to get Anna back."

"And put those sleazes in jail," Cory said.

He had that right.

APPARENTLY MY LITTLE PEP TALK—OR maybe the food—was enough to get the troops in line. Me—I had my coffee. I was good to go all day, and all night too, if necessary. Whatever it took.

Anna had been missing for a week. It was time to bring her home.

"Ramon, you're not sure where the meeting is, right?"

"No. I would guess the back room. It is the only private place. No-one else would go there during Artwalk."

I remembered how unnaturally tidy that back room had been. It could make a good meeting place. No windows, and it was closed off enough—probably an easy place to barrier against any kind of electronic eavesdropping.

"We'll need to verify that. If it is the back room, can you get us in there without Don knowing? During the day I mean?"

He nodded. "Yes. On Thursdays, he has lunch at the Vancouver Club. One p.m., without fail. He is never back before two-thirty."

Perfect. "Badger, how good is their tech guy?"

"Chadwell?" she said. "He's good. I'm better." She gave me a shrewd look. "You want to bug the place?"

"Yes. Both the backroom and the basement."

"The basement?" Ramon said. "You don't think he would take them down there?"

Quite frankly, I had no idea how Don thought.

"I can't rule it out," I said. "And I want us covered, no matter what. But if they regularly do business at Zanthus, and if Chadwell is that good…?" I glanced over at Badger.

Who nodded. He was.

"Then they'll have some sophisticated processes in place," I said. "And they'll check regularly."

She nodded again. She'd already figured that out.

"Can you do it?" I asked her.

"Yeah."

"You'll have enough time?"

"Yeah."

She was starting to look annoyed. I guess I either trusted her or I didn't, because judging by her expression that was all she was going to say on the matter. Okay then.

"I'll see if Sonya can keep Chadwell occupied then, too. But let's be really clear about this. We aren't trying to catch these guys," I said.

"We're looking for that one weakness so we can hand them over to the locals and Interpol. Who will all be waiting," I said, looking from face to face. "We need to be sure that we're in a position to get Anna out when she makes her move."

"If she's alive," Marie muttered so only I heard her.

I glared at her. She shrugged.

What had got into her? "Your sister's alive," I said, just as softly. "Despite everything she went through."

That shut her up.

And her expression had lightened, just a little.

Good thing she was an artist. I didn't think she was cut out for the P. I. business.

I ignored the irony in that thought.

"We're not there to put ourselves in danger," I said. "We're there to get information. Bringing these guys down is not our job. Finding Anna, getting her home safely"—I hoped—"is."

I glanced around the table. "Anyone have any arguments with that?"

If they did, they didn't voice them.

Cory looked relieved, though. Ramon just looked determined. Marie actually looked a little hopeful. It was a good—if unexpected—look on her. Badger was as enigmatic as always.

This was as ready as we were likely to get.

———

BY NOON, most of the plan was in place.

Ramon hadn't been able to confirm where the meeting would be held, but Artwalk Thursday meant Don James had to be at Zanthus most of the evening. Where we could keep an eye on him.

Badger was also keeping an eye on Chadwell's activities online. When Don went for lunch, she and I would pay a little visit to the backroom and the basement at Zanthus.

Ramon was working at the gallery all day, keeping an ear out for any further hints of what Don was planning.

Marie had set up as communication central, fielding calls and finding ways to connect us with each other. Including getting us all Bluetooth headsets and some program Badger had recommended, so we could communicate.

Under protest, Cory had spent the day at school, then rushed back to help as soon as he could.

By six-thirty, we'd done everything we could.

By seven, we were a mess.

We'd met at the office for sandwiches and a final debrief.

Somehow what seemed at least remotely possible this morning now felt like a disaster.

Oh, everything was in place, but compared to the sophisticated strategies that Don and his group used, we felt like amateurs. Which, basically, we were.

Not a reassuring thought.

If it weren't for Anna, I think I would have pulled us out. But Ramon was still sure she'd act today.

And none of us wanted to leave her out there on her own against this group.

For better or worse, we were committed.

CHAPTER FORTY

EIGHT P.M. SHOWTIME.

CORY AND I strolled slowly along Granville Street, lost in the Artwalk Thursday crowd. Or so I hoped.

Don James would recognize me easily. Spotting me anywhere near his meeting might be enough to make him change his plans, and we couldn't have that.

So it was Marie and Badger who were inside the Zanthus Gallery, ironically enough. And Ramon, of course, in his role as a gallery sales associate. Which meant his participation in our plans would necessarily be limited by that role.

Cory was protective coloration for me, in case Don did catch a glimpse of us. He'd never met Cory, probably didn't know I had a nephew. He'd be expecting to see just me. I was making sure he didn't.

Five major galleries on two blocks kept this section busy. Crowds surged around us, chatting happily. My eyes flicked from person to person, looking for anyone I recognized.

Mostly we were waiting for word from inside the gallery.

Which wasn't long in coming.

"Alan just met two friends," Marie said softly in my earbud. "No sign of any of the others." Alan was the name we'd assigned Don for the evening.

"His friends brought two friends," Badger added. "Near the doors."

Bodyguards. Guarding the entrance and exits.

"I've got Moneybags," Cory said beside me, almost making me jump. "North-east, headed for the Gallery."

I casually glanced across the street, to see Kevin Chadwell striding quickly towards Zanthus. What was he doing here?

And what did his being here mean for our plan?

"Watch him," I said to Cory, "but don't let your eyes linger on him. He'll have good radar."

"Got it," Cory said equally softly.

I let my eyes roam our side of the street. And caught a glimpse of a woman I was almost sure was Anna.

She'd done something with her hair—cut and colored it, or maybe bought a good wig—and was wearing a tailored coatdress. She looked older. And taller and heavier than I knew her to be.

She didn't look anything like her photo. But she did look like Sonya on a stressful day.

So I'd been right. Anna had come after Don.

And she was with someone. Another woman. The crowds surged again, and I got a clearer view.

Yes, it was Anna, had to be. And I knew the woman she was with. Roxy, the server from the Burrow Inn. The one who'd seen Anna on the Wednesday, after she'd "vanished".

Very cute. So that's where Anna had been hiding. I should have asked more questions as soon as Roxy told me she'd seen Anna that day.

The two of them had stopped and were looking in the window of the Omega Gallery, seemingly discussing a painting hanging there. Their backs were to Zanthus.

And to Kevin Chadwell. Had Anna recognized him?

Would he recognize her? Maybe. From what Badger had

unearthed, Chadwell made it a point to know everything he could find out about everyone their team dealt with.

"Moneybags is entering," Cory said.

I could hear him more clearly in my earbud than in person, despite the fact that he was standing beside me.

"I have him." Badger's voice. "He's avoiding Alan. But watching him."

Interesting. As the silent partner, I'd have expected Chadwell to stay invisible and leave Don to deal with the buyers. So what was he doing here?

"Alan plus two are headed for the basement," came Marie's voice.

"And our tech is working," Badger's voice added.

Good. Though how she could be sure of that from inside the gallery… "And Moneybags?" I asked.

"Checking his watch," Badger said. "He may have the basement wired too."

Uh oh.

"Something's making him nervous," she added. There was a pause. "He's spotted the friend's friends. Uh oh."

"What?" I asked.

"They gave him a nod. Moneybags is going down."

Moneybags knew the client's bodyguards? Was trusted by them? That made no sense.

What was he up to?

Half a block down, I could see Anna and her friend turn decisively away from the window they'd probably been using as a mirror and dash across the street. Too fast for me to stop them.

They were headed for Zanthus. And she'd be walking straight into the arms of those bodyguards.

———

"INCOMING," I said quickly. "Debra and friend." Debra was our code for Anna. "Don't let her go downstairs."

"Copy," Marie's voice, sounding determined.

I held my breath, waiting. Nothing happened.

I peered across the street. The big plate windows had been set up with a solid backdrop to showcase several large pieces. I couldn't see into the gallery itself. Through the double glass doors I could see movement, but the elaborately scrolled iron that protected them meant that was all I could see.

And the doors stayed resolutely closed. No-one else went in. No-one came out.

"Where's Debra?" I said urgently.

"We have her," Marie said calmly.

I let out a relieved breath.

"Check your phone," Badger said.

After a quick glance around, I pulled back into the doorway of a closed shop, pulling Cory with me. Safely out of the stream of art lovers—and unobserved—I pulled out my phone, checked the app Badger had installed that afternoon.

I was looking at most of the interior of Zanthus's main gallery, surprisingly sharp despite the size of the phone screen. I could clearly make out Badger, Marie, Anna and Roxy to the right of the main doors.

I could also see the two bodyguards, their protective stance unmistakable, one standing close on the left of the entrance door, the other to the left of the door leading to the backroom, with its access to the alley and to the basement. The latter man was almost invisible in the crush of people. Both were watchful.

Marie had one hand on Anna's arm, the other on Roxy's, as she guided them to a fairly quiet corner away from the doors. The view was too zoomed out to make out expressions, but Marie's body language clearly expressed pleasure at an unexpected meeting with old friends.

Anna's posture looked a little stiff, but Roxy had apparently caught on and was reacting to Marie's overtures with a friendly openness.

The bodyguards were no longer paying the four of them any attention.

I let out a breath of relief. Anna was safe. At least for now. And Marie seemed determined to keep her safe.

My assistant had unexpected depths.

Suddenly my phone screen flickered, and I was looking at a zoomed-in image of Don and his two clients down in the Zanthus Gallery basement. Marie wasn't the only one with unexpected depths. How was Badger managing to manipulate images on the fly from the cameras she'd planted only that afternoon?

A small box lay open between Don and his clients. I couldn't quite see what it held. But Don looked like he'd received a horrific shock and was trying to hide it.

Another flicker, and I could hear them, too. They were arguing fiercely. But not in English. Spanish, perhaps.

And with their strong accents, my Spanish wasn't good enough to understand everything. Something Don had promised and not delivered?

The shorter of the two clients pulled a rock out of the box and thrust it towards Don, yelling all the while.

A rock. A medium-sized, very ordinary grey rock. It was clearly heavy.

Had Ramon been right that Anna had tried to hide the artifact Don planned to sell? Maybe even replaced it with a rock to hide what she'd done?

Clever of her. But when had the switch been made? Obviously after Don had satisfied himself with the contents, if he hadn't checked it again before today.

On my too small phone screen, Don was waving his hands, talking quickly. He'd turned red.

The other two looked angry. The taller of the two clients had a hand at his hip. A gun?

But where was Chadwell? He'd followed them down, and I couldn't see him.

Don threw up his hands and started towards the far wall. The image on my screen expanded to follow him. The shorter client barked something.

And drew his gun.

Don laughed. Said something.

Just as I'd expected Don to be shot, the shorter man grinned, shook his head. And lowered the gun.

With a quip, Don disappeared behind a shelving unit. A nod from the shorter man—clearly in charge—and the taller man followed him.

Don emerged with another box in his hands. From the way he held it, it was heavy.

He opened it carefully, passed it to the shorter man. Who holstered his gun to accept the box. Looked inside.

Beamed.

And drew out an exquisite pre-Columbian carving.

The Mexico heist. We'd been right.

"Make the call," I said to Cory, who'd been keeping one eye on the street while watching the action on my phone in fascination.

While Cory was punching in the numbers, I watched on my screen as the taller man re-emerged from the shelving unit in the basement of the Zanthus. Carrying two more identical boxes.

One of them was open. He circled around Don, and showed the open box to his boss.

Who looked at it for a moment, then at the carving he still held.

"Fraud!" he yelled in heavily accented English. "You try to cheat me!" Lobbing the carving at Don, he pulled his gun.

Don ducked instinctively, and the small statue crashed against the edge of a shelving unit before tumbling in pieces to the floor.

I just hoped it was the fake. One of the fakes.

His gaze locked on his would-be client, Don froze. "No, you don't understand. I can explain..."

"Oh, I do understand. *Hijo de puta*," the shorter man swore, raising the gun until the barrel centered between Don's eyes.

And Chadwell came down the stairs behind them, a small gun in his hand. "Freeze."

But the two clients had seen Don's eyes rise to the stairwell, and the taller of the two was already in motion, spinning to face Chadwell with his own gun drawn.

The shorter man, the one in charge, had moved so he could watch both Don and Chadwell. And his gun covered both of them.

Normally I'd have bet on the two clients against either Don or Chadwell. I'd thought of the latter as soft. Thinkers, not doers.

But there was Chadwell's interaction with the bodyguards to consider.

And the cold, hard look on Chadwell's face as the camera zoomed in again changed my mind. There was no sign of the nerdy programmer he showed the world.

I was looking at evil.

Melodramatic? Maybe, but the willingness to kill was clear on his face. There was no doubt in my mind he'd been the one to murder poor Mona.

It didn't seem to worry the shorter man. "He is ours," he said. "I suggest you leave."

"But I have a beef with him too," Moneybags said, with his eyes on Don.

Who suddenly went from complacent to more frightened than he'd been when Shorty threw the artifact at him.

"He was attempting to cut me out of your deal," Moneybags—Chadwell—said. "I can't allow that. And I can sell you the real artifact. Not one of his fakes."

Now that I hadn't expected. I held my breath.

Beside me Cory was open mouthed, his eyes riveted on my phone screen.

And across the street, the unmarked black SUVs started to pull up.

———

CHAOS ENSUED.

There was a shot, then another that I heard clearly over my smart phone's speakers and dully from across the street.

Then the image on the phone screen vanished. I could still hear muffled sounds of a violent fight, but I couldn't see anything.

Had someone shot out the electronics? Or had Don turned out the lights again?

I glanced up to see dark-suited figures in bullet-proof vests pouring out of the three identical SUVs parked in front of Zanthus and into the gallery.

"Stay here," I snapped at Cory, pushing him further back into the doorway we'd been standing in.

"But…" he began.

I gave him a hard look, then dashed between the cars that had stopped in front of me and across the street.

Art lovers were being herded out the front doors of the Zanthus Gallery. I fought against the tide, made my way almost to the doors.

A very large gentleman in a dark suit tried to convince me I was going the wrong way, but when I told him I was looking for Adrien Keller he let me by.

Inside, I looked first for the two bodyguards. Who weren't there. As I'd expected, they'd probably run after their boss at the sound of the shots.

Next my gaze sought out Marie and Badger, who were against the far wall with their two charges. All safe. And out of any possible line of fire. Thank God.

Badger had her head bent over her tablet. Probably trying to get the feedback from the basement. That could wait.

I surveyed the room, crowded now with law enforcement of various kinds. I didn't see Nick or Jerry, but I spotted Keller from Interpol. And headed straight for him.

"I'm Barbara O'Grady," I said as soon as I got close enough. "You have to hear this," and handed him my smart phone.

He'd started to turn away, but at the mention of my name he gave me a strained smile and reached for my phone. "What is this?"

"Live from the basement. There was video, but it went to black right after the shots," I said.

"How many?"

"There were four. Two thieves, two clients. At least three handguns. And the client's two bodyguards must be down there now."

"Six, then."

"Yes."

For a moment we listened to the thumps, grunts and crashes of a violent fight. It was impossible to tell how many were fighting, or to recognize voices in the harsh breathing and harsher sounds they made.

There were no further shots, which was a mercy.

Either they couldn't risk hitting the wrong person at close quarters, or they couldn't see to shoot. Hard to tell from up here, and the soundtrack told me nothing.

Obviously it didn't tell Keller much either. He looked over at a solid looking man standing at the entrance to the back room, gave a small circular motion with his fingers. The other nodded back, said something into his mic. He probably had officers in the alley.

Then he glanced at the officers clustered around him, and nodded. Eight of them headed through the open door to the basement in a rush.

I could hear them thundering down the basement stairs. Without them, the room felt almost empty.

Seconds later the video reappeared on my phone.

I held it so Keller could see it, and glanced over at Badger, who had just looked up from her tablet. I pointed at my phone, raised an eyebrow. She shook her head. Not her doing.

Don must have turned off the lights earlier.

Which had probably saved his life, though I could see blood staining the sleeve of his right arm. No-one else seemed to be bleeding. Yet.

As I watched, the last of Keller's team streamed in. The basement was now full of angry men, all of whom held guns. Some of them were the good guys. Most weren't.

If I'd been Don, I'd be surrendering immediately.

I wouldn't put it past Chadwell to kill his erstwhile partner, then the clients, if only so none of them could implicate him. Then claim self-defense.

Though I'm not sure how he'd have explained his presence in that basement.

But where was Chadwell?

I looked harder. And where had Don vanished to?

Even with the lights on, that many bodies meant that the image was zoomed way out. Which made it hard to identify any particular body.

I caught a flicker of movement as someone moved towards one of the shelving units. Disappeared behind it. The way he moved made me pretty sure it was Don. He must have a private exit.

I wondered if Kevin Chadwell was privy to the secrets of the basement. Had Don trusted him that far? Maybe not.

But I had an uneasy feeling that Chadwell would have uncovered everything anyway, whether Don had showed him or not.

Keller had seen the same thing I had. He was giving low-voiced commands over his mic. On my phone screen I could see two of his men fade back and make their way along the wall towards the shelves. Then they too vanished.

Presumably the guys in the alley would also be waiting for Don and Chadwell.

If Don's exit ended up in the alley.

And if it didn't?

I glanced over at Marie, who was in low-voiced conversation with Anna and Roxy. With both Don and Chadwell both on the run, Anna was probably safer here than anywhere else. For right now, anyway. Badger and Marie, too.

But I'd left Cory out across the street. On his own.

"Cory? You there?" I said into my mic.

Nothing.

CHAPTER FORTY-ONE

IT FELT LIKE I COULDN'T get my breath as I dashed out of Zanthus and across the street, dodging cars. No Cory.

I spun around, my eyes seeking that familiar face. Maybe he'd got caught up in the crowds around another of the galleries.

Still no Cory.

I looked back at the Zanthus Gallery, took in the wide, cleared space around the front door, the massed crowds all around it. All staring at Zanthus, chattering excitedly.

As I watched a news van pulled up, double parking next to the SUVs. In the distance I could hear a police siren. Then another.

The situation was getting out of hand.

And there was no sign of Cory.

Then my headset cracked, and I heard his voice. The first bit was garbled, then I heard, "…alley…," then more garble.

Oh no.

I didn't stop to think.

I ran for the end of the block, and the quickest entrance to the alley, swerving and ducking to get through the clusters of art-goers everywhere. All of whom seemed to be out on the sidewalk, gawking and gossiping at the action across the street.

I didn't care about that. I needed to find my nephew.

———

IT WAS GROWING DARK, and the lengthening shadows kept me from seeing what was going on in the alley. Down at the far end I could see the flashing red and blue lights that told me the police had set up a barricade. Good.

No one was blocking off this end yet. But the sirens I could hear growing closer probably meant they were about to. I was just in time.

They'd be set up soon.

Watching my footing – the alley was uneven, and I couldn't afford to sprain an ankle in the heels I wore so seldom – and with every sense on full alert, I ran. Blessing all those years and all those miles of early morning running.

If I'd stopped even for a moment to think, I'd have gone for help. I wasn't armed, and both Don and Chadwell were. And there was no shortage of armed responders here.

But I didn't stop. My nephew's life could be at stake. And I'd been the one to bring him here. My only thought was to get him out of this.

My mind was focused on finding my nephew, but years of training kicked in. My eyes scanned every shadow, watching for every movement.

I was looking for Don. For Chadwell. And for Cory.

For anything that didn't belong.

A skittering in the shadow had my shoulders tensed, then the smell of stale pizza told me I was hearing rats, scavenging in the bins. Another stealthy movement to my left was too low down to be anything two-legged.

Then I saw a bigger shadow, clinging against the wall next to what had to be the loading bay for Zanthus. I stopped abruptly, moved into the shadows. Tried to get my breathing under control before it gave me away. All the time watching that shadow, and the building, for any movement.

I felt almost sick for a minute—I'd been running hard. I ignored the feeling, and it passed.

There was a soft crackle in my ear. "Barbara? Where are you?" Badger's voice said.

I didn't answer. Couldn't take the risk of being heard. Not here. Not now.

I'd muted my phone earlier, now I glanced down at it. The basement looked like a standoff between Don's thuggish clients and Keller's team from Interpol.

I couldn't see Don. Or Chadwell. They'd gotten out in the confusion.

But where had they gone?

And where was Cory?

I glanced back at the shadow I'd been tracking. It was starting to move, creeping very slowly towards the back exit of Zanthus. That couldn't be Don or Chadwell. Back into the building was the last place either of them would go.

But it could be Cory.

And if it was, it was worth the risk. I started to move in the same direction, just a little faster than the shadow I was tracking.

"Hold it right there," said a soft, vicious voice from behind me. The barrel of a gun pressed against my ribs.

———

"NOW PUT your hands where I can see them," he continued. "Slowly. No sudden moves that will draw attention to us. You'd be dead before any of them could get here."

I did as he said, my mind racing, looking for options. And not finding any. I felt cold and sick inside.

I hate guns. Especially when someone's holding one on me.

"So you're the trouble-making investigator that Don's so sure he's fooled," the voice said.

Chadwell. It couldn't be anyone else.

"Don always was an idiot," he continued. "Useful, though. He'd take risks no sane person would have considered. Now, walk," and the gun nudged me back in the direction I'd come.

Why was he telling me this? It probably meant he intended to kill me.

I swallowed hard.

Still, it useful information. It meant I too would take risks that no sane person—or at least not one who expected to live out the evening—would consider.

I just needed to wait for an opening.

Chadwell apparently had no intention of giving me one. He stayed just behind me, out of reach, the gun prodding me forward at the same time it reminded me how vulnerable I was.

My headset. I'd forgotten I was still wearing it. I had no idea if I was out of range back here, but I could at least try to let Badger and Marie know I was in trouble.

It was time to stir things up.

"You won't get away with this you know, Chadwell," I said. Hating that all I'd come up with was a cliché.

He chuckled.

Which was just wrong. This man had no business chuckling.

"They know who you are," I told him. "Even if you manage to get out of this alley, you won't get far…"

Apparently under stress I talked like a TV show.

"With enough money, anyone can vanish," he said. "And I assure you, I have enough."

Of course he did.

"You have to get out of here first," I said.

"You're my ticket out," he said. "The cops aren't looking for a couple. And I'm sure you have car keys in that purse of yours."

So I had a little time before he killed me. Good.

I gave a little twitch, as though his words had unnerved me.

"Thought so," he said smugly.

"You can't expect me to drive you," I said, just in case anyone was listening.

Actually, I hadn't brought my car, I'd walked. My place is just a few blocks from here. But anything he got wrong could give me an advantage.

And I badly needed an advantage.

CHAPTER FORTY-TWO

MY BRAIN WAS RACING. WHAT did I know about Kevin Chadwell? He was really intelligent, probably equally arrogant.

And he was deadly.

He was also a games programmer. And a good one. Which meant he was strategic, and a planner.

I cast a glance back over my shoulder, trying to see his expression. Hoping to gauge what he intended.

"Now, now. None of that," he said, poking me with the gun. "Just keep walking."

There weren't a lot of women programmers, even now. It wasn't the easiest industry for a woman. Sonya was proof of that. He must hate the fact that he essentially worked for her now.

Maybe I could use that?

And maybe he'd underestimate me, too. Like Don had.

But what did I do with that?

I scanned the alley. We were walking away from the action at the other end. No-one had spotted us. And it was getting darker now.

I didn't hear any sirens, nothing to indicate anyone knew I was out here. And there had been no response from Badger or Marie. My headset was probably out of range. So no help there.

And we were nearing the far end of the alley. My chances of getting away from him on the side street might be better than they were here. There were more people around.

Which might mean that I got more people shot.

It was darker in the alley. Chadwell wouldn't be able to see any better than I could. But he might know this alley better than I did, if he'd spent any time at Zanthus.

I was guessing he'd made a habit of checking up on Don—his partner, the one he called "an idiot." And he'd known exactly where the basement was.

And, apparently, how to escape from it.

Still, I'd spent my share of time on Gallery Row. This was my neighborhood, after all.

In fact, Beans was just a few doors up. And their entrance to the alley had a solid steel door. One that was impossible to open from the outside. Unless you knew the trick to it...

It might work.

Or it might get me killed.

But in his mind, Chadwell had killed me already. I had nothing to lose.

I gauged the distance. Slowed my steps a little.

As expected, he prodded me with the gun. "Dawdling won't help you. Walk faster."

I walked slightly faster with each step for six steps, made sure I was on the right foot.

Then launched into an all-out sprint, bearing slightly to my right.

Then zagging on a shallow angle to the left, heading arrow straight towards the door to Beans.

Behind me I heard a sharp inhale, a curse. Running footsteps.

I'd taken him by surprise.

The first shot went right, and I'd already changed course.

The second shot was left, but low and wide. Nowhere near me.

The footsteps stopped. Uh oh. He'd be aiming carefully now.

I hoped he wasn't a marksman.

Fighting the urge to duck, I powered everything I had into extra speed. If I could just clear that big garbage bin...

I rounded the corner of the bin just as a bullet pinged off the edge of it.

That was too close. I fumbled with the keypad beside the door. With an effort, I smoothed my ragged breathing.

Right now, I'd make a perfect target. I had to get inside before he could get around the bin and take another shot.

For a bad moment, my mind blanked on the combination.

Then my fingers slipped.

I had to try again.

And I made it.

I slammed the door behind me just as a bullet pinged off of it.

———

I DASHED into the bright lights and chatter of the coffee shop, drawing in a deep breath of that rich coffee smell. I glanced frantically around me, my brain still in overdrive, and every sense focused on any sound from the alley door.

I didn't think Chadwell would come after me. But if he did...

My headset buzzed to life. The sudden sound in my ear had my heart hammering even louder.

"Barbara? Barbara? Can you hear me?" Marie's voice. Frantic.

"I'm here," I said.

"OMG. When you didn't respond, we thought you were dead! We've passed your information on to Keller. His men should have Chadwell by now."

Apparently the eternity I'd just spent with a gun pressed in my ribs hadn't been long at all.

"Cory?" I asked. Dreading the answer.

"He's here. He's fine. His mic died," she said.

Oh, thank God. He was safe.

"And Anna?"

"Also here. Also fine."

Okay, then.

I glanced back at the rear door. I hadn't heard another gunshot, so either Keller's men had Chadwell, or he'd run as soon as I got through that door.

I was safe, too.

Trying to calm my breathing, I scanned the coffee shop. People were clustered in little groups, and the tone was excited. But not afraid.

No-one was panicked.

Whatever was going on down the block must be under control.

My favorite barista was on, and glanced my way. Her eyes widened a little and she left her station and brought me an espresso. Which was unheard of.

Some poor schmuck was going to have to wait for his coffee.

"You look like you need this," she said.

She was right.

"Thanks," I said, downing it. Wondering just how bad I looked.

Not much caring.

"You need help?" She was still hovering.

"No, I'm good. But I need to get back. I'll just pay for…"

She waved it off. "It's on me. Go. Do what you need to do."

"But…"

She grinned at me. "And when it's all over, I want to hear about all this"—and she waved towards the windows, where blue and red flashers lit up the street.

I'd forgotten she knew I was a P. I.

"And why you look like you just ran a marathon. In heels," she added.

I gave her a wry grin, glanced down at my heels. Yup, they were still there. Who knew I could actually sprint in them?

"Done," I said.

"You need another espresso?"

What I needed was to know how all of this ended. And to see that everyone was safe.

"I'm good," I said. "Thanks. Really."

She patted my arm, which stunned me. "Go."

I headed back to Zanthus.

Where this had all started.

———

ZANTHUS WAS STILL CORDONED OFF, but they recognized me and waved me through. The main room was still full of cops of all stripes, but the tension was gone. People were in mop-up mode, you could feel it.

I glanced around for my team, found them huddled in the far corner where I'd last seen them. The difference was, Cory was with them.

I arrowed towards them. But I'd been spotted.

Adrien Keller hurried towards me. "O'Grady. You okay?"

"Fine. You have Chadwell?"

"Yes. We have the bastard."

"And Don James?"

"We have everyone. Chadwell shot James, but it looks like he'll make it. "

Something inside me settled.

"Now we're tearing apart that basement. And you wouldn't believe what we're finding," he added

Oh, yes I would. "Good. Then I need a minute with my team."

"Of course," he said, and stood back.

I thanked him with a nod, but my eyes were on Cory.

Who looked drained, with dark circles under his eyes.

I ran my eyes around the little group. They all looked like that.

They should be celebrating. We'd done it.

Marie spotted me first, let out a little squeal. Next thing I know her arms were around me and she was hugging me like I was her favorite teddy bear or something.

"Eep," I managed to get out. Trying to get my breath.

"Oh, sorry," she said. "Too tight?"

And she loosened her grip a little, but didn't let go.

Next thing I knew, Cory was hugging me from the other side.

"Uh, guys…" I said. I needed to get free so I could hug him back.

And we were drawing a lot of attention. This wasn't exactly professional behavior.

It didn't help. First Anna, then Roxy had joined our hug-wich. With me still in the middle. Barbara-as-filling.

That's me, the hard-edged P. I.

At least Cory looked less strained.

So did Marie, but she was babbling something about the mics, and she was trying to save money, and she was so sorry…

Anna was crying, but in a happy way, and saying she hadn't thought it would work, and he'd have killed her…

At least Roxy wasn't talking. But she was still hugging me.

Badger, bless her, didn't join in. She just gave me a wry grin from the sidelines. But her eyes were dancing.

Yup, she was my kind of people.

CHAPTER FORTY-THREE

THE FOLLOWING MORNING I WOKE before the alarm. Which had almost nothing to do with the set of claws that were resting on my forearm.

I opened a reluctant eye.

"Mrrt?" Cat said.

Which translated to "Are you going to feed me breakfast now?"

"Just wait," I told him, and stretched lazily.

Why was I feeling so relaxed? And so exhausted at the same time. I glanced at the clock.

Quarter after eight? I'd slept through my alarm? Then it came back to me.

The hectic planning. Finding Anna. Losing Cory. The alley. The case.

For a moment I felt frozen. It could have gone so badly.

But it didn't.

I'd come home late—I'd seen the others home, then gone back to Zanthus. I hadn't left the gallery until nearly two a.m.—turned my alarm off and fallen into bed. And slept better than I had in weeks.

They'd found everything in that basement. Stolen art of all kinds. Forgeries of those works. Copies of things that hadn't even been reported stolen.

And documentation. Lots of documentation.

"Sometimes I can't believe how stupid even the cleverest criminals are," Keller had said, waving a dusty folder at me.

"Without these printouts, I'm told it would have taken our experts years to crack their systems. I guess somebody couldn't keep it all straight themselves without a reminder, either."

"That sounds like Don James," I said, with an inward grin. Good thing Badger wasn't there. I couldn't have resisted the urge to exchange glances with her.

"Probably," Keller said. "James seems to have been the one who was using that basement as a hiding place. And the printer in his office might be a match."

It was. Right down to the paper. And that hadn't been easy to arrange, either.

"Good," I said.

"They are all turning on each other. And with Anna Lang's testimony? This is one gang that is going away for a long time."

I held back a smirk at the thought of Don's face. "Happy to hear it."

A knock on the door had me scrambling into my robe. Now what?

It was Nick. Who immediately gathered me into a deep kiss.

Which I returned with fervor.

"You could have called," he said.

"I was busy," I said with a grin. "As were you. Quite the night we had."

I ushered him in, closed the door behind him. Fell back into his arms.

"Between us all, we've wrapped up almost everything. Chadwell looks like my killer in the Gruen case, as well as the solution for a number of cases Interpol's been working for years. Your Don isn't much better off."

"I heard something about that," I said with a straight face.

"And when I heard later that you'd ended up confronting Chadwell in that alley…"

He shook his head, kissed me again.

"That wasn't my idea, believe me."

"I know. It never is." He broke off, held me back so he could see my face. "I wasn't even close…"

"No, you were deployed further back. As part of the team that brought him down," I said.

"Yeah. But I had no idea you even were in danger." He swallowed. "You…"

"I got out of it."

"Barely. You don't even carry a gun."

"I'm fine."

"You were supposed to be across the street. Out of the way. What happened?"

"I had to warn my missing woman she was in danger. Then Cory went missing and our communications went down," I said.

He nodded. He knew how that went.

"I couldn't see any other options."

"Yeah."

"But I'm fine. Really. And it's done."

"This time."

"Yes. This time. For both of us."

He didn't say anything for a moment. We both knew it was true. Both our jobs were dangerous, his more than mine.

Though somehow I'd been the one getting shot at recently. At least he hadn't pointed that out.

Though maybe that was a bad sign. Nick always seems to know how to lighten the tense moments. If he wasn't joking about my getting shot…

"Of course, Interpol and the VPD are taking all the credit," he said with a lopsided smile.

At least he was trying. "Do you care?"

"Nope. Just wanted it solved. We have more than enough on our hands with the recent spate of gang killings."

That's what I'd thought. "You're welcome."

"And I don't know if you heard, but in addition to the murderer and his buds, they also arrested one of their clients. Who might be the key to cracking an international drug ring Interpol have been working on."

He paused, watching me.

"Chadwell seems not to have trusted this guy. Or maybe it's his own partner he didn't trust. He collected some pretty damning evidence on this client, and is busy negotiating to trade it for his own skin."

Had Chadwell bought off the client's bodyguards? Was that why they let him by?

"That must have happened after I left. It won't help him, though. Not with a murder charge hanging over his head."

He grinned. "And James is busy fingering Chadwell for murder, in hopes of reducing his own charges. Which means I can take a bit of overtime. I'm off until Monday. You want to take a long week-end, go somewhere?"

"Pretty short notice," I said.

"Blame yourself. You're the one who set this all up. Which meant I solved my impossible case in the middle of the night."

"Hmm. Guess I did at that."

And I could use some downtime. Especially downtime spent with Nick. "Let me think about it."

"Think about it? Just how late a night was it?" He glanced around. "Wait a minute. I don't smell coffee. And why is your cat glaring at me?"

"He's not my cat," I muttered.

"Haven't you had breakfast yet?"

"No. I just woke up."

"No coffee either?"

I shook my head.

He looked properly horrified. "I'll put it on, and make you some breakfast. You go have a shower."

Maybe living together really could work. Not to mention the side benefits.

"Join me. Coffee can wait."

———

WIDE AWAKE after a truly energizing shower and properly caffeinated, my brain started functioning again. I ate another mouthful of a really good omelet, and looked across the table at Nick.

"I can't go," I said. "I have paintings to finish. I need four new ones by the end of this month."

"Is that an excuse?" Nick said.

Now where had that come from? "Of course not. Why would you even think that?"

He looked sheepish. "You'd said you were getting painting done in the mornings. I was curious."

"You looked?"

Once that would have felt like a betrayal. Now I didn't know what I felt. I'd shown him stuff before, and the sky hadn't fallen.

He nodded. "You have at least five new paintings in there."

I definitely knew how I felt about that. "I couldn't show those. They're either not finished, or they're too awful to show."

"What? They all look good to me."

Nick was no art critic, but his judgement wasn't usually that bad. I put my fork down, grabbed my coffee mug. "I'll be right back."

He had the sense not to follow me into my second bedroom. I probably should start calling it the studio, now that I have plastic floorcloths covered with cotton drop cloths all taped to the floor.

I looked around. He was right. There were five completed paintings sitting there. Two were ready to package up and send to Margaret Courtland, as is.

Three of them? Well, they were finished. They might even be good. But they were the result of all-nighters when the case was at its worst.

And they were—powerful was the best word I could think of. I wasn't sure if that was in a good way, or a bad one.

Would they even sell? Part of me just wanted to paint right over them. Immediately.

Part of me was really impressed with them in a disconnected way, as though I was considering another artist's work. They didn't feel like something I'd painted.

Though I was sure I'd never want to hang them on my walls. I gulped some coffee. It helped.

Clearly the only thing to do was send them all to Margaret. Let her make the call.

Leaving me free to take a long weekend with Nick?

I started to grin. I just had a few loose ends to tie up. First I went and told Nick the good news.

Then I poured more coffee, and checked on Cory. He was fine, and still enthusiastic about the case. I was just glad it was over, and that nobody else got killed.

I told Cory I'd be away for the weekend, that I'd see him Monday, and to let Badger know.

Then I sent Sonya a terse email letting her know I'd found Anna, she was safe, and that my report would be on her desk by mid-next week. Along with her final bill.

Draining my coffee, I emailed Keller, telling him I'd be unavailable until Monday. Called my answering service, asked them to take the office phones until then.

Emailed Marie, gave her the day off. And set up a meeting between Cassandra and Marie.

Maybe Cassandra would end up hiring my would-be assistant, and solve that problem for me. Though I was beginning to appreciate Marie's merits in a way I'd never expected.

Thanks to Marie, I had five finished paintings I wouldn't otherwise have painted. Even if they were—well, different. I might even miss her being my assistant if she left.

But this afternoon, Nick and I would be driving to Seattle. Where I planned to hole up in a hotel room with him for most of the weekend. With the phone turned off.

Everything else could wait 'til I got back.

ACKNOWLEDGMENTS

Many thanks to all those who were part of my journey with this book. Particular thanks go to Linda Roggeveen for an amazing copy edit and Colleen Cross for great feedback on the beta version.

www.ingramcontent.com/pod-product-compliance
Lightning Source LLC
Chambersburg PA
CBHW061555190726
48288CB00007B/2036